BANKING ON TROUBLE

KATHI REED

ISBN-13: 978-1511675901
ISBN-10:151167590X

This book is dedicated to
Helen and Fred Lehnartz

ACKNOWLEDGMENTS

I've wanted to write a book since I was 12. Now at the age of (blank), having finally published one, it seems like a small miracle. But it is due, in large part, to the editorial acumen of my son, David Reed, and the laser eyed professionalism of my copy editor friend, Sandy Koppen. Other people who have been invaluable to me in my writing are Brian Andersen (for sharing his knowledge of southwest Ohio history); Cincinnati Police Department Detective Jeff Dunaway (for imparting his wealth of experience in police work and the world of crime), and in no particular order for their support and friendship: Bill Clark, Jim Grate, Barbara Heyward, Joe Luca, Susan Overman, Team America Plus One; and especially to my family for their support through my whining and whimpering.

Prologue

A QUESTION BEFORE WE START. Have you ever seen a dead body? I don't mean a body that has died of natural causes. Nor do I refer to the type that was killed and later gussied up by a funeral team, laid out in a coffin, looking more like Keith Richards than themselves. Not that kind of dead body. I mean the freshly murdered kind. I have. Four of them. And I can tell you each time I clap my eyes on one it's a shock. I don't know if morbid curiosity is a normal reaction to shock (probably not), but that's how it is with me. The story you are about to read is about my fourth corpse. Okay, the first dead body I didn't see in the flesh, but I saw it being murdered on a kinky VHS tape, so I count it.

I'm sort of like the hero in an Agatha Christie novel if you can imagine Bugs Bunny solving crimes in rural English parlors. Jane Marple and I do have one thing in common though—we're both inquisitive, or, if you're a stickler, nosy.

My name is Annie Fillmore, I'm 50 years old, the divorced mother of two children, ages 22 and 20. I work as a mortgage loan officer for EFB (Everybody's Favorite Bank) in Cincinnati, Ohio. Why the mortgage business? I just stumbled into it like most everything else in my life. I envy those kids who at 12 or 13 know exactly what they want to do when they grow up (or at least their mothers or fathers know). Or those people who say, "I knew the moment I saw her/him we were going to be together the rest of our lives." How nice for them. As for me, it's been potluck.

1

I was aided and abetted with the solving of the first three murders I stumbled upon by my younger friend, Marilyn Monroe, nee Klotzman, who became a dead movie star when she married Mike Monroe. I would like to say she was my Dr. Watson, or even my Archie Goodwin; but because I am no Sherlock Holmes or even Nero Wolfe, I'll say she and I are more like Laurel and Hardy. *We* have most of the laughs though. The audience seems unamused, especially when it includes cops trying to do their jobs and solve crimes.

I don't believe in voodoo, or sorcery, or witchcraft; I don't even know if those are the same thing. But I was brought up by two aunts who are true believers in all of the above and more, and that belief has manifested itself in my daily life. No matter how hard I try to free myself from it, like static electricity it takes hold of my skirt and rides up my tuchis, leaving me both trapped and exposed.

Aunt Helen's and Aunt Emilie's favorite admonition to me was "go with your gut." I was about three the first time I heard it, and I didn't even know where my gut was. From some of my choices you'd think I still don't know where it is, but every now and again my gut guides me to some good surprise endings.

I'll tell you about the other murders later. I read magazines from front to back, too, so you'll have to read about the last first. Heck, maybe there will even be more dead bodies. I think there could be. I feel it in my gut.

Chapter 1

Friday, April 5, 2013 (morning)

THE AROMA OF FRESHLY BREWED coffee from my timed machine wafted up to my loft at the same moment my Bose radio went off playing NPR's *Morning Edition*. Six a.m. Way too early for my natural clock. But I need both of those dastardly coffee and clock technologies to root me out of my favorite place—bed. My aunts used to wake me: "Annie dear, Annie dear, Annie dear," until getting out of bed was less irritating than their annoying sing-songy insistence. My ex-husband sometimes roused me—and almost stopped my heart—by kicking the bed soundly. A real charmer. The only thing that ever got me out of bed in one bounce was the crying of Humphrey or Ingrid, my two delectable infants. When they visit these days, I have to wake them: "Humphrey dear, Ingrid, dear."

This morning, I drifted in and out of sleep until *Storycorps* came on the radio. What's the United States' problem with Mexicans? This morning's story was about this natural-born American guy who was deported from the United States eighty years ago at the age of six because he was a child of Mexicans. He was only able to return when he joined the U.S. Army. That pissed me off and got me on my feet. It also helped that it was Friday and I had a lovely, leisurely weekend to look forward to.

Or so I thought.

~

I wheeled my black Honda Civic into the parking lot of

EFB about 8:30 that morning, a little earlier than usual. I like to get in as late as I can without being fired; but I had to re-lock some loan rates so they wouldn't expire. After ten years of working there, I still felt that I was pulling into the parking lot of a funeral home. The building is an enormous mansion built circa 1903 in the Italian Renaissance style and too ornate for my simpler tastes. I wouldn't have been surprised if one of the Addams Family emerged from the porte-cochère that shadows the massive carved double doors, but, alas, it was just normal looking employees who came in and out, not Gomez or Morticia.

I made my way from the parking lot across the circular driveway and through the ornate door under the portico. The two guards sitting at the decidedly un-Renaissance-like security desk nodded their good morning hellos in unison as their one-size-fits-all security-guard hats bobbed up and down on their heads. Their starched grey uniforms didn't match the grandeur of the entry hall with its red-wool carpeted staircase and soaring columns that reached the gilded ceiling.

The upper reaches were for the executives like our chief honcho, Homer Doukas. The rest of us made our way to a descending metal staircase down the hall to the left of the grand entry into the "rabbit hole," so named by my associate and friend, Sophie Sugarman.

I autopiloted my way down the stairs to the mortgage department door, where I fumbled with my security badge to swipe myself into a land of cubes, "home" to about 160 workers. About 50 of us were mortgage loan officers—others were processors, underwriters, closers, and support staff. Some of the operations team was located on a loft that hung over the main floor. Wasting no space, two office cubes sat under the wide staircase that connected the loft to the floor. It being a balcony, there was the joker who would occasionally call out, "Romeo, Romeo, where the hell are you?" to the entertainment of the busy workers below.

First things first: I locked the two loans that were set to expire that day. Then as I was stuffing my purse into my drawer, I looked up from my cube and caught a glimpse of a dark smudge in my peripheral vision coming from Al Markey's office. Revelers had filled it with black balloons to celebrate his 60th birthday that day. Although loan officers' offices were open-air cubes, the VPs desks sat in what looked like fish tanks. Some of these tanks in our corporate aquarium might have held barracudas, but I'm afraid Al's held a toothless shark. I think his teeth were extracted the day he started working at EFB.

The night before, there had been a bit of hoopla about the advent of Al's birthday, and folks were tapping black balloons over the glass walls of his office as I was walking out the door. Al was our VP of Mortgage Sales and was well liked for his humor and conviviality; but his title might have been The Messenger (as in, don't shoot the…), since he was so often the bearer of bad news from upper management. For the rest of us, younger women with a lot more enthusiasm for celebrations than I have, typically would hang black crepe paper and a skull and crossbones motif over desks, even if the celebrant was only 30 years old.

Al was returning from vacation that day for some important meeting upstairs and to celebrate his birthday with his flock no doubt.

"Morning, Annie. You're early," said Chad, my team manager, who was always at his desk at 8 a.m. "What brings you here on time?"

"Ha ha. I'm usually pretty close, aren't I?" Knowing darn well I wasn't.

"If you call nine-thirty close, I guess so," he chided. "You know Kevin is here at seven every day?"

Kevin was one of those hotshots who were at their desks improbably early to get a head start on making money. I wasn't one of those hotshots. I found it worthwhile in the morning to sit on my couch, put my feet up on the coffee table, enjoy a cup of coffee, and read *The New York Times* before slogging down 71, the highway that turned a 20-minute jaunt into an hour ride due to the pain-in-the-ass bumper-to-bumper traffic.

We early birds mingled outside Al's door, waiting for the birthday boy while swapping family news and regular news that was pretty much all about gun control that morning. I inched away from the conversation about arming teachers.

"Look at the shoes under the balloons," hissed Jessica, a Beyoncé look-alike on our team.

Sure enough a pair of brown shoes pointed out from under the balloons toward the ceiling like a wing-tipped banker Wicked Witch of the East.

"Maybe somebody got tanked in there after they found Al's bottle of vodka," chortled Rick, our team's self-appointed spokesman.

"Like anybody could get into the glass vault without a key or sledge hammer," Jonah chimed in. Jonah was our team go-to guy for anything we didn't know about mortgage minutiae.

As more team members trickled in, they joined us outside Al's door, waiting to kid him about turning 60 and for a few good laughs.

Sophie Sugarman whooshed in about 9:10 with her four bags and her purse. Sophie was our most senior team member at about 65. As for the bags, she said you never knew if we might get stuck down the "rabbit hole" and would need supplies to survive the stultifying air and fluorescent lights that were more than likely ruining our eyes day by day. As it was, Sophie wore sunglasses and a green accountant's visor "to forestall blindness." We never knew what she carried in those four bags, but I personally hoped that if we were imprisoned by a natural disaster, Sophie would have something with her to save me. I'd known Sophie before EFB. She was one of my favorite customers at the video store I owned. We were both from New York City, and we shared a special bond and understanding of each other and the world. I seemed to have lost most of my New York accent, but Solphie's Yiddish expressions persisted, along with a hint of Brooklynese.

"What's goin' on heah?" Sophie asked as she elbowed her way to the middle of the rubberneckers.

"Somebody filled Al's office with balloons and put his shoes under them like in the Wizard of Oz," offered Rick.

"Oh, yeah, they were puttin' the balloons in there when I left last night," Sophie said. "It was Noah and three of his gals."

Noah was the Manager of the Loan Officers' Assistants, and, believe it or not, the Assistants' Assistants. Management wanted to improve the process of getting loans from the Loan Officers' original application to closing, and hiring assistants for assistants was one of their clever solutions for expediting the operation.

Noah was also the go-to guy for unhappy customers, and there were plenty of them. If Noah couldn't assuage the customers' anger, the call would go up the chain to the complaint line, coyly named "What's on Your Mind Line". The acronym WOYML translated on the floor to the "Why Me? Line."

As CEO of the Mortgage Division, Homer Doukas would take the flak from the top brass, and taking the blame for anything wasn't Homer's cup of hemlock. To wit:

TO: SALES

FROM: Homer Doukas

I take no comfort in informing you that our Customer Displeasure Quota is through the roof and the WOYML has had to field calls from customers who are not happy with <u>your</u> inability to get their loans closed. I understand that there are some issues in the process of getting the loans to close, but it is your responsibility to see that these problems are overcome. I have zero interest in having to explain loans not getting closed due to your inefficiency. I don't care how you do it, just do it.

If you would like to discuss this further, please contact Al Markey, he is aware of my feelings on this subject.

Seriously? The fault fell right in corporate's lap. They had no idea how things worked down on the sales floor, but they came up with quick fixes to problems that weren't fixable by their quick fixes. Then they quickly fixed it again with another hare-brained idea the following week. Right. Nothing gets fixed.

"So, who put the shoes under the balloons?" somebody

asked Sophie.

"I left at eight, and they were still blowing them up and shooting them over the wall. I didn't see them throw shoes over, but I was on the phone so I probably missed it." She nudged her way closer to the glass, "Well, they're shoes, but they ain't Al's shoes." she said in exaggerated New Yorkese.

"Huh?" somebody grunted.

"Al never wears brown shoes; they're black shoes every day whether it's jeans day or suit day."

That's the kind of thing that Sophie would notice. She paid attention to the sartorial fillips, but not as much attention to the endless daily loan updates and changes made by EFB or Fannie Mae or Freddie Mac.

Phones began to ring, and we retreated from the puzzle of the glass office back to our cubes. We figured Al's plane had arrived late. He's sleeping in we thought. He's entitled. And there was that important meeting at 3 p.m., so we guessed he'd be in no later than 2.

But the birthday boy didn't show up at 2.

The day wore on in the usual way. Fridays weren't as busy as earlier in the week, when home owners would often come to the realization that they should call to see if they could get a lower interest rate (interest rates *were* historically low) after reading the Sunday papers or listening to the news.

My phone rang, and I gave my usual spiel when I punched in to take the call: "Thank you for calling EFB. This is Annie. How may I help you?"

"Who's Jackson?" said the brash voice on the other end of the line.

"Jackson? Is that a last name or a first name, sir?" I asked.

"How the hell should I know? Would he call himself by his last name?"

"We don't have a Loan Officer with the first name of Jackson, sir," I said.

"Okay, then his last name is Jackson," he stated.

I quickly looked at the alphabetical list of the fifty Loan Officers on the floor, but there was no Jackson.

"I'm sorry, sir, there's nobody here with the last name of

Jackson either," I said.

"Jackson, Jackson," he yelled in my ear.

*1MUTE: *Michael Jackson? Janet Jackson? LaToya Jackson? Tito Jackson? Gimme a break.*

"He's from Chicago. Look up the name of Jackson in Chicago. Are you smart enough to do that?"

MUTE: *Smart enough to get you off my phone, you blockhead.*

"One moment, sir, I'll transfer you," I said, which meant he'd have to be rude to Noah.

At 2:50, Al breezed in, and folks started blowing party tooters and throwing confetti. He checked out his balloon-infested office and made a kind of "aw shucks" face, not that easy for a guy about 6' with slicked-back black hair, killer tan, and grey pin-striped suit; but he pulled it off.

"Oh, you guys are the best. Who could ask for a better crew than you? I have to get up to the third floor for the meeting, but I'll be back down, and we can really celebrate," he said.

An hour later, Al re-emerged through the door into the "rabbit hole," and said, "Homer was a no-show. I've never known him not to show up for a meeting without any notice. What the hell?"

Noah stepped up to the plate and said, "Well, let's at least get these balloons out of your office so you can get to your desk."

Sadie and Angie obediently followed him into the office to remove the balloons they had spent a few hours putting in there the previous evening.

As it was, the balloons were starting to deflate, and they no longer reached the top of the glass wall. Noah and the assistants started to punch the balloons that were near the top over the wall; they floated to the floor like swollen black vultures. They popped the rest of the balloons and shoved them into a black plastic garbage bag.

---

1 *Mute: It was the custom of some Loan Officers, me included, to press our MUTE buttons on our phones to make comments aloud for each other's amusement when customers got abrasive or in some other way pulled our chains; and I have taken to thinking "Mute" whenever I have a thought I know I should keep to myself.

I don't remember exactly how long they were in there getting rid of the balloons before a high-pitched screech discharged like a siren from Angie's open mouth. Everyone who sat near Al's office bolted to the door, only to see that the brown shoes under the balloons were not a gag or a prop but worn by Homer Doukas's now-dead feet. Homer's white hair matched his egg white pallor, and his stocky body looked as if a taxidermist had gotten to him. The other people on my team, who probably had never seen a dead body up close and personal, seemed to have an even more dramatic reaction than my gulp, with our hotshot, Kevin, hitting the floor knees first.

"Get out of the office, stand away," Al said calmly. But his robust tan had faded, and from the sweat beads on his forehead, I thought he was going to faint. We stood back, but by this time almost everybody on the floor had gathered around those of us who were up close and able to see the hideous look on Homer's face and a dagger sticking out of his chest; the blood, looking like a map of Texas on his white shirt, pooled down onto the grey pebbly carpet. We were like pillars of salt, unable to move—except for Sophie, who ran to call 911 as soon as she saw what had happened.

There's no corporate protocol for waiting around for police to arrive when the CEO of your company has just been found dead under a jumble of balloons. Al stood outside his office door with the rest of us. Nobody said a word, which was mighty unusual. There wasn't a sound except the unanswered ringing phones. Finally, Al made a call on Jonah's phone to someone to have the phones turned off; then there was dead silence until a policeman pounded on our door, ignoring the sign on the door saying, DO NOT KNOCK. YOU MUST HAVE A SECURITY BADGE FOR ENTRY THROUGH THIS DOOR. To be fair to the officer, I always knocked, too, every time I forgot my badge.

Al opened the door and showed the cop to his office and Homer's dead body. Officer Creighton, as he announced, got on his phone immediately, and it seemed like only minutes before a phalanx of police poured in. The man at the head of the brigade and clearly in charge introduced himself as Detective

Aaron Jamison. He was about 5'9", stocky, and looked as strong as one of those bulls you see running the streets of Pamplona. He had fierce blue eyes.

Shortly after Detective Jamison assessed the situation, the Coroner arrived. The Coroner was a woman, and all business. She and Detective Jamison conversed, and I sure wished I had supersonic hearing to hear if she was giving him an estimate of time of death. That would have been interesting, and, maybe, telling; but, as I've already established, I'm not Sherlock Holmes, or even Columbo; and I don't know what I would have done with that information.

A police photographer was snapping his camera over what seemed like every inch of Homer's body, Al's office, and the surrounding area. The office was no longer a pristine crime scene—Noah and the girls had been in there, Al was in there, and potentially 160 people may have tread on carpet that could have presented clues. That was surely going to muck things up.

It was a toss-up between whether I wanted to get the heck out of there or stay to see the developments. What if someone ran up and screamed, *"Yes, I killed him. I killed him for money and for a woman. I didn't get the money and I didn't get the woman. Pretty, isn't it?"* like Fred McMurray said in *Double Indemnity*. I did mention I owned a video store at one time, didn't I? I've seen lots of movies.

The ten of us on Chad's team were told not to leave the building until we were interviewed, because we were the first ones who had seen the body discovered under the balloons. We hunkered down for what we thought would be a long wait, and I, at least, eyed Sophie's four bags.

Detective Jamison commandeered Room A-7, halfway down the hall to the Bra, as an interview room. The Brasserie, aka the Bra, was our cafeteria, which was at the end of what seemed to be a football field-length hall, with meeting rooms along the way. We all stood around not knowing exactly what to say after being so traumatized.

As names were called to go down the hall to be interviewed by Detective Jamison, the rest of us tried to talk through what could have happened (and how the hell Homer

Doukas ended up with a dagger in his heart under a mountain of balloons). To be one hundred percent honest, the fact of the dagger through Homer's heart was less of a mystery than was how someone got him under the balloons. Homer was hated by just about everybody except those whose asses he kissed, i.e., those above him in the pecking order. He was a loud-mouthed bully, and just about everybody I knew would walk a mile to avoid meeting him face-to-face, because invariably he would have something nasty to say.

Names were being called alphabetically, and I finally walked down the hall to A-7 about 7:00 o'clock.

Detective Jamison stood when I entered the small room, and asked me to take a seat.

"Miss Fillmore?" he asked.

"You can call me Annie, but I guess I go by Ms. Fillmore," I said.

"Ms. Fillmore, can you please tell me exactly what you saw, starting the minute you came to work this morning?"

"Well, I came in about eight-thirty, a little earlier than I usually get here," I said.

"Why was that? Why did you come in earlier than usual?" he asked.

"I had some loan rates I had to lock. If the rates expire, then customers have to take the rate of that day even if it is higher, and customers don't like that as you can imagine," I said.

"Right. So you came in to lock your loan rates, then what did you do?"

"I noticed that Al Markey's office was filled with black balloons to celebrate his birthday and a few people were standing outside his office, so I went up to join them for a few minutes," I replied.

"What did you notice when you were outside of Mr. Markey's office?" he asked.

"As someone pointed out, there was a pair of brown shoes sticking out," I said.

"Did you think the shoes were a joke?"

"Yes, I thought it was a joke about the Wicked Witch from

the *Wizard of Oz*. Kind of making a joke that Al was a witch, which he wasn't."

MUTE: *A witch which he wasn't? Time for a drink.*

"Then what did you do?" he asked.

"I stood with the rest of the guys outside Al's office waiting for him, and then Sophie came in. She noticed the shoes were brown, and she said that Al never wore brown shoes, only black shoes, which I guess is true if she said it, because she notices things like that," I said.

"That would be Sophie Sugarman?" he asked.

"Yes."

"Did you still think at that point that the shoes were just a joke?"

"Yes."

"Then what happened?" he asked.

MUTE: *"Listen, Jocko, you got things all tangled up. You don't ask me questions, I ask you. See? See?"*

"Then we waited until Al came in, and he did, I think about two forty-five," I said.

"Okay, let's go to when Mr. Markey returned from the meeting that Mr. Doukas didn't show up for," he said.

"Noah and Angie and Sadie started getting the balloons out of Al's office, and I heard a shriek, and looked up and saw there was a body on the floor of the office. I still thought it was just shoes until I got to outside of the office and saw that the shoes were attached to Mr. Doukas."

"How long, approximately, do you think they were in the office getting rid of the balloons?" he asked.

"I don't know, it couldn't have been long, maybe five minutes, or seven minutes, something like that."

He stood up. "Thank you, Ms. Fillmore. Please make yourself available over the weekend if more questions are required of you. I'm sure it won't be until next week, but just in case," he said, shaking my hand.

I was so happy to be out of there, I practically flew up the stairs and out the door to my car, happy to have the drive time to decompress before I got home. Or better, to Marilyn's, where I would surely receive the commiseration to which I was so indubitably entitled.

You'd think.

Chapter 2

Friday, April 5, 2013 (evening)

I CALLED MARILYN ON MY cell from my car. The conversation went something like this:

"Marilyn, you'll never believe what happened today. Can I stop by on my way home to tell you about it?"

"Oh, God, Annie, I'm so glad you called. Archie disappeared."

"Okay, we have a lot to talk about, but I have to say right now, we may see Archie again, but we'll never see Homer Doukas again."

"Do you want to see him again? Whatever, get here as fast as you can, but drive slowly."

At 8 p.m., 71 North was a piece of cake but for the annoying semis hogging the left-hand fast lane, and I got to Marilyn's in Mason by 8:32.

Twenty-eight fifty-eight Chandler Lane looked like Coney Island on the 4th of July. Every light in the house must have been on. You didn't have to feel your way gingerly up the walk, because with the spotlights, path lights, and carriage lights ablaze it seemed like you were on a Hollywood red carpet.

Jackson, age 6, opened the storm door; the house door already stood ajar. "Hi, Annie," he said, running in front of me. "Archie ran away. Even if he's in heaven you can still talk to him, you just can't see him."

Jackson had no sounds when he was born; he learned to

speak with the help of a speech therapist at about 3 years. He has other disabilities that he has to deal with, but he also has an interesting point of view and a hell of a sense of humor.

Andrew, age 5, came up, hugged my legs, and said, "Aren't you sad, Annie, we don't have Archie anymore?"

I never figured having your boss murdered a few feet away from you could take a back seat story-wise, but this is just what was happening: A missing dog took precedence over a dead Homer.

I made my way to the kitchen, sidestepping whatever obstacles were on the floor. Marilyn's house is the most consistently messy home that I visit, including my neighbor's with the five cats. She has her face in a book when she isn't seeing to piles of laundry, scouring bathrooms, tending kids who look and sound like they were about to kill each other, running around doing errands for Mike—who is a builder—and, of course, taking Archie for walks up the nearby trail. Picking up doesn't make the short list. They have one of those invisible fences, and she has to remove the collar that comes with the fence and replace it with a regular collar when taking Archie for walks. I always think it has to be confusing for Archie, and although I know other dogs who understand the drill, I've seen Archie try to make his way through the invisible fence, only to see him bouncing back as if he had run into a glass wall. He's a beagle with strong hound tendencies, and my guess is he would like nothing better than to roam around the world sniffing for food.

While Marilyn is good at keeping the boys on the straight and narrow, when it comes to Archie she is insufferable. Whatever trouble he gets into, she finds a good reason why it is okay.

"Well, he's a hound, for heaven's sake, that's what he's bred to do, find food," she'd said when he was found grazing on the turkey ON the table one Thanksgiving. I know she loves those three boys and Mike as much as a mother and wife can, but I always wonder if Archie isn't #1 in her heart.

A word about the boys' names: Mike had discovered through his mother's crack at genealogy that he may have been related to Andrew Jackson on his mother's side of the family. He named the first two boys after his supposed ancestor, and then Marilyn decided she wanted her shot naming the third. She decided to pay homage to her glamorous namesake, even though it's her married name, and called their third Norman after Marilyn Monroe's real first name, Norma Jean.

I found her in the kitchen sitting at the table with her head in her hands, crying, with 3-year-old Norman playing with his cars at her feet. She looked up as I entered the kitchen; her eyes were red and puffy, and she looked bedraggled.

"What happened?" I asked.

"He's gone." She sniffed. "My golden boy is gone."

MUTE: *She must have let her membership lapse in the Optimist Club.*

She called him her "golden boy" because he was a lemon beagle, not the normal white with brown and black spots, but white with pale tan spots.

"How long has he been gone?" I asked, trying to sound hopeful.

"I think since around the time the plumber was here this morning, about 10 o'clock. He was asleep under the oak tree the last time I saw him." She sniffed. "I drove around the neighborhood, walked up the trail, asked everyone I saw if they had seen him, and nobody has. He's gone."

"He's been gone before, Mar, before you had the electrocuting fence," I noted.

"Electric Fence," she corrected me. "It's probably the fence that kept him safe this long."

She was probably right. Archie would run any time he had a chance and could be away for as long as a few days. Once he came back with a fully packaged ham in his mouth. When he threw up a pile of beans the next day, they knew he had at least had the pleasure of several courses. They thought the electric fence was their only defense against a wayfaring beagle.

"I've called the police, and they told me that when an animal whose lot is protected by an electric fence is missing, it has sometimes been a dog-napping, or a wild animal has come on the property," she said, even more agitated.

"You don't have bear in the neighborhood, and Archie is pretty fat to be whisked away by a squirrel or a raccoon."

Archie definitely could have benefited from Weight Watchers. Marilyn's teenage neighbors called him Electrolux, and there was a resemblance.

"I don't know what else to do," she said.

"Did you call the plumber to see if he hopped into his truck?" I asked.

"No, actually, I didn't think of that. I'll call him right now," she said.

The noise emanating from Jackson and Andrew playing their video game in the TV room was so loud that I could barely hear her on the phone, but I got the drift that the plumber's lunch was missing from his van.

"Are you sure he wasn't in the van when you left, Drew? Can you please look to make sure he's not locked in there?"

"Okay, I'll wait," she said, turning to me with her fingers crossed.

"No? Okay, well, please keep a look out for him in case he did go for a ride with you, and you didn't realize it," she said.

She plopped her lanky 5'8" frame down in the chair, her short blond hair looking like she had taken an eggbeater to it.

"What's this about never seeing that jackass Homer Doukas again?" she asked, finally changing the subject.

"He's off to join the big bank in the sky."

"What?"

MUTE: *Dead, bought the farm, gone to meet his maker, pushing up daisies, kaput.*

"He was found murdered," I said more seriously.

"What?" she shrieked, "What do you mean, murdered? Oh, my God, Annie, dead bodies find you no matter where you are, even in a bank."

Her scream must have scared Norman, because he started stuffing the mini cars in his pockets, and carried the rest in his pudgy little hands to the less threatening racket of the TV room and his yelling brothers.

I spun the whole story for her: Balloons, Al's return, Homer's body, the questioning by Detective Jamison.

"What kind of questions did he ask you?" she asked, her eyes wide-open.

"Did you kill him?" I exaggerated.

"They think you did it?" she asked.

"They think everybody did it until they can find out who did do it, just like in those thousands of crime novels you read."

"Maybe it's like the plot of the *Murder on the Orient Express* where everybody took a shot at him," she said.

"I don't think so. I think it was one lone crazy like Oswald."

"You think Oswald was alone?" she asked.

"Marilyn?"

"Right. How are we going to find the killer?"

MUTE: *We're going to need "hints and allegations." And if Paul Simon can't find him for us, we might just be out of luck.*

"Marilyn, *we* are not going to do anything. *We* are going to leave it in the very capable hands of Detective Jamison," I stated with finality.

"You're just being coy. You know you're going to nose around and find out what happened, and I, of course, am here to help, as always," she offered.

I stifled a guffaw, because Marilyn's idea of helping me is to ask a million questions and nudge me into danger while she is safely hiding behind the proverbial bush. But she is a faithful Indian companion, for sure.

"Have you eaten dinner? At the very least let me get you a glass of wine," she suggested, heading for the refrigerator. "Mike had to give a quote to a potential client after work, so he hasn't eaten yet, and I've saved him dinner. I have plenty, you know, from the Crock-Pot," she said.

She ladled out a heaping spoon of chili into a bowl, grabbed some crackers, and I was set. When you live alone like me, it's mighty nice to know you have an alternative home or two so that you can count on a meal that's not in a wrapper.

Norman came running back into the room, "Mommy, where Archie?"

Then Marilyn's tears started again.

I tried to console her, rocking her on my shoulder, but the

tears kept coming, until a blood curdling scream came from the TV room.

"Mommy, Mommy, help," cried one of the kids.

Marilyn and I ran into the room to find Andrew with his head stuck between the metal slats of a dining-room chair back.

"Oh, my God, are you okay, can you breathe?" She crouched down eye-to-eye level with Andrew. "No, I can't breathe," he screamed, clearly breathing.

"Just be calm, sweetie. Mommy will try to slide your head out," Marilyn said.

But no matter which way he turned his head, he couldn't get it out from between the slats.

"Maybe if I butter his head," she said.

"Butter his head? You mean like you put butter on your finger to get a ring off?"

"Yeah., Do you think that will work?" she asked.

"I guess it's worth a try. But what time will Mike be home? Maybe he can jimmy the slat to loosen it," I suggested.

"I don't want to be a butter head," Andrew screamed.

"It's okay, honey, it won't hurt. It will feel like Mommy's washing your hair," she said, hugging the part of his body that wasn't stuck in a chair.

MUTE: *Butter the kids head? He'll feel like he's about to be cooked, not like his hair is going to be washed.*

"How about lotion? I think lotion will have the same slippery effect, won't it?" I asked.

"I don't want lotion. I want butter," Andrew sobbed.

I got the tub of butter from the refrigerator and brought it in to Dr. Monroe to perform the "chair-ectomy."

"I don't want butter," yelled the, by now, fully agitated Andrew.

"It's okay, Andrew. Mommy will be sure it doesn't hurt," Marilyn cooed.

As Marilyn was buttering Andrew's head, Mike walked in.

"Don't tell me. Let me guess. Uh, you were taming a lion with the chair, the lion shoved you into the chair slats, and, uh, the only thing that will make you feel better is butter on your head?" said Mike.

"Noooo, Daddy, that's not what happened," cried Andrew.

Jackson and Norman were standing by, quietly for the first time ever, I think, mouths hanging open.

Mike walked over to the chair and bent the slat about an inch, enough for Andrew to slip out his head.

The boys ran back into the TV room, and started playing Super Mario; even Butter Head.

I said my good-byes, so tired I was sure there wasn't any way I could drive without dozing off.

Thank God, the next day was Saturday so I could sleep in and take a brisk walk around the lake my condo sits across from. It's about a two-and-a-half-mile walk, and surely that would get rid of some of today's tension. When I first moved to Lakeview and Humphrey came to visit after a summer in NYC, he clearly frowned upon the lake. "It's man-made," he said by way of objection. "Oh, I forgot that the Empire State Building sprouted up from the ground like organic wheat."

Anyway. What a day: a murder, a missing dog, and a buttered head.

Chapter 3

AND I MIGHT HAVE BEEN able to sleep late had I not received a hysterical call from Sophie on Saturday morning at 7 a.m. I'm an early riser, but a call at 7 a.m. always sounds like a blade screeching down a guillotine.

"Oy Gevalt. They think I did it, they think I killed Homer," she said, stifling a sob.

"What? Why on earth would they think that?"

"It wasn't a dagga' like we thought, it was one of my antique letta' openers," she replied.

Everybody decorated their cube in their own way, most with family photos, or team slogans, but Sophie's only decoration was a rectangular box that held knives that Sophie used for her elegant if lethal, apparently, letter openers stuck into some kind of silicone stuff in a wooden base.

"I put one of my openers on Al's desk as a birthday gift. The one with the bone handle I bought when I was in New York last year. I wrapped it in black ribbon around the handle, you know, keeping with the theme. Oh, my God, my letter opener killed Homer," she sobbed. "He was such a schmendrik, but I still don't like it that my opener killed him."

"Well, you didn't kill him, and aside from his being dead, that's all that matters right now. Try not to worry about it. I know we are in good hands with Detective Jamison, but if it makes you feel better, it won't hurt to snoop around a little on our own. Please try not to think too much about it anymore today," I said.

"Are you meshuga? I'm not going to stop thinking about it until they find out who did this," she said obstinately.

"Oh, and Marilyn's worried, too. Archie ran away, or was taken, but he isn't at home, and she's frantic, so I have two worried friends."

Archie? That annoying mutt? She should be glad he ran away. And how can you compare a runaway dog with being a murder suspect? Marilyn may be worried, but I'm freaking out."

"Okay, freak out, Sophie. I'll see you Monday morning."

MUTE: *What am I saying? I'm going to be a butinski? Again? Sophie put me in a Yiddish mood.*

I got out of bed, parted the cream-colored Ikea bedroom curtains to determine what the weather was like in southern Ohio on April 6. Flat grey skies reached over the trees across the fields to the horizon. "The Beast" loomed like the skeleton of a hunched dinosaur. I live within spitting distance of Kings Island Amusement Park (if you could spit a quarter of a mile) where a roller coaster named The Beast resides. I squinted to see the burgeoning buds on the trees that line the condominium property. Yep, the portent of a full spring put a smile on my face. Crocus had already bloomed, the daffodils had sprung, hyacinths were about to pop up, and the forsythia were yellowing the neighborhood. With the pear and crabapple trees flourishing, I had to wonder what precisely T.S. Elliot meant by "April is the cruelest month." Let's just say it's open to interpretation. He may never have been in southern Ohio in February.

I padded down the steps to the kitchen to pour my coffee before I dared to even think of what might have happened to Homer. Sudden banging on the front door made a chill run up my spine. What now?

Marilyn stood in the doorway holding Archie's "electric" collar in her hand.

"Mike found this under one of the shrubs at the front of the house, so he really is dead or going to be dead, maybe already made into an Archie pie," she howled, with tears starting to flow.

Marilyn could go from A to Z without any stops at any of the other nice letters in the alphabet. Her reasoning was direct: from good to horrible, there was no in-between for her.

"Mar, there could be a lot of reasons why his collar is off, and only one of them is the worst possible one. Before you start saying your Novenas to St. Anthony, let's think of what else might have happened besides Archie being ground up into a pie," I said.

"Don't say anything so terrible," she cried.

MUTE: *Jeezle peats as they say in this part of the world.*

"Maybe the first thing you should do is contact all the animal shelters in the area to see if he was picked up and being held," I said. At the very least this might keep her from abandoning her family in a global search for Archie. "He had all his tags on, right?"

"Wrong," she answered. "They were behind the shrubbery along with this collar."

"Then just tell them what he looks like when you call, and they will know if he has been picked up."

MUTE: *My description: yellow beagle looks like a canine zeppelin.*

"That's what Mike said, too, but I wanted to see if you had any other ideas," she said.

"I think that's your best bet right now. Also, I'm trying to help Sophie out as well. The dagger that killed Homer turns out to be one of Sophie's antique letter openers, and the police are looking at her."

"Well, I guess you have two awful crimes on your plate right now, so I'll let you do whatever it is you do to solve crimes," she said, "and, of course, I'm here for you when you need my help."

MUTE: *Eye roll.*

You would think with the specter of the murder of Homer Doukas, the possible suspicion of my friend Sophie as murderer, and the drama of the missing Archie, I would have cancelled my haircut appointment. But, alas, you would be wrong.

Joe Luca at Harrigan and Crew was the guy who has cut

my hair for several years, and a nicer guy you could never meet, not to mention a great hair cutter. He cuts a lot of expensive heads in Cincinnati, mine not being one of those, but I am convinced he did every bit as good a job on me as he did on the wife of the president of EFB or any of the other luminaries in Cincinnati whose hair he might have cut.

Once seated, I let out a whoosh of air.

"What's up?" Joe asked, looking at me looking at him in the mirror.

"You'll never believe what happened yesterday at EFB," I said. "Actually, I'm surprised it's not all over the news already."

"What?"

"Homer Doukas, the president of the Mortgage Division of EFB was murdered," I said, just waiting for his expression of amazement in the mirror.

"No, he wasn't," was his surprising answer.

"Yes, he was. I saw him," I said, with a bit of triumph in my voice that I couldn't cover.

"I just cut Mrs. Doukas's hair, and she didn't say a word about it. She said she was going to a special event tonight," he said. "Maybe she's in shock."

"Maybe she's just going out to celebrate," I said uncharitably.

"Why? Isn't he a nice guy?"

"No, he wasn't a nice guy. How old do you think his wife is?" I asked.

"Hard to say, but she's lovely, maybe mid-thirties," he offered.

"Yikes. Homer is, I mean was, late sixties and not a looker," I said.

"These people aren't like you and me, Annie. Money can buy things like a thirty-year-old wife when you're in your sixties."

"Did she seem upset, or nervous, or different than she usually seems?" I asked.

"No. She is always a little quiet and reserved and calm, and that's how she was this morning," he said.

"Valium," I muttered. "She'd need it being married to

someone like him."

"That's just a guess on your part," he ventured.

"Maybe. But I wouldn't be at all surprised if I were dead-on—excuse the expression."

"Do you know anything about them?" I asked.

Joe was not the kind of hairdresser who would gossip about his clients, unfortunately, but this was different. I never asked him about his other clients, but if he knew anything that could help the police, or help me help the police, he needed to fess up.

"Honestly, I know nothing about them except that they live in Indian Hill. Crystal has spent almost two years remodeling the eight-bedroom mansion to her taste. She said it's been a nightmare getting the kitchen countertops just right. She had them install and remove granite tops three times and then found out that poured concrete was much trendier, so she had them install that: the poor builder. But that's all. She's not one to share, or even talk to me at all except complaining about the redo of the house. I have to say it's unusual, because most women and men whose hair I cut divulge something about their lives. But, wait a minute, she did say she'd come right here from the airport, that she'd spent the week in Chicago."

That made sense, the police probably wanted to let her know first that her husband had been murdered before the news went public.

"Can you believe we're even having this conversation?" I said.

"If it's true," he replied, putting the finishing spritz on my hair.

"I wish it weren't true, but it is."

"Remember that time you told me Sofia Vergara was killed by a falling icicle from the Empire State Building?"

"That was just a very vivid dream. This is a real life nightmare."

My hair looked great. Joe agreed not to say anything to anybody until the news broke for the rest of Cincinnati, and knowing him, he wouldn't.

I hated spending the day cleaning my house with my hair

looking so good, but I had to bite the bullet, and I put the cleaning time to good use thinking about who could have had the opportunity to kill Homer.

There was probably a murderer walking around town, and that was no joke. There were so many people who probably wanted Homer dead, but who could have been able to do it? Of course, I didn't know at this point what the police knew, and I was pretty sure they weren't going to share that information with a busybody who could very well be a suspect herself. The most likely suspect would be his wife, but how could she have killed him in Al's office? Why would they have been in Al's office? It might have been a ploy that she was in Chicago, but easy enough for the police to check out.

My brain hurt from the mental meddling, and my back hurt from all the uncharacteristic deep cleaning, so about 4 o'clock I took a break to go to a mindless movie: *Identity Thief.* Movies take my mind off reality, but they seem more real to me than the fact of sitting in a cube all day working as a mortgage loan officer in a bank. Although most identity thefts do not end up with people taking a road trip together; most that I know of end up with people trying for years to get their lives straightened out again.

~

The phone was ringing when I returned home at about 6:30. I picked it up in my office. It was the Cincinnati Police Department "requesting" I come down to pay them a visit; they had a few more questions they wanted to ask me.

"You mean now?" I asked.

"Yes, ma'am, now."

"What if I hadn't answered the phone?"

"You did answer the phone," he stated.

"I live up in Warren County. What station do you want me to go to on a Saturday night?" I didn't add, on date-night Saturday night, because it was just too pathetic.

"Please announce yourself at our District 1 Headquarters downtown," he said.

"Okay. I'll be down as soon as traffic will allow," I said. I also didn't say I'd be there more quickly if they actually enforced no trucks in the fast lane on 71, but I thought I'd better leave that for the nonce.

I arrived at District 1 about twenty-five minutes later. The building was right across from the back of the stately Music Hall, and I thought about all the criminals who walked through those police doors, but would never walk through the gorgeous Music Hall doors to be uplifted by one of the country's finest symphony orchestras.

It looked like a typical police department that I saw on TV or in the movies, not glamorous; but once I was there I would have liked to have explored to see what the police dealt with every day.

Detective Jamison greeted me cordially, and was nice enough not to show me to an interview room where "perps" were questioned, but to a more civilized, carpeted room.

"What can you tell us about Sophie Sugarman?" asked Detective Jamison. He bent his head slightly forward and looked at me with what seemed to be a laser focus, and I could imagine that even if someone dared lie to him, he would know instantly.

"I can tell you she is a very good person: kind, funny, divorced, is a grandmother, has a great family. Is that what you mean?" I asked.

"We've heard from a few others that she does not follow orders very well and parks in no-parking zones."

MUTE: *No-parking zones? Get out the leg irons.*

"Well, I don't know about no-parking zones; she has been known to park in the executive spaces if the weather is bad. Her thinking is she is older than any of them, and they should be courteous enough to allow her to park nearer the building," I said, trying to sound reasonable.

"But she's breaking the rules."

"Okay, she's a bit of a rule breaker, but definitely not a murderer," I said.

"Do you think she's a little bit off?" he asked.

"What do you mean by a little bit off?"

"Somebody said she writes messages on cardboard and

holds them out of her car window," he replied.

"Oh, that. Yes, she is a bit batty about traffic. You have to understand that she's from New York City, and anybody who has lived in New York City is going to seem odd to a conservative midwesterner," I explained. "I should know, I'm an expatriate New Yorker myself. Anyway, the messages at first were kind of a joke that she found worked pretty well. Like most of us, she doesn't like it if somebody is riding on her ass, I mean bumper. We were discussing it one day at lunch, and she said she wished she had one of those digital signs on the back of her car that she could program to let people know what she thought of their driving. She did have the good sense, however, to admit that it would be just as dangerous to be typing messages as it would be to send text messages while driving. But then one day when I was following her for lunch, she held a cardboard sign out her window that said, GET OFF OF MY ASS, YOU MORON. We had a good laugh about it when we were sitting at lunch over our soup."

"But she has continued with it," he said.

"She told me after that she was going to try it to see if it had any effect, and it apparently did, because the car riding on her back one day slowed down and backed off, so she decided to write a whole bunch of different signs for what she calls "infractions." She wrote them on white poster board instead of the cardboard because she thought it would show up better," I added.

He shook his head as if I were talking about some lunatic.

"We will deal with that later. Does she have any other eccentricities that might mean she was confused?" he asked.

"If you mean is she eccentric enough to murder Homer Doukas, I'd have to say definitively, categorically no," I said, trying to look as aghast as I actually was.

"And, you are not aware of any psychological disorders she may be suffering from?"

"None. She's as sane as the rest of us," I said.

MUTE: *That should leave some room for interpretation along with* The Waste Land.

"Had she and Mr. Doukas had any run-ins?" he asked.

29

"None that I know of. They weren't best friends, but nobody I know was friends with Mr. Doukas."

I wondered if I should mention that Sophie told me that what we thought was a dagger was really her letter opener. What the hell, if Jason Bateman could go after an identity thief, I could ask this simple question.

"Sophie called me this morning very upset that you discovered that the dagger was really one of her letter openers," I brazenly ventured.

"Why do you think the letter opener was in Mr. Markey's office, as she states," he asked.

"She tied a black ribbon around it, and gave it to Al Markey, as a birthday gift. She and Mr. Markey got along very well, and it was a nice gesture on her part to give him something she liked so much," I said with a hint of indignation.

"She didn't exactly give it to Mr. Markey, did she?"

"No, she put it on his desk I believe," I replied.

"There was no card or note with it, was there?"

"I have no idea, but he would have known it came from Sophie, because everybody kidded her about her collection of letter openers when we almost never had any letters to open," I said.

"Why do you think she collects letter openers?"

"Everybody finds beauty in different things, Detective. Sophie finds it in antique letter openers," I answered.

One of my aunts would have argued that a letter opener held an important place for her in a past life. I felt confident that Detective Jamison would not share this view, and I kept that little notion to myself since it might have diverted the subject of Sophie's being peculiar to my being peculiar.

He asked me some questions about my familiarity with ways of getting in and out of the building, and I told him that the only ways I got in or out were by the main front entry or by the rear near the Bra.

Talking about it got me wondering whether someone could get in and out by a window that wasn't covered by alarms. Maybe they could have gotten in on the first floor, but the second floor is too high to scale. I would have to pry a little to find out if the windows could be opened.

I was free to go, and happy to comply. It's just not pleasant sitting in a police station on a Saturday night being grilled about the sanity one of your best friends.

MUTE: *Sophie, that ganef.*

Chapter 4

Sunday, April 7, 3013

I DIDN'T SLEEP IN AGAIN on Sunday morning due to Marilyn's 7:30 a.m. wake-up call.

"I know you're up reading *The New York Times*," she said.

"*The New York Times* doesn't arrive in my driveway until eight on weekends, so, no, I'm not up, and no, I'm not reading *The Times*," I answered groggily.

"Oh, sorry. Anyway, do you want to come with me to the animal shelters today? None of the shelters I called yesterday had Archie. Please?"

"Okay. Do you want to head out after ten o'clock?"

"Ten? Oh, all right. You folks without children sure know how to take care of yourselves."

I didn't bother to remind her that I had already raised two children, who were happily living on their own, and that's what happens after they fly away. You get to enjoy mornings, wake up in the middle of the night and walk around your house naked if you want, and have wild and crazy sex in any room at any time. Okay, that last one never happens, but, I suppose it could. My luck on Match.com and eHarmony has not delivered anyone who might meet the requirements for wild and crazy sex. I know lots of people who have met partners online; and I have met some nice men, but none with whom I'd like to dangle from a chandelier, if that's something people actually do. I peeked through the drapes to see another grey day, but the open window let in some pleasant warm air. One of the things I like about Cincinnati is that the winters are shorter than the New York winters I knew. That April morning turned out to be a soft 60 degrees, and a pale sun managed to spill a little light onto the southern Ohio day. Mind you, when I look out the window in April, I am very happy to see only grey skies, because it wasn't that many years since a tornado touched down within a half mile of my bed; so grey skies are fine with me, with or without sun.

Marilyn was knocking at my door at precisely 10 a.m. with a list of Cincinnati animal shelters in one hand and a map in the other.

"Where should we start?" she asked.

I looked at the map, and the closest shelter to Lakeview, where I live, seemed to be the SPCA on School Road in Sharonville, about ten minutes away.

We made our way down Montgomery Road, busy with traffic even on a Sunday morning, and made our first stop at the shelter.

It's an impressive place with a large lobby; it even has a fireplace at the end of the room. And it's spotless. Marilyn asked the gentleman at the desk if they had picked up a lemon beagle in the last few days.

"Not that I know of, but you're welcome to look in the kennels to see if he might have snuck in when I wasn't here. I'm only here Sundays and Tuesdays," Bob said, or at least that's what his name tag said his name was.

He pointed to the dog kennels, and we made our way into kennel #1 where the barking was loud and insistent.

"Oh, my God, these poor puppies!" exclaimed Marilyn.

It was overwhelming at first, but as we walked past the cages, none of the dogs in them looked like puppies to me. They were, for the most part, big, and the tags showed they were a mix of mixed breeds. They all had lovely faces, and even in just a few minutes you could tell they had different personalities. It was a heart-breaking tour to see them jumping and wagging at us. One huge brown-and-white-spotted pit bull jumped so high, he reached the top of the glass door of his cage. A golden retriever had her face pressed against her glass door, looking at us mournfully as we passed. I had to read every tag just to show I cared, though we weren't going to be leaving with any of these deserving dogs.

"I'm going to take a quick look in all the kennels to see if Archie may be in one of these cages," Marilyn said. "I'll meet you in the lobby."

I couldn't see myself spending an entire day crying over every dog in Cincinnati that needed a home, but I felt guilty even thinking of myself instead of the needy dogs. What about them? The one who got to me the most was a large white boxer mix whose tag said DEAF. He had one brown eye with the white showing, and the other eye totally black. He just sat there, looking sweet, not being bothered by the howls and barks of his fellow inmates.

I reluctantly left the kennel and made my way out to the lobby to meet Marilyn, who was nowhere in sight.

"Have you seen my friend?" I asked Bob.

"I did see her come out, but I don't know where she went. Maybe in to see the cats?" he ventured.

I went through to the cats, mostly kittens, but she wasn't there either.

Just as I was about to check the car, I passed a window to a large room where, I assumed, volunteers would spend time petting and playing with the animals, and there she was on the floor with one kitten on her shoulder and another in her lap.

I knocked on the window, and she put her finger up for me to wait. I quickly went around to the other side, opened the door, and had to block a kitten from escaping.

"It's going to be a long day, Marilyn, if we spend as much time at each shelter as we have spent here," I said.

"I know, but look at these sweet babies," she said holding the tiniest one up to her face.

"But that's not what we're here for. We have to move on if you want to find Archie," I stated.

She reluctantly rose and walked with me out the door.

When I turned the key in the ignition I looked at the car clock. It read 11:33. It was going to be a long day.

"Okay, the next place is the Scratching Post on Plainfield," said Marilyn.

"The Scratching Post?" I asked.

"Yep."

"Do you think the Scratching Post might just be for cats?"

"Oh, yeah, right, that makes sense," she replied sheepishly.

"The next one is Save the Animal Foundation on Red Bank."

About twenty-five minutes later, we found ourselves outside a shelter that wasn't open: this one was open on Thursdays and Saturdays. I was getting the idea that these shelters were run by volunteers who otherwise have full-time jobs.

"Before we move on to the next one, why don't we call ahead to make sure they are open," I suggested.

"Good idea. But since we are so close to Indian Hill, do you want to drive by the Doukas's house to see what it's like?" Marilyn asked.

"Why? Why do you want to do that? The guy's dead, and his wife is probably entertaining a new lover as we speak. Why spoil her fun," I said in jest.

"Oh, you are a mean bitch."

"And you are a nosy one," I countered. "And I have no idea where he lives in Indian Hill."

"Two three four five Pudding Lane," she said. "It's off of Indian Hill Road someplace."

"Wow, you have certainly been a busy little detective, haven't you?"

"I figured you needed a little push, and this is a good place to start," she said, looking very pleased with herself.

"What kind of a street name is Pudding Lane?" she asked.

"Maybe it was named by someone who went to Harvard and belonged to the Hasty Pudding Club," I suggested.

"You're just making that up," Marilyn scoffed.

A lazy Sunday drive through Indian Hill isn't the worst thing, unless the sight of nothing but sprawling mansions and horse farms depresses you. The gentle sloping hills and massive trees sequester the stately homes nestled into at least three or four acres apiece. The budding trees and new spring growth was amplified in this setting, and it seemed as if some of the roadside plants were lit from within. Knowing what these homes cost, the light was probably from gold nuggets.

"Can you believe these places?" asked Marilyn. "I've never seen houses like these except in magazines and movies."

"I've never lived in one, but I've been in a few, and I've been through this neighborhood many times," I replied.

"Can you imagine living in one of these places?" she asked.

"Not really."

And why couldn't I imagine myself having the maid fix me a small, freshly squeezed orange juice before I took off in jodhpurs for a morning trot through the estate? Or would it be an amble, not a trot? Hell, I don't even know the difference. I wonder if it's as simple as *really* wanting to be rich that would thrust you in that direction. "Never mind" I told myself, I should keep my mind on the less fanciful facts of life, like finding a missing beagle.

"Annie, do you hear me? We just passed Pudding Lane," Marilyn said, interrupting my reverie.

"I guess I was daydreaming," I said.

"Daydreaming while you're driving is not exactly a safe thing to be doing," complained Marilyn, whom I'm surprised doesn't actually read while she drives.

I drove a few miles before I could find a driveway to turn around in, and it was a shallow turn at that because of the wrought iron gate defending the home from the onslaught of the masses. I headed back, slowed up, and took a left onto Pudding Lane per Marilyn's screeching insistence.

We drove another mile or so before we saw the 2345 on the imposing post that held the mailbox, and I pulled over short of the driveway due to the red and white barricade tape that cordoned off access.

"Here it is," I said. "Is this what you wanted to see?"

"We at least have to get out and look around, don't ya think?"

"No, I don't think. You've seen the house. It's way too big for two people. It's even too big for a family of six. Isn't that enough information? I'm not going a step farther."

"Come on, what's the harm of a little peek in the window?"

She was uncharacteristically brazen despite the tape at the end of the driveway.

"It would come under the heading of trespassing, and I wouldn't be surprised if there are police cars hidden somewhere."

"Okay, you stay here and keep watch. I'll skirt around the side to see if I see anything out of the ordinary," she whispered.

MUTE: *Whispered. I kid you not.*

She made her way around the right side of the house, where pristine lawn abutted a woodland. She kept to the edge of the woodland, and when she was directly across from the middle of the house, she tiptoed over and peered into the window. She must have read all the Nancy Drew books as a young girl. Then she let out a silent screech à la Edvard Munch and motioned me over. I didn't waste any time daintily sidling at the edge of the grass; I just bolted from my lookout position. I fully expected that she was seeing Crystal Doukas hanging from a mahogany ceiling fan; but in fact it was something much less dire, at least to my eyes. We were looking through white plantation shutters into what seemed to be a dining room, but there was nobody there, nothing that I could see that was alarming.

"What are you so excited about?" I asked.

"Look at the wallpaper," she jeered.

"What about it?"

"Wha-at? It's wallpaper bookshelves. Have you ever seen anything so tacky? The books aren't real; it's just wallpaper," she said.

She had a point, but I don't think I would have alerted the guard on watch with such frenzy.

"Different strokes," I murmured.

"But in a house this huge?"

"Hey, you don't have to be poor to have lousy taste," I said. "Let's get the hell out of here. I do not feel good about this at all."

The wallpaper must have done her in, because she left without another word. We got in my car and started back down

Pudding Lane, headed for Indian Hill Road, when I spotted a black Escalade right on my tail. I could see two guys in the front seat, both with sunglasses, and they followed much too closely.

MUTE: *Where were Sophie's infraction signs?*

"Mar, don't turn around. Look in your side view mirror and check out these guys behind us. I think they're following us," I said, with my eye on the rearview mirror.

She turned around.

"Can you see their license plates?" I asked.

"They're too close. Can't you speed up?" she replied.

I put my foot on the accelerator, and Marilyn said, "No front-end plates; they must be from Kentucky."

"Or Indiana," I said.

"It's probably Kentucky. They look like they're from Kentucky," she said, eyes now glued to the side view mirror.

"What makes them look like Kentucky?"

"They're wearing sunglasses, and it looks like they're smoking."

They kept up with us, and I took a right turn into the next driveway and thanked God there was no privacy gate. I drove right around the circular drive up to the front door. Marilyn and I leaped out of the car, and I rang the doorbell. The Escalade stood at the foot of the driveway.

"May I help you?" asked the guy at the door, who sported a light blue velour jogging suit.

"Yes," I gasped. "That Escalade at the end of your driveway has been following me and my friend, and I think they are up to no good, and I need to call the police. May we come in?" I asked.

Thank heavens he wasn't a fraidy cat and let us right in.

"Do you need to use my phone?" he asked.

"I have a cell. I can use that, but thank you so much," I replied.

"No, I insist, please use my phone right here," he said, pointing to a discreet phone on a small carved table that abutted the staircase. "Actually, just push the POLICE button, and it will patch you right through. While you're calling, may I offer you a beverage? Coffee, soft drink, wine?" he said gallantly.

That blue velour jogging suit was growing on me.

"Wine would be nice, what with the shock and everything," Marilyn replied.

MUTE: *Just the bottle with two straws, please.*

I was indeed "patched through" to the police, and I briefly told them my problem. They were well aware of my location and said they'd send someone right over. I didn't even think, at that point, to look to see if the Escalade was still there as I was so taken with my new surroundings. Although the carved crown molding, engraved ceiling, and marble floor were impressive, what struck me the most was that it was all so shiny and clean; I bet there was not one speck of dust to be found.

Marilyn gawked at the two-story sweeping staircase with a niche halfway up the stairs displaying a carved figure of a supine woman. "Can you guess how long that little lady would last in my house?"

"Until one of the boys put her in their Lego fort, or Archie bit off her head?"

Our host came out with a tray with three glasses and a bottle of wine.

"Please go on through to the family room," he said.

Straight ahead was the family room with a floor-to-ceiling stone fireplace that had a fire in it, with two plush, paisley-covered couches sitting to either side of the hearth. Our host set the tray on a mahogany coffee table with graceful carved legs.

"I'm Stu Jenkins," he said.

I introduced myself and Marilyn, and there was the usual jocularity about Marilyn's name—always an icebreaker. I didn't mention that we'd been trespassing at his dead neighbor's home, but did say the Escalade was at my bumper for about a mile, and when I sped up it sped up, and we were frightened.

"Very sound decision coming into the drive, very sound indeed," he said.

Unless, I thought, way too late, he was the one who murdered Homer: They *were* neighbors.

"Do you live in the area?" he asked.

"No, we're just out for a Sunday drive, enjoying the balmy weather," I replied.

Conversation about the weather in April ensued until the doorbell rang and a policeman arrived.

"Do come in, Officer," I heard Stu say. He was gallant to everybody, probably too old for me, but I did wonder if there was a Mrs. Jenkins.

"Good afternoon, sir. I'm Officer Eufer. I'm sorry for the disturbance you've encountered, but I don't see the Escalade at the end of the driveway that the lady mentioned," he said.

"Thank you for being so prompt, Officer. I'm glad that I was home to let them in. I decided to stay behind when Mrs. Jenkins went off to see the grandchildren this morning."

MUTE: *So much for my Indian Hill future.*

"Do come in and meet Mrs. Fillmore and Mrs. Monroe who have endured the incident," he continued.

Too bad about the Mrs., I really was getting used to Stu's charming ways, and the wine didn't hurt.

We told Officer Eufer as much as we could. I didn't tell him we were snooping, but I did tell him about my closeness to the Doukas murder and said I wondered if being followed by the Escalade had any relevance. That snapped him to a level of attention to which he hadn't ascended earlier.

We said our good-byes to Stu, thanked him profusely for his help, and made our way back down Indian Hill Road out to 71 North toward the more pedestrian parts of town.

On the way home, the thought of a guy like Stu in my life reminded me that I had a date Monday night with a "connection" from Match.com.

"Did I tell you I have a date with a guy from Match?" I asked Marilyn.

"It's about time that paid off. Is he the first guy you've met on there?"

"No I've met others; but I haven't met this one yet," I said.

"What's he sound like?"

"His name is Marlon; he looks kind of cute from his pictures."

"Marlon? Like Marlon Brando?" she asked, sounding more enthusiastic.

"Brando in his early years would be fine, but too much to love later on."

"Stella. Stella," she said. So delightfully predictable.

By this time it was 2:30; Marilyn needed to get home to her family, and I needed to get home to the Sunday *Times*. Marilyn without Archie, me without Stu.

Chapter 5

Monday April 8, 2013 (morning)

THE TRAFFIC WAS BUMPER TO bumper Monday morning as I got off 71 and started toward Incline Street and EFB. The pleasant 63 degree temperature brought a shroud of humidity that seemed to be the hallmark of warm Cincinnati weather. It curled my hair as if I were on a bayou. When I finally reached EFB at 9:17 a.m., the only parking place that was not filled was Homer's, and I thought it might be in bad taste to take that one. I pulled over on the grass as a few others had done and got out of my car. A media ant colony swarmed over the property—I didn't watch much local TV, but I recognized a few familiar faces talking into cameras, while others were rushing EFB employees to interview them. I was almost instantly accosted by a reporter, from a Dayton station if her badge was to be believed.

"Good morning. Were you present when they found the deceased's body on Friday?" she asked.

"I'm not at liberty to speak to the press," I answered, guessing I wasn't at liberty to speak to anyone.

Snaking my way among the crowd, I heard, but did not see, Sophie saying, "This is a crime scene he-ah, no questions please." You have to love a New Yorker, or at least I do.

I made my way through the great doors, and the lobby was as busy as the parking lot. Three security guards at the front desk were on their feet, conferring, and I would have bet they were saying "Murder? That's above my pay grade." But, I'm sure they didn't have to worry about solving Homer's slaying.

I ambled along the hall and down the steps, into the "murder chamber" as I now thought of it. It seemed the whole floor was on its feet powwowing.

Troy Whitman, who sat across from me, said, "Don't get comfortable. We're all going down to the town hall at nine-thirty for a conversation with Detective Jamison."

In truth, Troy could have been considered a suspect, because he and Homer did not get along. Not too many weeks earlier, a customer called in to the What's on Your Mind Line and said that Troy had told him that his loan process was going to take a long, long time and may not even close. The conversation was reported to Homer, who came down and stuck his finger in Troy's face, saying, "Don't you ever tell our customers that their loans may not close." Troy, the nonchalant sort with a simmering anger underneath, replied, "The loan *may* not close, so why not give them a heads up? And, if you don't take your freaking finger out of my face, I'm going to shove it up your nose."

Homer said, "You have not heard the end of this, Mister. Your days here are numbered."

Troy replied, "I think there are enough people around us who just heard what happened, and I'm only too happy to go to HR about it. In fact, that's just where I'm going after you get out of my face." Nothing came of it as far as I know, but it was common knowledge on the floor that Troy would have happily decked Homer if given the chance—and vice versa.

Now, as we were waiting around for the 9:30 meeting with Detective Jamison, Troy said, "Heh, heh, looks like somebody beat me to it."

"That's not funny, Troy, and I'm pretty sure you don't want to be heard saying that to anybody else," I said.

"Whatever, he got what he deserved. Let's get going down there to see what the cops have to say."

I pulled Sophie out of her cube, and she, Troy, and I walked down the hall, to the Town Hall, which was located across from the Bra. We must have made quite a trio from behind: Sophie about 5'2" in heels, with her nicely coifed blond bob, me also about 5' 2"in flats with my humidity-prone brown curls bouncing as I walked, and Troy about 6'1", shaved head, and slinking between us looking like Kojak between an aging Cagney and Lacey.

The Town Hall auditorium was already packed, so we grabbed the only available seats in the back row. Detective Jamison was on the stage with four other police personnel. Al Markey and Erwin Richter, Vice President of EFB Consumer Bank, were in the first row with other "suits," whose names I didn't know.

After about ten minutes it was standing-room only and Detective Jamison called for attention.

"Good morning, ladies and gentlemen; I'm Detective Jamison, and I'm heading up the investigation of this heinous crime that has befallen EFB and its employees. Mr. Doukas was a respected officer of the bank, and our Criminal Investigation Section is doing everything possible to find out who is responsible for this atrocity. In this particular case, we are going to rely heavily on employees of EFB for any and all information you may have no matter how inconsequential you think it may be. I refer to this crime as a "closed door crime" because on the face of it, it appears it had to be perpetrated by someone inside the building. I am not ruling out an outsider, but our early investigation points to an inside crime. With that in mind, please be ready to speak with me or one of my officers when requested. We, of course, want to bring the murderer to justice as quickly as possible. I want to remind you this isn't a television show, this is a serious crime; and to think in terms of TV police dramas would be counter-productive.

"Also, sadly, one of EFB's maintenance staff, Rodney Wilkins, has been missing, we believe, since at or about the same time as the murder of Mr. Doukas. Again, any information you might have about Mr. Wilkins's whereabouts should be brought to my attention immediately. At this time, Mr. Wilkins is listed as a Missing Person.

"I can be found in Meeting Room A-Seven. I will be calling individuals to interview, but I will be available to speak to each of you if you have information, or if you noticed anything out of the ordinary, no matter how small and insignificant it may seem.

"Thank you, ladies and gentlemen. That's all for now."

The room came alive with a loud hum, as more than 160 of us poked our way across the seats and up the aisles, exchanging speculations on who might have done in Homer, while making our way back to the cubes.

When I got back to my desk, I took a deep breath, started my computer, and went directly to my e-mails. There were hundreds of them since 3:30 on Friday when the unthinkable had happened. The last was from Detective Jamison:

Please come to Room A-7 immediately.

"Uh oh," I don't know why I thought "Uh oh," but I always seem to; and in this case there was a valid reason for an Uh oh, thanks to Marilyn Monroe.

Al Markey was seated opposite Detective Jamison as I knocked on the glass wall. The detective said something to him, and Al got up; as he came out the door, he gave me a hug. "These are smart guys. They'll get to the bottom of this," he said. He looked like hell, and I can't say that I was surprised—it was his office where Homer was found.

"Please have a seat, Ms. Fillmore," Detective Jamison said, motioning me to the chair Al had just vacated. He sat there and looked at me for what seemed like five minutes, but was probably more like a few seconds. "Ms. Fillmore, I've heard a lot about you this weekend," he said with an expression I was trying to pinpoint.

"Yes? All good, I hope," I said, well, hopefully.

"I guess that depends upon your point of view. Some of it could be construed as good, some of it I would construe as not so good," he replied, with an expression that was easier to understand—deadly serious.

"So good news, bad news, is that what you're saying?" I asked.

"Not exactly. Let me get to the point, because as you know we have a murder to unravel." He pulled a folder in front of him with my name on it. Geez, it looked as thick as my folder at my doctor's office. "First, I see you called in an incident to the Indian Hill Police from a Mr. Stuart Jenkins's residence on Sunday, yesterday," he said looking at me intensely.

"Yes. As soon as I had a chance, I was going to speak to you about that. It was pretty scary."

"We are, of course, interested in why that car was following you seemingly out of the blue, but for the fact that Mr. Homer Doukas's home is next to the Jenkins property." He continued, "Do you want to explain to me how you happened to be on Mr. Doukas's street, when you live in"—he looked at the folder—"Lakeview, roughly twenty miles north of the Doukas's home?"

I could have said I was out for a Sunday drive, and I could have gone into the fact that I was out looking for a missing beagle, but I thought better of it. "I have a good friend for some years who has been through a lot with me, and when I told her about Mr. Doukas's murder, she decided we should pay a visit to the home to see if we could see anything out of the ordinary," I stammered.

"Ms. Fillmore, I'm sure that explains the other information I have gathered about you that you have been involved with not one, not two, but three other murder cases. Am I correct?" he asked.

MUTE: *As Jane Marple might have said to him: My reputation, Detective Jamison, if I have one, and how very kind of you to suggest I do, is neither here nor there.*

"Well, yes, it is strange, I know; but it's true."

"And in these other murder cases, am I to believe you also decided to see if you 'could see anything out of the ordinary'?"

"I guess it depends upon which murder you are referring to," I replied.

"Sweet Jesus"— he ran his fingers through his salt-and-pepper hair— "the way I look at it is that you were very, very lucky in three other instances not to become collateral damage—that, incidentally, means harmed. You were lucky you weren't killed. And besides you could have complicated each situation to make even more work for the police you were trying to help," he growled, looking as if he were at the end of his tether. "That's not going to happen in this case. Do you understand?"

"Yes, sir."

"So, let's go back to when you were followed by this Escalade whose license plates you were unable to make out," he said.

"When we left the Doukas residence, I immediately noticed this Escalade on my tail. I sped up in order to get away, but also so my friend, Marilyn, could jot down the license plate numbers, but there were no front-end license plates. When the Escalade didn't back off, and I knew my Honda wasn't going to get away from them, I pulled into the first driveway I saw, and, luckily, the gentleman, Mr. Jenkins, was hospitable and invited us in, and let us call the police," I explained.

He wasn't taking notes, but maybe I was being taped.

"We will attempt to find out who the Escalade belongs to. We are, of course, talking to Mrs. Doukas, and it seems that the Escalade might have thought you were Mrs. Doukas. She is staying at a safe place at the moment, because we don't know the motive behind this murder. "However"— he continued— "that Escalade does not know you are not Mrs. Doukas, so you may be in danger. I want you to put my personal number on your cell phone, and if you see that car again, I want you to call me immediately while getting to a safe, populated area as quickly as you can. If that fails, I want you to drive to the nearest police station. Until we know who these folks are, I would advise staying on main thoroughfares. Am I clear?" He scratched his cell phone number on the back of his card and slid it across the desk to me. "In the meantime, as you seem to have an eye and an ear for murder, what is your first thought about who might have wanted Mr. Doukas dead?"

"He wasn't well liked within the Mortgage Sales Department, and I can think of a lot of people who didn't particularly like him, but I can't think of one of them who would stoop to murder. "Also"—I continued, hitting my stride— "I wonder if they not only wanted to get rid of Homer, but also to frame Al Markey. It was his office, and even though he was on vacation, I'm sure that puts him in a bad light," I said.

"Yes, we are investigating that closely. I understand you can't imagine anybody you know who might have killed Mr. Doukas, but what I would like from you by the end of the day is a list, in writing, not via e-mail, of those people you know who really didn't like him." He stood, extended his hand, and said, "I'll be back in touch, but I couldn't be more serious when I tell you, do not get involved in this. I don't want to have this meeting again with somebody else about who may have killed you."

MUTE: *So gloomy.*

The first thing I wanted to do when I returned to my desk was to write the list for the detective, but as I thought about it, there were so many people who really hated Homer. I, myself, didn't like him for his anger issues and his lack of respect for what I believed loan officers, processors, and underwriters did to make the bank money. He was a greedy bastard. Giving names to Detective Jamison also had the stink of McCarthyism, that revolting blight on our history back in the 1950s, when thousands of people were named as Communist sympathizers and ratted out by their friends. Nope. Somebody could give names, but it wasn't going to be me. However, I did take the opportunity to write a list for myself of those people I knew who really, really didn't like Homer. Troy Whitman, for reasons I have already stated. Jan Mulligan, the head of our Underwriting Department, was constantly in battle with Homer about denying loans. Loan officers did jokingly refer to the Underwriting Department as the No-Sale Department. But we were fully aware of the hundreds of guidelines loans had to adhere to in order to be sold to Fannie Mae or Freddie Mac, the government-sponsored enterprises to which big banks sell their loans. Gender was no deterrent for Homer, he was as nasty to Jan as he was to Troy—one conflict ended in Jan telling Homer to "Get stuffed." Naturally, Homer didn't hear her, but that was the measure of her dislike for him.

There was also a customer, Mr. Harlans, who, after having a loan in the system for over 120 days, couldn't close on the purchase of his house with EFB because his credit score had gone down in those four months, making him ineligible. When he found out he couldn't close on the house, he called and left a message for Rick that said, "I'm going to come up there and kill you, and then I'm going to kill the guy in charge, and it won't be a quick death." It would have been a stretch for him to get to Cincinnati and get into EFB, as he lived in South Carolina, but stranger things have happened. Others could be on the list, but these were the three with the biggest ax to grind, or letter opener to thrust. Mrs. Doukas, of course, and whoever was driving the Escalade were honorable mentions.

The phones did not stop ringing for the rest of the day, some from callers wanting to refinance or finance a new home. But most of the calls I received were from people wanting to know the scoop on our murdered CEO. About 4 o'clock I received another e-mail from Detective Jamison:

Ms. Fillmore, please come to A-7 at your earliest opportunity.

I dropped everything, and headed over to A-7. This time Alice Mayview was in the hot seat. Alice was Homer's administrative assistant and had arrived at EFB the same day I did. We went through a three-day training period together and remained friendly, occasionally having lunch together in the Bra. She was a nosy Nora; knew a lot, but kept it to herself. I again knocked on the glass wall, and Alice rose and came out the door. "Sorry," she whispered to me as she passed.

No preamble this time; he got right to the point. "Do you remember what you wore to work last Thursday and Friday, Ms. Fillmore?" he asked. I was stunned for a moment as I tried to think what this question could mean. I searched my wardrobe memory.

"On Thursday, I believe I wore black pants, grey sweater, and a grey blouse. On Friday, I wore a black pants, black sweater."

"The reason I'm asking," he said, "is because…"

"May I?" I interrupted. He nodded for me to proceed. "The reason you are asking is because Alice Mayview, told you I sometimes wear the same clothes on Thursday and Friday. Right?"

"Correct," he said.

"On Thursday nights, I sometimes go down to Dee Felice on Mainstrasse in Covington to hear a little jazz, The Lee Stolar Trio to be precise, with my friend Jim Grate. He owns a two-family house. The rental part is unoccupied, and he graciously offers me a bed for the night so I don't have to drive all the way back to Lakeview. That's probably more information than you need to know, but just to be perfectly straight about it, I didn't go last Thursday evening."

"What did you do last Thursday evening?" he asked.

"I picked up some Chipotle, went home, and read."

"Did anybody know you were at home?" he inquired.

"I guess my e-mails could be traced for date and time. I'm sure I wrote e-mails."

"Thank you. Do you have the list we spoke of earlier?" he asked.

"I don't have the list. I'd have to name everybody in the department, and that just doesn't seem helpful," I replied.

"I will decide what's helpful," he insisted.

"I don't have the list you want unless you want me to write everybody's name in the department," I said, hunkering down.

"That won't be necessary. I get your point. Thank you, again, Ms. Fillmore; I'm sure we'll speak again," he said, standing to let me know I was dismissed.

Chapter 6

Monday, April 8, 2013 (evening)

INDEED, I DID SEE Detective Jamison again, several times; but not that Monday.

My cell phone rang in my car on the way home. It was Debbie Markey, Al's wife. We took a Yoga class on Wednesday evenings, so we were yoga friends.

MUTE: *Hot yoga on Wednesday, cool scotch on Thursday.*

"Annie, what's going on?" she asked.

"I probably know less than you know, Debbie," I replied. "It's been terrible, and I can't imagine how Al feels or is taking it."

"He's pretty banged up about it. I've never seen him in a worse way, and we've been married for thirty-eight years. Of course, nothing like this has ever happened to us, or to him— and in his own office." She let out a whoosh of breath.

"I'm so sorry, Debbie. Is there anything I can do?" I asked.

"Can you meet me for dinner? The police are all over the house, and I just need a break."

"I'm just leaving work, so I'm close to Hyde Park if you want me to meet you there," I offered.

"How about the Wild Ginger place on Edwards, do you know that?" she asked.

"Sure. I'll head that way."

I found a table at Wild Ginger, a great little Thai restaurant with charming décor that also offers great sushi, and waited for Debbie.

She arrived at the restaurant about ten minutes later, looking harried. Debbie was about the same age as Al, I would guess, and has taken very good care of herself. She's a platinum blonde, and a woman who looks like she's from Cincinnati; I can't put my finger on it exactly, but women of a certain social class in Cincinnati dress well, but cuter than what I was used to in NYC: pastels vs. earth tones.

"I took the liberty of ordering you a white wine," I said.

"Oh, my God, thank you; white wine, perfect," she said, exhaling.

"What are the police doing at your house? Do you know what they are looking for?" I asked.

"I think they are looking for anything that might implicate Al or rule him out. I don't know when they think he would have been able to do it; we got home late from the airport, and he was asleep next to me until we both woke up the next day about eleven o'clock. They've been very thorough, and it really does feel like an invasion of our privacy even though Al gave them his permission. I mean they don't have probable cause or anything like that."

"I know that a murder not only affects the victim, it has arms that grab just about everybody who knew the victim, and then fingers to pinch people around those people," I said.

"The ripple effect," she stated, much more succinctly than I.

"I probably shouldn't be telling you this, but last weekend when Marilyn and I were out looking for her missing beagle, we were followed by a black Escalade that, for some reason, I thought may have had something to do with Homer's murder," I offered.

"You're probably just paranoid, but I know something like this can play tricks with your mind. When the police asked Al if he had a license for the gun he kept in his bedside table, he said he did have a license, but when the police held the gun up, it wasn't the same gun that I had seen in there a few months ago. It always gives me the shivers whenever I see the gun in there; it looks so menacing. The one I saw was a little silver thing, but the one the policeman held up was brown and black. I think it was a revolver, because it had one of those round barrels you see in Westerns," she said, leaning back in her chair. "When I asked Al about it, he said he has a few different guns, and he likes to change it up once in a while. Anyway, Homer wasn't shot, so it makes no difference I guess."

"Well, the police are looking into the Escalade, so who knows," I said. I didn't mention the little tidbit about Marilyn and me looking in Homer's windows, so she wouldn't think it had any relevance.

"Poor Crystal, she's in a terrible way, too," Debbie said.

"Have you spoken to Crystal? Detective Jamison told me she was in a safe house, or at least a safe place."

"Yes, she is, and I have no idea where that is, but she did call me to ask me what was going on," she replied.

"Does she have any idea at all who might have done this?"

"No, she doesn't, but she did hint that there were things about Homer nobody knew, and that she thought he had secrets he even kept from her."

"Has she told the police this? Did you ask her if she had?" I asked.

"Yes, I asked, and no, she hasn't shared this with the police. She's afraid that anything she tells them might incriminate her as well. Well, she didn't use the word 'incriminate.' Did you know Homer met her at Hooters? She was a waitress there; she's only about thirty-four. They've only been married about five years," she said.

Hooters has a bad rep, and when she mentioned it, she lowered her voice as if she were saying something shameful.

"I know a few girls who made their way through college working at Hooters," I commented.

"Well, she wasn't one of them," she allowed.

That might explain the bookshelf wallpaper.

Once we ordered our sushi and were served, we chatted a little awkwardly about other things that were going on in our lives. But, really, when I asked how they enjoyed their trip to Aruba, it was hard not to think of Homer lying in Al's office with Sophie's black beribboned letter opener in his chest.

When I left, I thought I'd scoot around the corner and go

to Whole Foods in Rookwood Commons to pick up a few items. My refrigerator was looking even more than usual as if I were a 25-year-old bachelor—without the beer. I've tried to eat as healthy at home as I do when I'm eating out, but I've thrown away enough kale and spinach and fish to feed a small country. I finally gave up. It's a handicap: I can't cook for myself.

No sooner had I pulled out of my space on Edwards than I spotted an Escalade ahead of me doing an illegal U-turn. I went the back way to Whole Foods, and I found the closest place to the store as I could. Luckily, I found a space where I could pull through, so my nose was facing out in case I needed to make a quick getaway. I got down on the floor of the front passenger side and speed dialed Detective Jamison; but the call went to his inbox. I was hoping the Escalade guys would think I had already gone into a store and wouldn't look in my car to find me cowering on the floor. I raised my head the tiniest bit to see if I could spot them, and sure enough, they were parked directly opposite me in a handicap spot; they *were* criminals. I grabbed the first piece of paper I could find, a gas receipt, and with my eyeliner wrote down the license plate numbers. Marilyn was right, they were from Kentucky.

As I remained hunkered down, my cell rang and it was Jamison.

"Where are you?" he asked.

"I'm on the front floor of my car, and the Escalade is parked directly across from me," I whispered.

"Where?"

"Rookwood Commons. I'm in the row directly across from the entrance to Whole Foods, second car in, and they are across from me."

"Don't move. I'll have somebody there in a few minutes," he said.

I started to say, "I can't move," but he had already hung up.

It didn't seem like any more than two minutes when I heard a police siren getting nearer and nearer to me. Was this a good idea? I thought this was going to be a stealth visit; but sure enough I heard the Escalade start up, back up, and bump my front end. Bastards.

I disentangled myself from the floor and managed to lurch my way out the passenger side, feeling like I was a 90-year old arthritic—more yoga, less scotch. The police car pulled up directly in back of my car, and I walked around to the driver's side.

"Hi, Annie Fillmore. I assume you were here to find the Escalade that is following me?" I said to the policeman.

"Yeah. Where did he go?"

"Don't know. I think your sirens scared him away. He backed hard into my car," I whined.

"Huh."

"Here are the license plate numbers. Can you read them?"

"Yep. Got it. Let me call them in, then I'll follow you home. Jamison's orders," he said.

"I haven't gone shopping yet. Can I do that now?" I asked.

"Which store?"

"Whole Foods."

"Fancy. I'll come in with you just to be safe," he said.

It's just not the same going through Whole Foods with a cop. I felt a little funny about stopping at all the freebie food stations with him beside me. My Whole Foods always has samples of guacamole and chips that are impossible to resist. I can tell you from experience that if you were starving in Lakeview, Ohio, you could count on that guacamole and chips to get you through.

Even though I just ate, I can't resist free goodies, but it being Whole Foods and not Kroger I didn't feel as guilty.

I bought my few supplies, and the officer followed me up 71 and waited until I was in the door of my condo before he took off.

It was now about 8:30, and I needed to sit in a bathtub and read, or at least get my mind on something other than the miserable mess all around me. It was a nice thought until my cell phone rang, and things got a lot messier.

"Hi, is this Annie Fillmore?" a young girl asked.

"Yes, this is she."

"I hope you don't mind my calling you. This is Crystal

Doukas, and Debbie Markey said you might be able to help me." She sounded like a kid. Yuck, the thought of somebody as young-sounding as her in bed with Homer Doukas made me want to gag; actually, any woman, any age, with Homer wasn't a good visual. He had been about 40 pounds overweight and had one of those dark-lipped mouths that collected saliva when he spoke.

"Hello, Crystal. I'm so sorry for your loss, but I don't know what Debbie meant when she said I might be able to help you. What could I possibly do?" I asked.

"I don't want to talk to the police, so I'd like to hire you," she answered.

"Crystal, you can't hire me. I'm a mortgage loan officer, not a private detective. I don't have a private eye license, and we would both be breaking the law," I said, and thought Detective Jamison might just break my neck.

"I asked my attorney if I could use you, and he said there might be a loophole we could find that could cover it. He tried to get me to use a guy he knows, but I just have a good feeling about you. Debbie said you are very clever and have helped in other murder investigations."

MUTE: *Loopholes? Loopholes? I blame everything wrong with our country on loopholes; I don't want to be a loophole.*

When did I tell Debbie about the other murders? It must have been after one of our hot yoga sessions. I'll say anything after one of those as I'm sipping coconut water. Or maybe Marilyn, who also takes the Hot Yoga class, spilled the beans.

"I'm sorry, Crystal, it's just not something I feel comfortable doing, and you should probably go with the guy your attorney recommends; or, even better, speak to Detective Jamison."

"I'm not going to the police, and I don't want to use a private eye I don't even know," she said.

I didn't want to say that she didn't know me either, because for some reason she felt she did know me.

It sounded like she was whimpering when she said, "I had to live through five years of hell with that asshole, and it isn't any better now that he's dead."

"I'd like to help you in any way I can, Crystal, but I cannot do detective work," I insisted.

"What do you mean by detective work? I don't want you to find anybody. I'm not asking you even to find out who murdered Homer, but that would help. What I want you to do is to find out the secrets Homer had and let me know. I think if we know those secrets, they might lead to who killed him. But I definitely don't want to ask the police. What if it involves me in some way I may not even know about?" she said.

"What secrets would Homer have about you that would involve the police? Homer is dead, Crystal, and I think you're overreacting. How would I unearth secrets if he's not alive to divulge any?"

"He has a secret stash of stuff under some tiles in front of the hearth in the dining room. I know it's a metal box, and I know there's a key, because I saw him lock the box and put it down there," she said. "I can't remember how big it is, so either you can find a key or take the box."

"Do you have any idea where the key is?"

"I don't know. That's what I'm asking you to find out. My attorney said, legally, anything in the house is mine, so it's not like I'd be stealing it."

"No, but it is like *I'd* be stealing it," I said.

"But it's mine, and if I want you to get it for me, it's okay, right?"

"Your driveway is cordoned off with red-and-white barricade tape, so I don't think CPD is going to let me go waltzing in to take a look around. You get that, don't you?" I asked.

"Oh, I know. I hear the neighbors are furious about the tape," she said.

"But back to the fact that the police are not going to let me go into your house."

"I was hoping you would be able to figure out a way to get in without being found out."

"I don't know, Crystal, let me think about it, okay?"

"When can I call you back? I have to call you, because I don't want my guards to know I'm calling out without their permission. I feel like I'm in prison," Crystal said, moaning.

"It's for your own safety. Why don't you call me Friday?"

"Friday? No. I can't wait that long. I'll call you tomorrow," she said, and hung up.

As I was soaking in the bathtub letting the Epsom salts work its wonder (as I had read it would on Facebook), I thought about that strange conversation. Crystal may not have gone to college, but lots of murderers didn't go to college. She could have masterminded this whole thing, and the "secret stash" may have something in it that could implicate her, and that's why she didn't want the police involved. Maybe she had a background that only Homer knew about, and if he came to harm, it would prove that his wife could have been responsible. If he were dead, nobody would know that he even had a secret hiding place, and if Crystal did him in, she wasn't going to divulge any information about it. Oh, good grief, if only I could soak my head in the Epsom salts, maybe it would leech out these crazy thoughts.

The fact remained that Crystal wanted me to get into that house to look for a key to unlock the mysterious box or take the box itself, and being the kind of person who comes alive when this sort of challenge arises and doesn't come alive on a day-to-day basis when faced with mortgage conundrums, it certainly was a tantalizing prospect.

I lay there thinking through how I could get into Crystal's house, with the police probably guarding the place and with Detective Jamison knowing my proclivity for snooping, when I looked down and realized Epsom salts or no Epsom salts I was pruning up. The bath water was now cool. As I was stepping out of the tub reaching for my towel I thought, and where the hell is Rodney Wilkins?

Chapter 7

Tuesday, April 9, 2013

ANOTHER WARM APRIL DAY GREETED me as I arose from my bed. I brushed my teeth, washed my face, got dressed, and came downstairs. I love the loft in my condo, but it's open to the living space below, so everything drifts upward; coffee—good; heat—bad; noise—worse. Even when someone is in the living room reading a book, I can hear the pages turning. I would like to say it's my excellent hearing, but my children would tell you otherwise.

There was nobody reading a book that morning, so I retrieved *The New York Times* from the driveway, made my morning protein shake (my only concession to making something healthful in the kitchen), and read the newspaper until I had to peel myself away and go to work.

I stopped by my mailbox, which is a colonial-looking affair with residents' mail and package cubbies, for the mail I didn't fetch the evening before. To my wonder, there was a big poster taped to one side of the box declaring LOST DOG, with vital information and a large picture of Archie. Marilyn lives about 15 miles from me, and, although not unheard of, I thought it was a bit of a stretch for her to be looking for Archie in my neighborhood. I wondered how far afield she had posted her LOST DOG posters.

"Marilyn, it's me."

"Hi, what's up?" she asked, not sounding much happier

than the last time we spoke.

"I just found your lost dog poster by my mailbox. Don't you think it's a little far from your house?"

"I posted them as far as downtown Cincinnati, so, no, it's not that far. You have heard of the *Incredible Journey*," she said a little huffily. "I'm going to visit the rest of the animal shelters in town today, just in case he showed up at one of them."

"Have you received any calls at all about him?" I asked.

"Yes, three, but unless he's turned into a rottweiler, pug, or pit bull, it's not him." She sighed. "Oh," she continued, "how was your date last night?"

"Date? What date? Oh, no, that *was* last night wasn't it? I hope that poor guy isn't still sitting at Delhi Deli. Debbie Markey called me and wanted to have dinner, and I completely forgot about him," I said.

How could I forget the only date I've had in almost a year? I was supposed to meet Marlon at my local hangout. Delhi Deli is owned by one of my other best friends, Neil Jakhar. Maybe my heart wasn't in it. You never know about Match.com guys; some are what is advertised; some are a figment of their own imaginations. Marlon, if that was his real name, seemed to talk straight, no goofy talk about loving moonlight walks, snuggling in front of the fire, dallying in the rain together, blah blah blah. He said he was retired at 60 from owning a Garden Nursery that he sold to one of the bigger nurseries in town. And I had stood him up!

"I'll stop by double D after work to see how long the guy waited. Besides, I don't think I told Neil about Homer. I didn't have a chance to. And I'll email Marlon and fall on my sword, I guess. Marilyn, are you still there?"

"I'm here, just listening to your teenage excuses why you missed a date."

~

I arrived at EFB at about 9:10; but so much was going on with the murder, I didn't think ten minutes late would matter, and I would make it up during the day somehow, I always do.

The first e-mail I saw when I opened my Outlook, was

from Ginger Townsend, one of our processors, asking for donations for Gladys Wilkins, Rodney Wilkins' wife. She was home from a stay in the hospital, but without Rodney she was running out of money, and she needed help keeping afloat. One of the good things about EFB was that employees never let other employees swing out there alone; somebody always comes forward to aid those in need. I had no doubt that Gladys would get a nice little account to help ends meet. One had already been set up in the banking center on the second floor, and anybody who felt inclined could make a deposit. Wanting to give Gladys a helping hand, I volunteered to bring her some flowers and the check, giving me the opportunity to find out if she knew anything at all about where Rodney may be.

The e-mail said she and Rodney lived in a walk-up apartment in Over-the-Rhine, a neighborhood in downtown Cincinnati that has been in the process of being gentrified from one of the poorest urban communities in the country to one of the most sought after for its ornate brick buildings, built mostly by German immigrants in the mid- to late-1800s. Walking around the area, if you look closely with a book of architecture in hand, you can pick out Italianate, Greek Revival, and Queen Anne styles. The name Over-the-Rhine came from the Germans who immigrated here and called the Miami and Erie Canal, the Rhine, as homage to their homeland.

I wasn't sure of the exact address of the apartment, but I would take Sophie along as support, and we would find our way, and, hopefully, not a widow.

I had two small mortgage refinance loans under my belt by 12:30, so felt okay about taking a break for lunch with Sophie, Katherine, and Jessica. If I ate lunch at the Bra, it was mostly with the three other women on our team, who were far more interesting than lunching with the guys whose topic invariably was either The Reds or The Bengals or their losses or wins at a casino.

As we were walking down the hall to the Bra, I noticed Troy was in A-7 with Detective Jamison. He was sitting, bent over at the waist with his head down. I wondered what was up with that. Detective Jamison had called some of us into A-7 to ask some questions, but the body language looked off for run-of-the-mill questioning. I had to check that out later.

We settled at our usual table nearest the windows to enjoy the daylight that is lacking in the rabbit hole.

"I wish I knew if they were going to arrest me or not," Sophie fussed, looking pretty depressed.

"In the end, Sophie, anybody could have picked up the letter opener from the desk. It makes less sense that you would put a ribbon around a letter opener if all you were going to do was kill Homer with it, don't you think?" I asked.

"That's right, Sophie," Jessica said, "they can't really think you did it, just that it was your weapon, I mean letter opener."

"And, think of it this way, Sophie," advised Katherine, "it would be too obvious for you to have killed him seeing as how much you hated him."

MUTE: *Thank you, Dr. Phil.*

"Oh, my God, this isn't making me feel any better," Sophie wailed.

"If they were serious about you as a prime suspect, they would have arrested you already, so you have to stop worrying about it. Besides, there are other suspects who have more reason than you to have killed him."

"Who?" They all turned to me.

"I don't know who they are, just that they must have somebody in mind," I said, not having a clue who the suspects would be.

After lunch, the first e-mail I opened was from Detective Jamison: **A-7 please**, it read.

I trotted down the hall, and found Detective Jamison alone this time. I knocked on the glass wall, and he motioned for me to enter. He had what looked like the plans of the EFB building spread out before him on his desk.

"Good afternoon, Ms. Fillmore. I wanted to let you know that we looked up the owner of the license plates of the Escalade that you jotted down, and they belong to a guy who works for one of the bigger loan sharks in northern Kentucky. On the face of it, the guy has done nothing wrong, and we don't know at this point why the car was following you. There is more to it, to be sure, but we don't know what it is at this time. I've alerted the Newport Police to talk to them and find out what they want with you. At the very least they will know you are not Mrs. Doukas, and that should stop them bothering you. If it is Mrs. Doukas they are after, we'll find out why."

"Thank you, that does make me feel better. How is the investigation going? Do you have any leads?"

He just stared at me.

"I guess that means no."

"It means it's none of your business."

"I understand," I muttered.

The rest of the afternoon was catch-up time with paperwork: getting it in for the loans I had taken that morning and following up on getting costumers' documentation that had not come in yet. It is a wonder to me why people think we shouldn't ask for bank statements to make sure they have money in the bank to actually pay their mortgage. Some people know exactly why we are asking and are quick to supply us with what we need to proceed, but others act like we are prying. There are a surprising number of people who actually do not have a bank account at all. They are outraged that we won't lend them money on the strength of their claim that they have $5000 under their mattress. That's how I spent the rest of my afternoon, coaxing people out of documents for proceeding with the loans they wanted.

On the way home, I swung by Delhi Deli, which is in a strip mall book-ended by a grocery store and a pizza parlor, and, happily, is about a half mile from my home in Lakeview. Delhi Deli isn't what you might think, or at least it wasn't what I thought when it first opened. To me a delicatessen means one thing, but to much of the country it seems to mean something else; and Neil Jakhar fell into the latter category. His parents were born in India, but Neil was brought up in a huge apartment building in Sunnyside, Queens, before moving to what he called "the cornfields of Ohio." He must have been in a NY delicatessen, but he didn't model his Ohio deli after one. In fact, it wasn't the kind of deli I was used to—it was something different, and I loved it. It was one of my favorite places to hang out. The name Delhi Deli suggests Indian food, but he serves a mixture of delights from all over the world. And Neil changes it up pretty often. My current favorite is his Falafel Wrap that has spinach, tomato, and cucumber-dill tzatziki. He offers a savory Portobello mushroom burger, and big, fat, American hamburgers. He's got Hungarian goulash and an amazing beet salad. I always find something I want to eat there, and hanging out with Neil over a glass of wine or a beer is the icing on the cake. See? Why do I have to cook at home when I can eat like this whenever I feel the urge? Standing at the register in his white apron, with one curl of his dark hair falling over his left eye, he looked more Middle Eastern than Indian; he is a handsome bloke, but I'm not sure he knows it. He wears the apron though he doesn't cook the food, just creates the dishes. One of his aunts, Samali, who also found her way from New York, is the head cook, and she is a star. They argue in the back, but it's civilized arguing, from what I can hear, about what they each think about ingredients, name, presentation; I'm not sure who wins, but it all seems flawless and mouth-watering to me.

Two college kids, Heidi and Jeff, also help out with serving, and doing odd jobs when Neil is away. His wealthy parents bankrolled the restaurant when Neil's future seemed shapeless. After he graduated from Miami University, he floated from job to job, playing his guitar in local bands with no future. One of the jobs he floated to was as the music buyer for my video/music store. It definitely helped; he knew his music, and he was a responsible backup if I had to be out of the store. He had no prospects that fell in with his parents' idea of him to have a life; that's when they stepped in and told him they would buy him a restaurant. It seemed to be just what he needed, because the place is always crowded and is a hip place to be seen. On Saturday nights, he has some kind of live music: blues, jazz, alternative rock, whatever he is in the mood for when he makes the schedule.

"Hi. What's up? I haven't seen you in a few days."

"Hey, I wondered what happened to you. Did you get my message on your cell?" Neil asked.

"No. You know I hardly ever even look at my messages, and forget about texts altogether. But there's big and terrible news since I've seen you last."

"What? There's a meteor heading for Ohio, and we're all going to die?"

He had a dark humor that I laughed at every time, although I had to remind him not to share this sarcasm with customers, as they may fear he was poisoning the food.

"Nothing quite as cataclysmic as that." I filled him in on the events of the last several days, including the Escalade tail.

"Zoinks!" Neil exclaimed.

"Oh, and was there a guy in here last night waiting for someone? With all the kerfuffle of Homer's murder, it completely went out of my head that I was supposed to meet this guy from Match.com," I said.

"Oh, that's who that guy was. He kept coming up to the counter asking if there was a call for Marlon. He sat here for about an hour or so and finally left. And he was waiting for you? Ha."

Even though Neil's and my age difference is significant, about 20 years, I think he had some wild notion that we should "date." He was too much of a gentleman to act upon this sentiment, but I am pretty sure that's what was on his mind.

"What's good today?" I asked, looking at the menu.

"We're just trying this caramelized onion and warm goat cheese tart. You want to try that with a green salad?"

"Heck, yes."

"What did this guy, Marlon, look like?" I asked.

"He was okay, if you like the fat, drooling type," he said.

"Funny. Seriously, what did he look like?"

"He wasn't my type, so I didn't pay too much attention. I like the type with breasts."

"Never mind. I guess I'll have to check him out for myself if he ever wants to meet me again after I stood him up."

The place began to get busy, and Neil drifted around, suggesting dishes for his customers, making sure everything was just so. For a one-time slacker, he sure was all business about his restaurant.

After the scrumptious meal, I drove home, and curled up with the book I was reading, *Bangkok Tattoo*. It's the second book in a series by John Burdett, featuring Detective Sonchai Jitpleecheep solving crimes in Bankgok that would make Sam Spade's toes curl. It was good to know that what was happening in my world was a stroll in the park by comparison, and he shared one of my aunts' beliefs.

I just read the complete chapter 16: "*Rebirth, farang (in case you're wondering). You are lounging on your magnificent balcony open to the starry sky, divine music is playing with such exquisite perfection you can hardly stand it, when all of a sudden something terrible occurs: the magical sounds break up into an obscene cacophony. What's happening? Are you dying? You could put it that way. That awful noise is the first scream of an infant: you. You have been born into a human body hardwired with each and every transgression from the last time around, and now you must spend the next seventy years clawing your way back to the music. No wonder we cry.*"

I knew this was too good to be true: the phone rang.

"Annie? It's me, Crystal."

MUTE: *Why, oh, why did I pick up?*

"Hi, Crystal," I said.

"I have to talk to you about getting into the house and about the loan sharks," Crystal began.

"Loan sharks? What do you know about them?"

"I know they are after me because Homer owed them a lot of money. A buttload of money from gambling on the boats, I guess," she said.

"Who told you they were after you? They haven't contacted you, have they?"

"No, Detective Jamison told me they were following you, thinking, maybe, you were me for some reason. Why would they think you were me?" she asked.

I let that one slide.

"Did Homer tell you he owed loan sharks money?"

"I knew it because of the calls we got at home. I asked him about it, and he went ballistic. He said they were a bunch of hoods who he met at the boats who knew he had money, and who wanted to get some. That didn't even make sense to me, but I know he thought I was stupid, and he would tell me any shit he wanted."

"Do you know how much he owed them?"

"No clue. But it must be a lot because the calls were coming more and more often," she said. "Hey, I wonder if I have to pay them back now that Homer is dead. How's that fair? Oh, my God, you don't think they killed him do you?"

"I don't know if you would have to pay that money back. You should probably check with your attorney. Or you could also ask Detective Jamison. They could have killed him if they were able to get into the building undetected. We don't know what Detective Jamison knows."

"I'm not talking to the cops, and that's it," she stated.

"You have to tell the police, Crystal. You are withholding evidence, and you are liable and could go to jail. Please call Detective Jamison and tell him you know Homer owed the loan sharks money. At least do that," I said.

"I'm not talking to the cops."

"Have you thought about how you can get in my house?" she asked.

"Yes, but let's talk about that tomorrow."

MUTE: *Before I reach through the phone and smack your lovely 34-year-old face.*

Chapter 8

Wednesday, April 10, 2013

"WE'RE HAVING A HEAT wave, a tropical heat wave" is what I sang to myself in the shower before heading down for the old coffee and shake. Balmy 75 degree weather after a cold winter sends the heart floating on clouds of hope, even though my inner cynic knows it won't last. A late frost could send me crashing back down to earth soon to be followed by dirty slush. Maybe that's what T.S. Elliot should have said, "April is a tease."

Even with my allergies in bloom along with the redbuds, I kept my car windows open on the way to work. What the hell.

~

I grabbed Sophie as soon as I got to the floor and asked if she wanted to join me on my visit to Gladys Wilkins' house at lunch to bring flowers, some food, and the money that had been contributed.

"Sure, I'll drive," she said.

"I'm good, and I've got a parking space close to the building, so we can take my car," I retorted.

MUTE: *Phew. Road rage incident averted.*

I settled myself into the day, checking my e-mails and looking at my to-do list separating the crucial from the procrastination-worthy; then I picked up my first call:

"Good morning, EFB Mortgage. This is Annie. How may

I help you?"

"I want to speak to your boss," the caller insisted.

"Perhaps I can help you," I replied.

"Perhaps you can't, miss fancy pants."

At this kind of snarky answer, many loan officers would hang up, but I liked a good snarky remark to see where it was going:

"Which boss are you looking for?" I asked.

"Your boss. What did you say your names is?"

"Janie." I lied, just in case.

"I have a letter here, and I want to speak to the guy who wrote it. I don't want to speak to you."

"The boss is out of the country, so if you want a mortgage or if you have a problem, I am the person you will have to speak with."

Marketing letters are sent out to bring the calls in and are signed by a fictitious vice president, so the caller really couldn't speak with the signee.

"Well, then put me through to the boss's boss," he demanded.

"I am going to transfer you right now," I said, transferring him to customer service.

What a way to start the day. There are a lot of alter cockers taking up space out there.

Troy stood up and motioned for me to come closer, which wasn't hard because he was in the cube next to me.

"What do you know about this Jamison guy?" he asked.

"As much as you do. Why?"

"He's on my case and doesn't believe me," Troy replied.

"What doesn't he believe?" I inquired.

"Do you want to take a walk?"

He led me up the stairs, away from A-7 and Detective Jamison. We made our way down the hall, up the plebian staircase to the grand lobby, and up the imposing staircase. He stopped at the end of the 2nd floor hall, past the ornamental rail that overlooked the grand lobby, and pulled me into a corner. He was pretty nervous going to this much trouble for privacy.

"You have to swear on your mother's life that you won't

say anything to anybody about this," he stated.

"I don't have a mother," I replied.

"Well then on your children's lives."

"I don't swear on anybody's life, but I promise I won't say anything if you have something that's important to share."

MUTE: *I don't like to press my luck with the juju.*

"I was in the office Thursday night. I left in the morning to go to the Reds game, and we stayed downtown to have dinner and party, but I had to lock a few loans and get a few things done, so I came back at about nine-thirty. I was the only one on the floor. I didn't notice if the balloons were in Al's office as Jamison keeps asking me. But I guess they were, I just didn't notice. He knows I hated Doukas, because someone told him of the time that I told him I was going to stick his finger up his nose. Christ, what a mess," he said, looking depleted.

"I assume they found out you were here because they checked the ingress and egress of badge activity, right?"

"Right."

"Troy, they'd have to have more to go on than you're being here. Did you see Homer, because he was probably here, too."

"No, I didn't see him," he said, looking down at his feet.

"You saw him, didn't you?" I asked.

"Christ, what are you, a mind reader? I didn't tell Jamison, because it would have sounded way too bad for me, and how would he ever know?"

"What happened?"

"When I was coming in, he was coming, I guess, from the Bra with a cup of coffee in his hand. He asked, 'Working late?' and I replied, 'Just catching up after the game.' He said, 'I'm glad I bumped into you, because I'm going to hand in your name on Monday for termination for insubordination, so you'll have all the time in the world to go to Reds games.' Jesus, what an asshole. I would have fought it, but I didn't want to have to go through all of that and then work under him," he said.

"Oh, my God, Troy, I wish you hadn't told me."

"Why, are you going to tell Jamison?"

"I have to say it puts you in a bad light, suspect-wise. Right now, in my mind, you would be the number one suspect, and, legally, I'm now withholding information."

"I didn't kill him, but I sure would have liked to. I swear, Annie, I didn't do it."

All I could think of was me saying to my aunts when I was accused of smoking at age 16, "I swear I wasn't smoking." And then again when I was in college, and a group of girls had beer in the smoker of the dorm, "I didn't drink any beer, Dean Bradshaw, I swear." I was a naughty girl, and I wondered if Troy was a very, very bad boy.

"I won't say anything, but if I find out something that proves that you are lying, I'd tell then. I'd have to, Troy. One more thing, what time did you leave?"

"I think it was about ten forty-five. Actually, it was ten forty-four according to Detective Jamison."

So much for the likeness to Jane Marple and her ilk; I just gave the possible murderer a good reason to murder me, too. I have to say this scenario gave me the gumption to get serious about finding Homer's killer. I was already constructing my rationale for Detective Jamison: I had to protect myself. It didn't sound that great of a rationalization to me either, but that's all I had at that moment.

After that trying morning, I collected myself for the visit to Gladys with Sophie, and I hoped I wasn't resonating the frequency that was vibrating in my stomach.

We stopped on the way downtown to pick up some food and some flowers for Gladys. The check we had for one day of collection was for over $500. I was sure there would be more.

As we were driving downtown, Sophie fumbled in her purse for the address she had written down for the Wilkins; it was on Main Street. Although the street was being renovated, there were some apartments that either hadn't been bought or the work on them hadn't started. Where were these people who have lived in the same place for years supposed to go? I'm all for progress, and Over-the-Rhine is a perfect place to be prettied up, but what about the people? Hopefully, wherever they went would be safer than the crossfire of drug deals gone bad, but I wouldn't bet on it.

With Sophie's help, I managed to find a parking place on one of the side streets.

"Grab a right, grab a right, I think I see a spot," she bellowed.

I squished into a spot that was barely long enough for my short Civic, but I'd worry about getting out when the time came.

Walking down Main Street was akin to what Scarlett O'Hara must have felt like in the rebuilding of Atlanta. Okay, a huge exaggeration, but that's the thought that went through my mind as Sophie and I picked our way under and over construction obstacles.

We found the Wilkins' apartment house to be a three-story Italianate building that must have been beautiful in its day and, from the signs on the ground-floor window, was soon to have a face-lift.

We had called ahead, and we announced ourselves on the intercom in the foyer mailbox area. The stairwell and stairs were spotless, and one could easily see why this place was going to be in demand once it was fixed up. I wondered how Gladys made her way up to the 2nd floor, having just been released from the hospital.

We knocked on the door, and a weak voice said, "Come in, it's open."

Gladys, wearing a yellow bathrobe and pink slippers, was sitting in a comfortable chair covered in a faded rose-strewn pattern. She was a handsome woman who looked like she had been deflated.

"Hi, Mrs. Wilkins. I'm Annie, and this is Sophie. We've brought you some flowers and some food, and Rodney's friends have collected some money for you until he gets back from wherever he is," I said.

"Oh, no, please call me Gladys. Thank you girls for coming to see me. Bless you."

"May we put the flowers in some water and put your food away in the kitchen?" Sophie asked.

"I hate to put you to all the bother," she answered.

"It's no bother at all. We just want to help you out until

you get back on your feet," Sophie said.

"Did somebody help you get up those stairs?" I asked.

"That nice college boy who drove my cab carried me and my case up. I felt like a princess. What a nice young man."

"Do you have somebody nearby to lend you a hand?"

"My neighbor is going to come in and cook me up something to eat later on. But the rest of my family have moved on up to the Hill, and I guess that's where me and Rodney will go when they finally kick us out of here. You know it's going to get all fancy here."

"So it seems."

Sophie was in the kitchen putting away the food, and putting the orange and yellow flowers in water.

"Would you care for a sandwich? We brought turkey bologna, cheese, lettuce, tomato, pickles, some chips, and ginger ale," I said.

"Mmm, that does sound good. Maybe I'll have a half of a bologna and cheese, and I can have the salad later. There should be some ketchup in the refrigerator if that's not too much trouble," Gladys replied.

This just wasn't a good picture. If we hadn't stopped by, I was betting that Gladys wasn't well enough to get to the kitchen to fix something. On top of that, Sophie told me later that there wasn't much to fix besides some grits, bacon with a March expiration date, and three eggs. We were going to have to set up a schedule for people to bring her lunch every day until Rodney got home.

Once Gladys had the chance to eat the sandwich, which she seemed to thoroughly enjoy, I asked whether she had any idea where Rodney might be.

"No idea at all. He came to the hospital that night and stayed as late as he could, then he was going to go home to take a short nap before he had to go in for work," she said.

"Did he leave anything, a note or something to let you know he was going away?"

"Going away? Where would he go? No, he didn't go away. He usually goes in about seven or eight to clean up after the day, but he was with me until eight, so I don't know what time he got there. He bought some food for the house the day before I went to the hospital, and it looks like he took some of that with him. We like them protein bars so we don't have to cook, and he bought some of them, and, of course, the Gatorade we like, and he took some of that, too," she said.

MUTE: *Good grief, these folks' larder looks like mine.*

"Did Rodney ever mention work or mention anybody's name at work?" I asked.

"No, just his boss, that Mrs. Flink, or Fling, or something like that. She was pretty pushy and made sure the cleaning staff did everything just the way she liked it, but really it sounded to me like all they had to do was put the wastebasket stuff into the big bin on wheels, so I don't know what they could have done that she didn't like. She's just pushy," she said.

"Gladys, either we will be here, or somebody else will be here tomorrow to fix your lunch for you. Is that okay?" Sophie asked.

"That'd be fine, just fine," Gladys said, starting to doze off.

We moved a small table over and put her feet up.

My car was almost impossible to move because a big SUV had managed to get in behind me in place of the Toyota sedan that had been there; but inch by inch I made my way out. I really hate SUVs. Why do people need these huge clunkers? Everybody managed just fine back in the 60s and 70s with station wagons and six kids. Some of the same people who are all up in arms about big oil are the people who don't mind paying the oil barons $100+ a fill-up. Maybe it's a penis thing, like midlife crises men buying red sports cars. I know it's a gross overgeneralization, and in Ohio a lot of the SUVs I see are driven by soccer moms, and why would soccer moms need a big penis? Never mind.

Sophie and I had stayed away from work over our allotted one hour, but inasmuch as it was for the benefit of an employee, or an employee's family, and we weren't out drinking martinis, Chad gave us the okay to take it as time worked. He was a great manager, because it hadn't been that long since he had sat in one of our seats, and he remembered how tough it was to pull those oars.

It was hard to get back into the swing of the job after seeing Gladys in that condition and wondering what happened to Rodney, but the phones rang. I picked up on cue and even managed to get a refinance from New York, which was always a big loan since even a small house on Staten Island was worth about $600,000. The trouble was getting those loans closed—you generally couldn't. The transfer taxes alone usually stopped borrowers in their tracks. On a loan of $600,000, transfer taxes would be about $8700, and that didn't include any of the other fees. Fuhgeddaboudit is usually the response I got when I passed on this bit of information.

I had decided to forgo my Yoga that evening with so much going on, when I probably needed it the most. But I was happy to get home and kick my feet up with a glass of cabernet.

I logged onto my computer for the first time since the previous week and found a ridiculous number of messages, mostly not personal, and several from Outlook saying I had too many messages. The message from Marlon was the one I was dreading, because, if *I* had been stood up, I wouldn't have been happy. I doubt I would have even e-mailed; but Marlon did:

Annabelle [I never give my real name] **I must have either had the wrong night or the wrong place, but I re-read your e-mail, and it did say Monday, April 8 at Delhi Deli, and that's where I waited. I hope you are okay and nothing has happened to you. Please let me know if you are okay. Marlon.**

Wow, that was a nice e-mail from a guy who was stood up. I let him know that an end-of-the world incident stood in the way of my showing up for our meeting, or something like that, without telling him I was involved in the murder that was all over Cincinnati media. We agreed to another meeting at Delhi Deli that evening, so I called ahead to let Neil know I would be in with someone I hoped was a Match.com cutie. Marlon said he was 6', but I have met guys on Match who have told me they were 5'8", and I practically had to bend down to shake hands, so I wasn't sure how tall he actually was going to be.

"Hi, Sam, is Neil out?" I asked because Samali almost never answers the phone.

"No, he's walking around and conscious. Do you want to speak with him?"

Everyone's a comedian. Samali was originally from London, so that explains the dry humor; it doesn't come often, but when it does, it's choice.

"What's up?" Neil asked.

"Hi. I'm going to be in tonight with the Match.com guy; can you fix us up a nice little table?"

"How about the one behind the silk curtains overlooking the Seine?" he replied.

MUTE: *He gets more sarcastic when he's in love. All right, I just made that up.*

"Anything you think will be fine. See you about seven."

I arrived at Delhi Deli on time, and Marlon was already there toward the back. When I walked in, Neil said, "Lover boy is here. Do you want me to introduce you?"

I ignored him and made my way back to the now-standing Marlon, who was more like 6' 4", or so he seemed to me. That is the most bumbling moment on these online dates, when you first meet. Neither one of you knows what to say, so you each kind of blabber until the wine or beer or coffee arrives, or at least that has been my experience. Think about it, in life you meet people you work with, live near, have gone to school with, or know somebody who knows them; you've got something in common. With Match.com, even after a month of e-mails, you really don't know each other, and it's awkward. The odds are long.

We kind of looked at each other, assessing what stood before us on the shelf.

"You look just like your picture."

MUTE: *Was that cause for a "thank you," or something else?*

I settled for "Thank you." He didn't look anything like his picture, where he looked like Sam Elliot; the guy seated across from me looked a little nerdy, the opposite of Elliot.

"You didn't say what you do," stated Marlon.

"Oh, I'm a mortgage loan officer. I sell mortgages for a lender," still not wanting him to know I worked for EFB, scene of the big murder in Cincinnati.

"I told you I'm retired from the nursery business, didn't I?" he asked.

"Yes, you mentioned it in your profile. How do you keep busy now that you're retired?"

"I know it sounds crazy, but I think I'm busier now than when I had the nursery. That may be a slight exaggeration, but my days are full. I volunteer for Habitat for Humanity, and I keep a big garden. Not so much in the winter, but then I went south this year to keep out of the cold."

All that sounded good, but I couldn't keep my eyes off the ginger-hair comb-over, and the big red- and-grey mustache.

"You said you're a big reader. May I ask what you're reading now?"

"I'm a Dan Brown fan. I've read all of his books, starting with *The DaVinci Code,* and then I read his first one, *Angels and Demons,*" he said.

I swear every third guy on Match says they've read *The DaVinci Code,* and, to me, it's not that impressive a read. But I'm nitpicking. He seemed like a good guy, a nice conversationalist, but no spark at all on my part. That's when I wanted to say, let's just leave it at one glass of wine, and take off. I'm sure there are men who feel the same meeting me, but this wasn't going the way I had hoped. I heard a guy on TV say that he met someone for lunch, and at some point during the meal, his date excused herself to go to the restroom and never came back. Now that's rude and spineless. I'd suffer to the very end, but I wasn't going on date #2.

I looked up to see Neil leaning against the wall next to the kitchen door with his arms folded, looking at me. I waved to him, but he didn't wave back, just shook his head slowly, which I interpreted to mean, "You idiot."

We ordered dinner: he the hamburger, I the falafel. Marlon had a lot to say, and I, mostly, listened. For me, that's saying something. If I like someone, I like to share; if I'm lukewarm or cooler, I'm just quiet. I might have said, "Marlon, you have ketchup and cheese in your mustache," but I didn't. After dinner, he said, "Would you like to go somewhere else for a drink?

I think we're hitting it off like gangbusters."

This is the part I hate most of all. I should say something like, "Thank you, but I don't feel the same way about it." But I'm a candy ass about these things, and usually smile. I did say, "I have to work tomorrow, Marlon, so I'll have to pass on the drink. But thank you for a lovely dinner. It was nice meeting you."

"When can we do this again?" he asked.

"I'm kind of busy right now, so I'll have to let you know." I was much braver on paper or e-mail than I was face-to-face. I'd have to work on that.

~.

I no sooner walked in the door than my phone rang. "You are not serious about this guy, are you?" Neil asked.

"No," I answered.

"Good. He looks like a dork." He hung up.

Just as I was hanging up, another call was popping in. Crystal.

"Hi Crystal, How are you doing today?"

"I'm doing lousy, thank you very much. I'm stuck in this house. I look like shit, and I have to get out of here. What did you come up with about getting into my house?" sounding as if she were near tears.

"I do have an idea. I thought if you could ask Detective Jamison if he could allow your cleaning people in the house, I could figure out a way to get in there with a friend to act as if we are the cleaning girls. How long does it usually take your crew to clean your whole house?"

"It's a big house, so I think it's usually about four or five hours."

"I guarantee my cleaning job isn't going to take any four or five hours. We'll go in for about two hours, tops."

"So you're not actually going to clean?"

"Do you want me to clean toilets, or do you want me to find a key?"

Chapter 9

Thursday, April 11, 2013 (morning)

I AWOKE TO MY RADIO announcing light rain, 69 degree weather, a chance of severe storms including quarter-inch hail, and a slight chance of tornadoes, which had wreaked havoc to the west. I called Marilyn to see if she was free to be a cleaning woman to get into Crystal's house. I felt as if we had as much chance of unearthing a key that may or may not fit a box that may or may not include paperwork that would shed light on the murder of Homer as I did of finding the diamond that fell out of my engagement ring in my house about five years ago.

"Marilyn, it's me," I said.

"Hi, you're calling early."

"I know. I have a proposition for you. I need to get into the Doukas house to see if I can find a key to the box Crystal told me about that might hold papers that might give a clue about Homer's murder. I told you about that, remember?"

"Yeah, I remember. How are we going to get into the house with all the police?"

"Crystal is calling Detective Jamison this morning to see if her cleaning people can get in to clean the house."

"And we are the cleaning people?"

"Yes."

"We don't actually have to clean the house, do we?"

"We're going to have to make a show of it, at least. If Detective Jamison agrees to it, can we use your SUV? We can bring your vacuum cleaner, and I'll bring some mops and other supplies so we look legitimate."

"Do we need shirts that say a cleaning company name on them?"

"Do you have shirts like that?"

"No."

"Well, then, no, we don't need them. But we should wear something that looks similar. How about jeans and a blue shirt. Do you have something like that?" I inquired.

"Who doesn't have jeans and a blue shirt?" she scoffed.

I jumped into the shower, but didn't do anything fancy with my hair, because with rain, storms, and possible tornadoes, my hair would look like Don King's by the end of the day anyway. As I was sipping my coffee, Crystal called to say she had the okay from Detective Jamison to have her cleaning staff clean the house.

"Staff? How many people usually come to your home?" I asked.

"Three girls. They're called Girls Gotta Clean."

"Did you tell Detective Jamison the name of your crew?"

"Yes."

"We're definitely taking a chance that he hasn't already vetted them."

"Vetted them? What's that mean?"

"Checked them out to make sure they are an actual cleaning service," I replied.

"They really aren't. They're just three girls I used to work with at Hooters who clean to make some extra money."

"Did he ask for their telephone number?"

"Yes, but I told him it was at home, and I reminded him I wasn't at my house."

"Just to be safe, call your friends and tell them the police might be calling to make sure they are who you say they are, and that they're cleaning your house this morning." I was probably being way too cautious, but I didn't want Detective Jamison on my bad side. "Oh, for Pete's sake, I need a key to get in the house."

"No, there's a keypad. You just need to enter the numbers

eleven-nine-one-nine-seven-nine."

"Wait, I need paper. Okay, eleven-nine-one-nine-seven-nine. Is that right?" I asked.

"Yep, that's it."

I didn't feel at all good about knowing the entry number to her house—what if all the silverware went missing after we had been there?

"You'd better change those numbers as soon as you get a chance when you return home," I suggested.

"Why, are you going to steal something?"

"Only the key and the box you want me to look for," I replied.

I called Marilyn and told her I'd be over in about a half hour; then I called Chad and told him I had an emergency and I'd be in about noon.

I arrived at Marilyn's about 8:30 wearing my jeans and blue shirt, carrying a bucket, two mops, and a caddy of cleaning supplies.

Marilyn's mother-in-law, Katy Monroe, lived in town, and was always thrilled to be asked to watch one or all of the boys. She had already arrived, so Marilyn was waiting in jeans, blue shirt, and a bandanna around her head à la Rosie the Riveter.

"Are you making tanks?" I asked.

"I think it adds an air of authenticity," she answered.

I didn't want to burst her cleaning-lady bubble, so I let it go.

We arrived at 2345 Pudding Lane in Marilyn's SUV about 9:15 a.m. The house was, indeed, surrounded by red-and-white tape, and there was a CPD police car at the end of the driveway. We stopped next to the police car, and I got out.

"Hi," I said to the police officer. "We're from Girls Gotta Clean, and we're here to do our regular cleaning for Mrs. Doukas. I believe she spoke to Detective Jamison about it?"

"Yep, he mentioned it. I'm Officer Blair. If you need anything just let me know. Go to it then, but I gotta say I'm glad I'm not you. How long does it take you to clean that place?" he asked.

"It usually takes about four or five hours, but Mrs. Doukas

asked that we just give it a light going over seeing as nobody's been there in almost a week."

"Must be nice. My wife would sure like to have you two come to our house once a week," he said, shaking his head in what seemed like disappointment in the wealth lottery.

"I hear you. I'd like to have someone clean my house, too."

We gathered our cleaning supplies, including Marilyn's huge vacuum cleaner, and made our way up the driveway in the drizzling rain and under the four columns to the arched double doors. The overblown doors each had two stained glass windows as did the arched transom.

"I'm not cleaning those windows," Marilyn said.

"Let's get in the house first before we decide what we are and aren't going to do," I said. But I wasn't cleaning those windows, either.

"Oh, my God!" Marilyn exclaimed. "Look at this place. It's huge. It's ugly."

"We're not here to critique the place, we're here to find a key." I took it all in, trying not to gasp. It looked like a cross between Buckingham Palace and Graceland. Or what I imagined those homes looked like: huge and cheesy. You can figure out which I thought was which.

I won't describe it all. But the enormous chandelier with pale pink crystals and beading looming over a round table covered with leopard-print cloth and animal heads more or less summed up the taste of the rest of the house.

"Where should we start?" Marilyn asked.

"Let's check out the rest of this mansion before we go to the dining room. That's where Crystal says Homer put the mysterious box. Why would two people want a house this big?"

"To get away from each other," Marilyn said knowingly.

We started up the winding staircase. It was carpeted in mauve wool and had gold filigree railings. The upstairs hall looked like a hotel. There were four closed white doors on either side of the stairs. The last one on the left turned out to be the master bedroom, which would have been drool-worthy had it not been for an overabundance of pink frills. On one wall were double French doors to a balcony that overlooked the lush grounds. Through another stained glass door there was a bathroom that had seemingly every amenity. A basketball hoop wouldn't be out of place at the opposite end of the clear glass shower with what looked like steam room fixtures. Next to it nestled a petal-shaped Jacuzzi tub.

Across the hall from the bedrooms were two more doors to capacious closets for linen and cleaning supplies.

At the end of the hall was a small door that opened onto narrow winding stairs that took us to an enormous attic. Alas, no old trunks no vintage clothes or hats, no Christmas ornaments or any other items were stored up there. It was just a long length of floor that gave the illusion of being even longer given there was nothing on it.

We climbed back down the stairs to find a small alcove off of which the stairs continued down to the kitchen. And an impressive kitchen it was, with what I guessed was the poured-concrete countertop that Joe Luca said Crystal wanted. It didn't look like concrete to me; it looked shiny and with blue gems in it. Marilyn said they could make concrete look like that by adding pigments and glass chips. Mike had been working with it for a while, she said.

Downstairs there was a living room, Homer's study, a solarium, and the dining room that had the bookshelf wallpaper and was, by comparison, not nearly as gaudy as the rest. The walnut fireplace and mantel were capped by a gold mirror. A step up to the hearth was inset with red tiles, I guess to match the red-and-white-damask covered Louis XIV style chairs, or vice-versa.

The red tiles looked like they were laid with white grout. How could we chip the grout out without a tool, I wondered? A chisel was what came to mind. I had no idea what I was doing when I started knocking on the tiles. I was copying what I saw in movies or read about in books when someone was looking for a hollow place. It all sounded solid to me. But one of the knocks upended a tile, and I soon saw that none of the tiles were grouted—just surrounded with what looked like grout—and were easily removed piece by piece. The tiles sat on a piece of wood that came out in one piece. Under the wood, I found an ornate metal box that was as almost as long as the hearth. The box was black, trimmed in gold, and painted with a nude woman under whom the words Pandora's Box were written in gold lettering. There was no key lock, but a combination lock over Pandora's private parts. I wondered if Homer designed this thing himself. It wouldn't have surprised me. The box itself was immovable, so it was either bolted to the base or secured in some other way.

Marilyn was gazing out the window at the estate while I was unearthing what we had come for.

"Marilyn, come here. You've got to see this."

I showed her the clever box with the double entendre. "What a pig," was her response.

Just as we started to put everything back in place, the police officer called out, "Girls, where are you?"

Marilyn went out to the foyer and said, "Whew, it's not easy cleaning a house this size in a few hours."

"I just didn't see any movement in here, so I wondered what you were doing."

"We like to start upstairs and work our way down."

"Where's your partner with the curly hair?"

"I think she's just checking out what we should do next."

"Officer, hi. Did you need something?" I asked, walking out of the dining room.

"I needed to see that you were cleaning the place."

MUTE: *Oh, look, it's the Spic 'n Span squad?*

"We're finished upstairs, and we're about to start down here. Shouldn't be that much longer."

"It already looks clean."

"We do a great job if you ever need a cleaning service," Marilyn piped in.

"Okay. I won't keep you. Carry on," he said, looking around the place himself. I wondered what *he* thought.

"I think we're going to have to at least look like we're cleaning if he looks in to check us out again; so why don't you vacuum in the living room where he can see you through the windows. You really don't have to do anything, because the place looks pretty spotless," I said. "I'm going to see if Homer has an office I can check out. I'll clean in there."

"Oh, sure. I can see how this is going to work."

"I'm lead here," acting like I knew what the hell I was doing.

Homer's office was off the dining room, with a splendid view of the verdant estate. His office was more conservatively appointed than the rest of the house. Much more. For starters, bookshelves were real, not wallpaper. The elegant mahogany desk had a burgundy leather inset on top, and sat on an oriental rug. The only item on the top of the desk was a gold frame with a photograph of Crystal and Homer on their wedding day. She was very lovely, indeed, and Homer, well, Homer was not.

I was looking for a combination and, maybe, a key, and I thought the desk would be the most likely place as there were no drawers in the room. There were some built-in bookshelves, a brown leather chair with hassock, a small side table, and a long, high console table along one wall. Where else would it be if it were in this room at all?

We'd been there for 1 1/2 hours already, so I was really hoping I would find something in the desk. I took out every drawer and looked through every item in them. Not much. In the long top drawer there was cream-colored writing paper with his name and home address embossed in black, matching envelopes, an unwittingly ironic monogrammed silver letter opener, a staple remover, and a Montblanc fountain pen complete with a small bottle of black ink.

The top left side drawer had a black-mesh drawer organizer with a calculator, four sharpened pencils, a ballpoint pen, paper clips, and a roll of Scotch tape. The second drawer down had two new yellow legal pads. Nothing in the rest of the drawers—nothing at all. Especially not a piece of paper with a combination on it. I wondered if he actually used this desk or if it was purely for show. It reminded me of The Container Store. Desks that pristine could only be unused desks. Even the most ingenious drawer organizers couldn't organize themselves.

I looked around the room at the bookshelves that covered one wall from floor to ceiling. Good grief, were we going to have to go through every book to see if one of them was har-boring a piece of paper with the combination?

"Marilyn, come into Homer's office, please," I called. She was running the vacuum cleaner so I had to go into the living room to fetch her. I found her moving her arm back and forth in a pantomime of vacuuming but not actually doing it. If I had asked her why she was *pretending* to vacuum instead of *actually* vacuuming with almost the same effort, the answer would no doubt have been longer than the time we had left.

"Marilyn, turn off the vacuum. We need to look in every book in Homer's study to see if the combination is in one of them, because it's not in the desk."

We fetched a stepladder we had seen earlier in the kitchen pantry, which turned out to be ideal: three steps, light as a feather, and just tall enough for me to reach the top shelf. Marilyn could reach that shelf without the ladder, but she was kind enough not to mention her advantage in this department. I started at the left-hand side, Marilyn started at the other end, and we worked our way toward the center. We'd pick out a book and turn it on its side. When nothing fell out, we'd flip through the pages to see if anything was stuck in the spine. As far as I could tell, there was no thematic order to the books; it seemed he organized them by size. Or more likely, a decorator did it by size and color, because there was a lovely visual rhythm to the wall. Looked like books bought by the foot to me.

The flipping and thumbing went on for some time, when Marilyn drew in her breath, "I think I found something."

She sure found something, but what the heck was it? In Edith Hamilton's *Mythology*, in a page about Pandora, was taped a small glassine envelope. In it was a piece of typing paper that was folded up small enough to fit into said envelope, about 3" x 5" maybe. When we unfolded it and stretched it out on the top of the desk we saw 12 square boxes drawn across and ten square boxes down. So 120 boxes. In one of the boxes—5 across and 5 down—was an X. What on earth could this be? It had to be connected to the box, because of the placement of the envelope in Hamilton's page about Pandora. I thought of what Pandora's curiosity had unleashed and what mine might. Not plagues, sorrow, and mischief, I hoped. Detective Jamison's voice came to mind, intoning, "I don't want to have this meeting again with somebody else about who may have killed you."

"Let's take another quick look around each room to see if we can find anything that resembles these boxes," I suggested.

We did, indeed, search every nook and cranny, but to no avail. By the time we were finished looking in the last place, the basement, we had been there 3 hours and 20 minutes.

"I'm taking this paper with me to ask Crystal if she has any idea what it might be, or if she can think of anything they had with 120 boxes," I said.

"I have to get home to change. Jackson has a play this afternoon that I have to go to. He's playing an Easter Egg," Marilyn said, winding up the cord to her vacuum cleaner.

"Easter was two weeks ago. Remember? I drove to Chicago to be with the Humphrey and Ingrid."

"I know, but the Easter Bunny got sick, so they postponed the play."

"Who was it, Anthony Hopkins?" I joked.

"What?" she said.

"HOPkins, HOPkins," I repeated.

"You've been looking at too many books. You're getting loopy."

We gathered up our cleaning supplies, and made our way back down the driveway to Marilyn's car, stopping to bid adieu to Officer Blair.

On the way home, Marilyn announced, "Oh, did I tell you we are going to look for a puppy this weekend?"

"A new dog? Archie hasn't even been gone a week," I reminded her.

"I know, but I just can't believe he'd be away for a week and be fine."

"Remember that time he was gone for over two weeks? And don't forget, he hasn't got any tags on him, so if somebody found him they wouldn't know where to return him."

"Maybe he found a new home. And I can only hope that

they are kind to him." She sniffled.

It was hard to believe that somebody would take in Archie and not try as hard as they could to find his rightful place. He was cute, but a scavenger, and, frankly, a pain in the neck.

"Why not wait at least another week."

"Maybe."

I picked up my car from Marilyn's house, drove home, took another shower, ate two protein bars, was still hungry, and made my way down to work.

I arrived at EFB at about 2:30, and the floor was abuzz with business. I had a ton more e-mails, one of which was from Sophie letting me know she and Katherine went to see Gladys at lunch and that she made a schedule for people to cover until next Tuesday.

She said Katherine was going to speak to her church to see if they could get people to help as a part of their Outreach Program: That made me feel good because I had forgotten all about poor Gladys.

These are some of the other e-mails I had in my in-box:

- Grant Brentworth from the Marketing Department wanting to discuss why my loans weren't hitting the $2 million mark. The lowest amount we could fund and still be paid commission was $1.5 million; if we didn't hit this number, we were paid $10 an hour. The e-mail didn't say that in so many words, but I had had this conversation with others so I knew: *Getting to Know You* wasn't going to be the subject of our meeting even if it was the subject of the e-mail. He set the appointment for 4 o'clock in one of the more intimate meeting rooms. I clicked YES.

- Alice Mayview, Homer's Administrative Assistant, asking if I could meet her for a drink after work. She was having a meltdown and needed someone to talk to.

- Al Markey asking "the floor" to hang in there during this difficult time and saying that if we need to talk to someone, he was there for us.

- <u>Troy Whitman</u> wanting to know if I had heard anything new.

- <u>Detective Jamison</u> informing us that today was his last
day in our building; he was returning to headquarters,
but the Doukas case was his number one priority.

The first call I took was about 2:50, and it turned out to be
a customer who had refinanced with me once before, Frank
Pickle—seriously. But he was the nicest guy in the world, and if
all customers were as pleasant as he, it would have been a very
easy job. After some conversation and a cursory look at what
his property might be worth with the market conditions being
what they were, we decided it would be better for him to wait.
There was no sense in taking up a lot of his time having an appraisal that wouldn't help him.

The next call balanced out the amiable call from Frank
Pickle. It was from Jerry from Cape Coral, Florida. I was in the
process of refinancing him when he found out that his appraisal came in much less than what he thought his place was worth.
That part of Florida took a heavy hit in the market downturn
starting about 2009. The homes that I saw appraisals for were
beautiful and in paradisiac settings. Some included covered
pools. But the original costs were upwards of $700,000, and
prices had plummeted. No matter how much you tell the bor-
rower what other homes are selling for in their neighborhood,
they do not think those unpleasant prices pertain to them. Until
they get the appraisal. Then the conversation goes something
like this: "I knew that appraiser didn't know what the hell he
was doing, he didn't even go downstairs where we have a completely finished basement.

"Is it a walkout basement?" I would ask.

"No, what the hell does that have to do with anything,"
they might say.

"The square footage is not included in an enclosed basement without a walkout capability," I'd explain.

"I'm going to sue you guys and the appraiser. You haven't
done your job," is an example of something I would hear. We
definitely had the conversation on the first call that a finished

basement without a walkout wasn't included in square footage. In fact, even if it were, the house wouldn't be worth $700,000 in that market.

"Put your manager on," was often the way these calls ended.

As soon as I hung up the phone, I realized it was 4 p.m., and I was going to be a few minutes late to "get to know" Grant. I ran down the hall past A-7, which was closed for business, and found my way to A-13, where the young Mr. Brentworth sat waiting for me. He looked like he could have been my son, except that he was dressed like George Banks, and Humphrey dressed, let us say, more artistically. He had on grey pants, a buttoned-down blue shirt, and a red-and-blue rep tie.

"Hi, Annie. I'm Grant Brentworth," he said, standing up and shaking my hand.

"Hi, Grant," I said, taking a seat across the table from him.

"The reason I wanted to meet with you today is because I have been commissioned to interview a few of our loan officers whom we think aren't living up to their potential. We want to help you reach your financial goals," he said earnestly, pinching his eyebrows together as if he were telling me I had taken poison and he might just have the antidote.

I wish I had a nickel for every time someone told my aunts or me they didn't think I had lived up to my potential. I learned back in high school that if I told them what I really thought, it would end up worse than it already was. So I just looked contrite and said I'd try harder. (*Not to be bored* I wanted to add, but didn't.)

This was not a case of being bored; this was entirely different. Loan officers received calls from all kinds of customers, not just those who had loans of $200,000 or upwards. Many had loans as low as $30,000. And just as many of them were paying the highest interest rate. How many loan officers took those low loan calls? I'd guess not many. I just couldn't let those people get stuck with interest rates sometimes as high as 7.5% when they could be paying 4.5%, for instance. Those loans weren't any easier to get closed, but we were paid by a percentage of the size of the loan, so you can figure it out.

I listened to Grant give me some pointers, although he had never sold a mortgage loan, or any other loan from what he told me of his background. This was his first job out of grad school about 18 months ago. You have to love the chutzpah.

After about 15 minutes he seemed to take a breath; I stood up and said, "Thank you, Grant. That was so helpful. I'm glad I brought my pad and pen so I could take some notes, and I can start putting those ideas to good use this afternoon."

I couldn't decide if his smile indicated that he was pleased or if he thought I was full of shit. Always leave them guessing.

Chapter 10

Thursday, April 11, 2013 (evening)

I CALLED JIM GRATE TO let him know I wouldn't be going to Dee Felice that night because I promised I would have a drink with Alice Mayview. Believe me, sitting at Dee Felice, sipping a glass of scotch with Jim Grate, was a lot more fun than sipping a glass of wine with Alice Mayview, but duty called.

Alice and I were going to Delhi Deli, because she didn't want to be seen, she said, at the usual pub where folks from EFB hung out.

She followed me up 71 North, and we parked next to each other at the other end of the strip from where Delhi Deli was located. It was raining hard, and we clung to the sides of the stores until we found respite under the Delhi Deli awning. Neil opened the door for us.

"Were you waiting for us? How did you know I'd be here tonight?" I asked.

"I saw you trawling for a parking place," he replied.

"Alice, this is Neil, the proprietor of this delightful establishment." I introduced him as I looked around to see if there was a free table.

"There's a table for one in the back, but I can fix it up for two. Otherwise, you'd have to wait. We just got slammed," he said.

"No, the table in the back is fine," I said.

We each ordered a glass of wine and settled in.

"This must be a hard time for you."

"You have no idea." She covered her heart area with her hand. "It's been a nightmare trying to decide what I should say and what I shouldn't. I know so much, and I just don't know what Homer would want me to divulge."

She looked harrowed.

"Homer is dead, and divulging what you know might help Detective Jamison find out who murdered him."

"It's so much more complicated than that," she said, her brow looking like a little bunched-up pink baby sweater.

"I think you should tell the detective everything you know. You don't want to be found holding back information."

Talk about calling the kettle black.

"My word, he had something on everybody. He was like J. Edgar Hoover," she declared.

MUTE: *The Director? Homer wore dresses?*

"What do you mean 'everybody'? Everybody in the Mortgage Division? Everybody in the Mortgage Sales Department? Everybody in the bank?"

"Everybody who if they knew what he had on them would have had a motive to kill him."

"Surely you're exaggerating. I know a lot of people at EFB, and I can't think of anybody venal enough to kill somebody, even Homer."

"That's because you don't know what I know," Alice retorted.

Neil interrupted the conversation by delivering a roasted vegetable quesadilla with a dollop of cilantro-laced sour cream. "We're trying this out tonight; let me know what you think."

It's just too damn bad he was so young. Who wouldn't love a guy who looked like Omar Sharif Jr. and who could come up with these recipes?

I picked up where our conversation left off. "What do you know? Why would Homer let you in on these secrets? He didn't seem that trusting."

"I'm not sure he did want me to know, but he fixed it so he did have something on me. I'm pretty sure he would have used it as blackmail if I felt the urge to share any of his secrets.

That's another reason I really can't tell the detective what I know," she replied.

"You're not making any sense."

"I can't tell you any more than that, or the police might consider me their prime suspect."

"Okay, but I think you should tell me everything you know. Whatever he 'fixed' probably isn't as incriminating as you think."

MUTE: *Maybe she bent over one day and he saw that she was wearing a thong.*

"Anyway, let's get back to what you know that you are willing to share with me, and who may have killed Homer."

"It could have been any of them."

"How many are there on your list?" I asked.

"Too many. Even one is too many."

"Just give me a number to work with. I assume you told me this so I would help you. Why else would you be telling me?"

"I guess so. Maybe that's true, but I just had to tell somebody or I was going to crack," she said.

She was already a little cracked, so something as monumental as this might have been the hammer it took to lay that chink wide open.

"Maybe I can help you," I offered.

"Okay. There are four people I know about, and I know what he had on them. But I think there were others that I don't know about."

"Of those you do know, could any of them been in the building at the time he was murdered?"

"I don't know. I have no idea."

"If we knew what Detective Jamison knew about who was in the building that night, it might help us cross some people off the list," I said.

"It couldn't have been Crystal, because she was in Chicago," she mused; then followed with "if she was on the list," spilling some of her beans.

MUTE: *I definitely wasn't going to have to threaten to pull her finger nails out to get the information.*

"Another glass of wine, ladies?" Neil asked.

"Yes, please," Alice replied.

"I'd like something to eat, too, Neil," I ventured.

"How hungry are you?"

"I'm not starving. Alice would you like to order something?"

"Sure, I'll have some more of those quesadillas," she said.

"Annie?" Neil asked.

"What do you suggest?" I replied.

"How about a bowl of the carrot and ginger soup with some raw rosemary crackers?"

"Sounds perfect."

"Back to business," I said to Alice. "If you want to feel safe, I think one, we have to find out who was in the building that night, and two, you have to tell me who is on your list and why. I don't seriously think we can find out from Detective Jamison who was in the building. Do you know anybody who works in the department responsible for the security badges?"

"I know somebody, but I don't know if I can get information out of them," she answered.

"See what you can do. We don't want anything to happen to you."

"That's a terrible thing to say," she protested, clutching her heart again.

It *was* a terrible thing to say, but it would be worse if she were murdered. I was beginning to sound like Detective Jamison.

We said our good-nights, and I went home, knowing that I'd be on the phone shortly with Crystal, who would be anxious to hear what *Girls Gotta Clean* found at her house that day.

"I've been calling you all night," Crystal said when I picked up the phone.

"I just got home, but I had some questions for you, too," I retorted.

"Like what?"

"How could you have seen Homer put the box under the fireplace tiles? The box I found was as wide as the hearth, and it seemed to be nailed down," I said.

"Maybe he put a smaller box in the box you saw," she suggested.

That made sense, because it was surely big enough to hold the size box Crystal had originally told me about.

"Also, the big box looks more like a horizontal safe with a drawing of Pandora on it," I said.

"Pandora? Like the music thing I get on my phone?"

"Never mind. I can't get into the safe because there's a combination lock. We found a drawing in a book in Homer's office that looks like it might be what we were looking for. It has twelve boxes across and ten boxes under each of those boxes. There's an X in the fifth box down and the fifth one across. Did you and he own anything that looked anything like that?"

"I don't know what you're talking about with boxes," Crystal replied.

"It looks like the combination of the lock in the fireplace might be someplace Homer indicated by the X, so I'm asking you, do 120 boxes sound familiar to you at all, even if they aren't the same size. They could be bigger boxes. They could be any size," I said.

"No, no clue. So I'm pretty much screwed is what you're telling me," she said.

"No, I'm not telling you that. Remember we don't even know if what's in that box has anything to do with his murder."

"Or has anything to do with my past?" she added.

She was definitely afraid of something coming out about her, given that I was pretty sure she was on Homer's *J. Edgar Hoover* list according Alice.

"You might feel better if you told me what Homer knew about you that makes you so afraid," I said.

"I might not. But what's your next step? Is it over, or do you think you can still find out something about what's in the box?"

"I don't know, Crystal. I'll have to think about what that drawing could mean. Maybe I'll have to see if I can get in Homer's office to look there. I'll let you know."

"I have news for you, too," she said.

"What?"

"Those scum bags that were following you? The guys from the loan sharks?"

MUTE: *Was this a statement or a question?*

"Yeah?"

"They called me on my cell phone. Don't ask me how they got my number, but they got it, and they called me, and they're not nice," she said.

"Were you expecting them to be polite?" I asked. "How much money did Homer borrow from them?"

"Hah! He didn't exactly borrow the money, but he owes them fifty k, and they want me to pay them back. I don't have any idea how much money I have. Homer gave me an allowance, and I have my own credit card."

"If he didn't borrow it, why does he owe it to them?"

"Do you know what an insider trading tip is?" she asked.

"Yes, I know what it is. Is this what it's about?" I replied.

"I guess. That's what he kept saying; it was an insider trading tip. A guy with a deep voice said, 'That bastard promised us we'd quadruple our money in about a month because he was going to put our fifty k on stock that he knew about that was going to go through the roof because of some bank deal,'" she said.

"Wow!" I exclaimed.

"So that's illegal?"

"Ask Martha Stewart," I retorted.

"She's not a banker," Crystal protested.

"Forget it. But it's giving out information that you are not allowed to give out. And if Homer were guilty of 'insider trading,' these guys would be guilty, too, for taking the information. I wonder if Homer actually was going to invest that fifty thousand or if he was just saying it because he needed the money. But he was sure taking a chance that these guys wouldn't come after him. Unless, of course, they did come after him," I said.

"But, do *I* owe them the money?"

"I doubt that you owe them the money, but this is something you absolutely have to share with Detective Jamison. It could save your neck."

"I guess I will then, but I don't like talking to the cops," she said.

MUTE: *Evidently.*

"I also have to talk to our money guy this week to find out how much money is actually mine, and if I can keep the house," she continued.

"Why would you want to keep that enormous house?" I asked.

"It's classy," she replied.

"How are you going to talk to your financial advisor? He's not coming to the safe house is he?

"No, we're gonna Skip."

"Skip?"

"You know, on the computer."

"Oh, Skype," I said. "It'll be good to know where you stand with your financials." I knew where I stood with my financials, if what I had could be called financials. It wasn't as good as she stood, by far.

We said good night, and she swore she would call Detective Jamison in the morning to let him know about the insider trading tidbit. If I could figure out how those loan shark guys could have gotten into the building or had anything to do with Al Markey, I would say they were good for the murder. I just couldn't imagine how it could have gone down like that, but there are a lot of things I can't imagine.

I thought I would quickly check my home e-mails to see if I had any from my kids or aunts, or anybody, for that matter. There was one from Marlon.

Hi Annabelle

I just want to thank you again for such a nice evening. I hope you agree we hit it off very well, and the 'chemistry' was sure there for me. How about getting together this weekend?

I think I'm in love with you. Marlon

In love with me? He doesn't even know me. This is the part I don't like about Match—matches. There seemed to be such a divergence in our take on the meeting. Again, I know there are thousands of people who have met their spouses this way and are wonderfully happy, but so far it wasn't happening for me, and I absolutely blamed myself. Someone would think Marlon was great, but it wasn't me.

Hi Marlon

Thank you again for a pleasant evening. You are a terrific guy, and I'm sure you will meet the woman you are looking for, but I'm sorry it isn't me.

The best of luck to you.

Annabelle

I checked out a few more e-mails, and BAM, another e-mail from Marlon.

Annabelle,

I am surprised by your response since you said how much you thought we were enjoying ourselves at dinner the other night. I'm losing faith in people on this website.

Good Bye. Marlon

See what I mean? I was polite at dinner, at best; but polite to some people must be the nicest anybody's ever been to them. No need to reply, I think he got it.

It was ten o'clock, time to read a bit and go to bed, I thought—until I heard the doorbell. Ten o'clock? Who's dead now?

I peeked out the side of my shade to see Neil standing at my door.

MUTE: *"When a great moment knocks on the door of your life, it is often no louder than the beating of your heart, and it is very easy to miss it."*

That's from *Dr. Zhivago* and a tad overly dramatic, but I was tired, and I opened the door to Neil standing casually with a bottle of wine in hand.

"Hi. Did I leave something there?" I asked.

"No, but you and your friend didn't finish the bottle of wine, so I thought you might like to have a nightcap," he replied.

Oh, boy.

"Come on in. I'm not sure about the nightcap, but I can have a cup of tea while you have some wine if you'd like. I have to get up earlier than you, and, of course, you're younger than I am," I said.

I put the water on to boil, and grabbed a glass for his wine while he settled on the couch.

"What's being younger got to do with having wine?" he asked. "You know, you mention my being younger than you are a lot. What do you think that means?"

I *so* didn't want to have this conversation, especially since I was tired and he looked so good.

"I don't know what I mean by it, if I do say it. I don't notice I say it, but if you say I do, I guess I do," I mumbled.

MUTE: *What did I just say?*

"Are you nervous?" he asked.

MUTE: *Hell, yes, I'm nervous. I'm trying not to jump your bones and drag you upstairs. Not quite as romantic as Dr. Zhivago.*

"No. I'm tired," I said.

"Why didn't you say so? I'll go home and let you get to bed."

He came over, kissed me on the top of my head, and tousled my hair. "Sleep tight, Annabelle. I'll tell you later what your boyfriend from the other night wanted when he called today."

"What? Boyfriend? You don't really think that guy was my boyfriend, do you?"

"I didn't think *you* thought he was your boyfriend, but I got the impression from him today on the phone that *he* thought he was your boyfriend."

He was standing with his hand on the doorknob, but I didn't want him to go until I made sure he knew Marlon was not my boyfriend.

"You know I met him through Match.com, and that date was the first time I had ever seen him, right? He seemed like a nice person, but nobody I could be interested in. In fact, I just told him that in an e-mail, so he is definitely not my boyfriend. And, boyfriend? I'm fifty years old. Is a guy who is going with a fifty-year-old woman called a boyfriend?"

"If he's lucky, he's called a lover," he said, and walked out the door.

Now how was I going to sleep?

Chapter 11

Friday, April 12, 2013

I WOKE UP SWEATY AND uncomfortable from the unseasonal April temperatures. It was 6:30 a.m. and already 60 degrees, and the radio was predicting rain, chance of hail, the possibility of dangerous storms, and not ruling out tornadoes. I don't know if since I turned 50 the weather has taken on more importance for me or if I just can't remember that it always did.

Friday meant everybody at EFB dressed more casually than usual. Dress codes had relaxed a bit since I first started working there. Al and the brass still wore jackets and dress pants; but there were those who didn't exactly look pulled together from Monday thru Thursday; and on Friday they looked like they were a) going to the beach b) working in their yard c) working a pole at a stripper club. This was no issue for me, since I wore pretty much the same kind of thing most days, i.e., black pants and whichever top was hanging nearest to the pants in my closet.

Even 71 traffic didn't seem so buttoned up on Friday morning. Even though I had to work that Saturday, Friday was a short day, and it felt like freedom. I found my way to my desk, checked my e-mails, and found another from Detective Jamison asking if I could meet him downtown at police headquarters on my lunch hour. I had a choice but decided to go, clinging to the notion that I might be able to find out what he knew. I think you call this being a Pollyanna. I concentrated on taking as many calls as I could that morning because: No calls mean no commission. No commission means no bills paid.

"Danken Gott!" whooped Sophie as she hung up the phone.

"What's up?" I asked her.

"That was Detective Jamison. I'm no longer a suspect in Homer's murder. My alibi checked out. I feel like I just lost fifteen pounds."

MUTE: *You don't want to connect those dots: More Salvador Dali than Andrew Wyeth.*

"Congratulations? Is that what you say when a friend has been exonerated as a murder suspect?"

"I'll take it," she said.

Phone alert.

"Good morning, EFB. This is Annie. How may I help you?"

"Yeah, hi. Is it Annie?" said the pleasant male voice.

"Yes, sir. How may I help you?" I asked again.

"I hope you can help me. You're not going to believe this, but I bought a house last month up here in Michigan for $15,000, and I put it on my credit card."

"Wow," I said.

MUTE: *Technical jargon is the hallmark of a true professional.*

"Yeah, I guess you don't hear that too much," he said.

"No. That's a first for me," I replied.

"Well, here's the thing—do you think I can refinance it with the bank, because the interest rate on this card is about seventeen percent, and that's a killer, if you know what I mean."

Generally, I would point somebody with a $15,000 loan to a local bank, where they are better prepared to work a refinance for such a low amount, but there was something about him that I liked, and, what the hell, I was curious what a $15,000 house in Michigan looked like.

"Yes, I do know what you mean. That's a high interest rate. I can take an application, and we can give it a try," I said.

"Great. Shoot. What do you need from me?" he asked.

I went through all the questions for the application, said we'd need an appraisal, and asked what he thought about the value.

"If the place isn't worth $15,000, I'd be mighty surprised: A house for $15,000!"

A few weeks later when the appraisal came back, I guess this nice guy was mighty surprised because it came in at $5,000 based on what else was selling in his neighborhood. The house itself was small, to be sure, but it wasn't in bad shape. But if your house is surrounded by foreclosures, it isn't going to have much value. That is the sad truth about this market.

~

Detective Jamison greeted me at the door and ushered me into the same room I had been in previously.

"Good afternoon, Ms. Fillmore," he said in his usual businesslike manner.

"Hi. How are you doing?" I asked.

"I have a few questions I'd like to ask you about Jan Mulligan."

"Jan?"

"Have you known her long?" he asked.

"I think she's been at EFB about five years. I know her from working with her. She's the head of the Underwriting Department, and that's a tough job I would guess. We want all of our loans to close, and the Underwriting Department wants to adhere strictly to either Fannie Mae, Freddie Mac, or, definitely, EFB guidelines."

"When you say, 'we,' I assume you mean loan officers."

"Yes, loan officers and our managers," I said.

"Do you know if she and Homer Doukas had any problems?"

"I think I told you almost everybody had a problem with Homer, and the Underwriting Department seemed to be one of the places he concentrated a lot of his anger," I replied, remembering the shouts coming from Jan's desk.

"Particularly Jan? He would get maddest at Jan?"

"Yes. She was in charge, so she's the one he would get

mad at. But, she didn't take much from him without giving it back, so I don't think there was any repressed bile on her part."

"Is there anything you can tell me about their relationship that isn't public knowledge?" he asked.

Was he asking me if they were getting it on? That would have been hard to believe. Jan was a very striking blonde, about 6' in the stilettoes that she wore every day, and was one of the people who didn't adhere to 'casual Friday' or casual anything. She dressed to kill every day in short skirts and body-hugging jackets, and received a lot of attention from the guys whether they needed to speak with her on business or not. She wasn't of the same ilk as Crystal, and I doubt whether Homer's money would have attracted her to him even if she needed money. "No, I don't know anything about their relationship, except that it wasn't friendly," I said.

"Okay, I'll let it go for now. I also wanted to thank you for having Mrs. Doukas speak to me about the guys we thought were loan sharks who were following you. We will be dealing with them when we have conclusive evidence that what she says they said is true."

"You're welcome. I didn't want Crystal, Mrs. Doukas, to get herself in trouble."

"Right. Have you uncovered anything else we should know about that might identify Mr. Doukas's murderer? Or have you any suspicion that might be helpful to me at this point in the investigation?"

Oh, man. I had to think of what I knew that he didn't know: the J. Edgar Hoover list of people Homer was more or less blackmailing: what I now knew about Alice Mayview, the hidden box at the Doukas's home that might hold evidence, my conversation with Troy Whitman. I also believed that Jan Mulligan must have been in the building that Thursday. Why else would Detective Jamison be questioning me about what I knew about her. But he knew that, too.

"No, I don't have any suspicion at this point," I said, not lying. "Oh, and Sophie was so happy to hear that her name has been cleared. That's very good news," I added.

"Well, then, thank you for coming down on your lunch

hour," he said, not even acknowledging my last statement.

"You are welcome, anything I can do to help. But I do have a question," I said.

"Yes?"

"I'm so concerned about Gladys Wilkins. A group of us have been helping her out during the day, but not knowing about what happened to Rodney can't be helping with her recovery."

"I wish I had an answer for Mrs. Wilkins, but, unfortunately, every road we have taken has been a dead end. I'm pretty sure, though, that once we find who killed Homer, we will find out what happened to Mr. Wilkins," he stated.

I think everybody thought the same thing, but that didn't help Gladys.

Although I was able to take half a day off on Friday, I didn't want to leave until I got back to EFB and had a conversation with Jan Mulligan. What I was going to say to her? I had no idea. I planned on winging it, the blueprint for the way I have led my life. First I checked in with Sophie to see how Gladys was doing.

"Physically, she seems stronger, but with each day that passes without knowing what happened to Rodney, she's lost. When I mention his name, she just gazes out her window looking so bewildered. I've told her that Detective Jamison has made this his first priority, but the longer it goes on, the less promise that holds for her," she said.

"I wish I had more time to spend with her."

"Hey, you've got a murder to solve, right? Right," she confirmed.

"I don't solve murders, but if I find something that may help, I'm only too happy to share," I explained.

"Yeah, yeah. Whatever."

Jan Mulligan was standing at her desk with a couple of loan officers, laughing convivially. It was hard to read her. She was glamorous for EFB and seemed to like the attention of the guys, but she didn't seem to be taken in by their flirtations. She was a tough cookie and could stand her ground against anybody, which she often did.

I waited my turn as Rick and Kevin fought their cause to try to save their loans; Jan told Rick, no way, and told Kevin that she'd look into the matter further.

"Annie," she said by way of letting me know I was next.

"Jan, I'm sorry to disappoint you, but this isn't about one of my loans."

"That is bad news. I was hoping I could wrestle one of the ladies to the floor instead of another guy," she said winking at me.

"You may or may not know that a few of us have taken it upon ourselves to help out Gladys Wilkins. You know, Rodney Wilkins' wife," I said.

"Oh, right. That's very nice of you. Can I do anything to help?" she asked.

"Not go to her home, but maybe you can help with this. I know you work late on Thursday nights; were you still here when Rodney came in that night?" I asked.

She was taken aback, and for the briefest moment I thought she was going to lose her cool. "I've gone over all of that with Detective Jamison, so why are you asking me about that night?" She quickly pulled herself together and gave me the haughty look she was known for.

"Well, Sophie just got back from seeing Gladys. She seems to be recovering from the hospital stay, but not knowing where Rodney is weighs on her terribly. I just thought I'd ask you so I could tell Gladys if there was anything that would put her mind at ease. I sure can't ask Detective Jamison what he talked about with you, but I thought maybe you could let me know," I explained.

"Hmm, I did see Rodney come in as I was leaving. It was on the late side. I didn't pay much attention to him; but, yes, I did see him. But I have no idea what time that would have been."

I'm pretty sure she knew what time it was, because I'm pretty sure Detective Jamison found her exit badge time, giving him a reason to call her in. I'm also pretty sure she didn't say hello to Rodney. Some people talk to the cleaning staff, others don't—she was one who didn't.

"Was there anybody else that you saw in the building that night?" I asked.

"I think we're done here. It's none of your business. If you are helping that guy's wife out, that's fine, but you're not a cop, are you? Why do you want to know who else was here? I don't like the way this conversation is going, and I don't like snoops," she declared, sitting down and turning her attention to her computer.

You definitely knew where you stood with Jan Mulligan: the No Sale Department.

I went back to my desk, logged off my computer, and told Chad I was leaving because I was scheduled to work on Saturday.

"Not a problem. But you better start paying more attention to the phones and taking some loans, instead of spending so much time on this Homer thing," he warned.

His commission was based on the team's commission, so he was covering his own butt, and I couldn't blame him. To me, finding out about what was going on with 'this Homer thing' was much more compelling than mortgages.

My plan was to go home, relax, and think about what my next step should be. I was honest with Detective Jamison—I didn't know who murdered Homer, but, without knowing what he knew, I guessed it was someone on the "J. Edgar Hoover" list. That was my plan, but my cell rang en route to Lakeview. It was Marilyn, in a dither because she had received a call from a guy who lived between Cincinnati and Dayton who thought he had found Archie scavenging in his field.

"I don't feel comfortable going to a strange guy's home, especially since it sounds like he lives in the middle of nowhere. Can you please come with me?" she begged.

The middle of nowhere was more or less where the guy must have lived if he lived between Dayton and Cincinnati. I knew this country from when I drove all over the mid-West in a job selling video software. You can get to that area via I-75 in about 40 minutes. Much better was to take the scenic route, which took about 25 minutes from Marilyn's house.

"I'll just run in to see if it is Archie so we won't spend too much time there. I know you have to work tomorrow," she said.

It was about 2:30. I drove straight to Marilyn's, where she was waiting at the door for me. I left my car in the driveway, and we climbed into her SUV. A 5'2" me getting into an SUV must look like Winnie the Pooh getting his head out of a honey pot—nothing but ass.

"I didn't know if you had a chance to eat, so I made you some soup, Lipton's Chicken Noodle," Marilyn said as she handed a thermos to me.

You can't quarrel with someone who is thoughtful enough to put anything in a thermos for you.

We made our way to Route 741, what I call the back road to Dayton. It doesn't take long before you are out of suburbia and in the country. This area is also known as the Miami Valley, and I've read that about two hundred years ago people believed it's where the West began.

When driving up that winding road straddled on either side by farmland and trees, I would not be surprised to see Indians in the break in the trees.

"Can you believe Archie would have wandered this far away?" Marilyn asked.

"Remember the *Incredible Journey*."

"But the pet found the people, not the other way around," she shot back.

She had a point.

"If it's not him, at least we've had a nice drive in the country," I commented. But the skies looked ominous. It looked like cone-shaped clouds were forming on the horizon.

"Gertie is saying take a left up ahead," she said. Gertie being her GPS system.

The left turned out to be a road surrounded by what I guess were soybean fields getting ready for the spring planting. It looked like hundreds of acres, so I figured this guy was a farmer.

But I figured wrong. More Gertie-directed meandering found us on a dirt road at the end of which was a single-wide trailer landscaped ornately with old tires and a collection of rusted objects that had outlived their use about 20 years ago.

"This doesn't look good. Why couldn't Archie find a nice place like we visited in Indian Hill?" Marilyn asked.

"I'm going in with you. This looks nasty," I said.

"No. I'll just hit the horn to see if he comes out."

Marilyn beeped the horn to let the guy know we were there, and we waited. The door opened, and swamp man emerged; you could smell him with the windows and doors closed. Marilyn opened the window and yelled, "Where's Archie?"

"Uh, he's inside sleepin.' Ya wanna come in?" he gurgled.

"No, thanks. Just bring Archie out," she replied.

"Ain't gonna work that way. You gotta come in and get 'em," he insisted.

"No, we're not getting out of the car."

He started toward the car, sashaying our way. "What's a matta ladies, don't like country hospitality?" he chided.

"Look, we just want Archie, and we'll be on our way," she said, closing the window until it was only a slit.

He was a big sucker, and by big I mean really, really fat. Afterward it took a while to get that piggy face out of my mind. He started hitting the car as if he were going to bang his way in.

I opened my door, with my pepper spray in hand, and got out. "Either bring Archie out right now or I'm calling the police," I warned.

"Heh, heh. You think you're scarin' me, girlie?" he gurgled, coming around to my side.

As soon as he got within a foot of me, I pointed the spray and let him have it. He fell to the ground so hard I thought he'd created a crater in his dirt driveway. I ran as fast as I could to the trailer, which made a NYC subway smell like Chanel #5, calling, "Archie, Archie." There was no Archie; there was nothing but filth.

By the time I returned to the car, the guy was lurching about with his hands over his eyes, burbling something I couldn't understand.

"No Archie. Let's get the hell out of here!" I yelled.

We started to back up but realized the slob had fallen again, this time almost directly in back of Marilyn's SUV.

"I can't back over him," she said, looking alarmed.

"Even this truck won't make it over that mound. Pull up and back up next to him, but we have to get out of this hell hole," I declared.

Adrenalin was surging in both of us, and with some backing and stopping, backing and stopping, she managed to turn around and jolted out of there as fast as she could, given the terrain.

We didn't say a word until we got back on 741 South. I turned to Marilyn and said, "Well that was a pleasant outing: We must do that again."

We started laughing, or it might have been hysteria, and we couldn't stop until we were almost back in Mason.

We pulled into Marilyn's driveway, happy to be back to civilization. It's hard to imagine people living like swamp man. There are probably fewer of them than there are soybean fields, but I wonder how many fewer.

"I'm sorry, Annie, for putting you through that."

"I'm glad I went with you. Promise you'll never go on a mission like that alone. Even Archie isn't worth putting yourself in danger."

"I guess," she sighed.

Once I pulled into my driveway, I made a silent promise that I wouldn't answer the phone, the door, or one single e-mail. And I didn't, despite the fact that there were three phone calls, one door knock, and a wacky number of e-mails, most of them were the usual suspects like Match.com, a politician asking for money, astrology, ArcaMax; a politician asking for money, and one from Ingrid; but that would have to wait until tomorrow. A promise is a promise.

Chapter 12

Saturday, April 13

I ENJOYED THE DELIGHTFUL CADENCE of the drizzle hitting my skylight until 6 a.m., when my radio alarm alerted me to the fact that I had to go to work that Saturday. I didn't mind it so much, because the hours of 8:30-2:30 are a lot better to me than 9-6. But that drizzle was beckoning me, like a siren song, to turn over, curl up, and keep dreaming.

No traffic on 71 that early on Saturdays, only one manager on duty at EFB, and phones ringing with fewer people to pick up meant more loans for me. Troy was working with me for our team, and he brought in a box of Krispy Kreme Donuts. Even though I needed a Krispy Kreme Donut like Chicago needs a swift breeze, I ate the glazed cruller and felt immediately hungry for another. Memo to self: Re: Gluttony. Never take a first bite of anything if you're not prepared to take a second bite.

Charlie Harris, the manager of another of our five teams, was also on duty that morning. His team and Chad's team were always dueling for first place in monthly funding, and I knew Charlie's team played dirty. To wit: one of my customers called one day to tell me he was withdrawing his $325,000 refinance loan because a guy named Sid (who was on Charlie's team) told him he could get him a lower interest rate and that he should withdraw his loan with me. It didn't happen. A customer can't withdraw and jump on a new refinance in less than 60 days, and by that time the rates could have gone up. But I knew this kind of skullduggery was fostered by Charlie.

I was surprised to see Al Markey at his desk when I arrived. He sometimes came in on Saturdays, but never much before 11 a.m. After I ate my donut, finished my coffee, and took a few calls, I knocked on his glass wall. He motioned me in, and I consciously avoided walking on the spot where Homer lay dead just over a week ago. Al didn't seem like the same man who had returned from Aruba freshly tanned and well rested. The guy I was looking at had lost weight, his face pallid, and looking like he had lost his best friend, whom I'm almost certain wasn't Homer.

"Happy Saturday, Al," I said.

"Hi, Annie. How are the calls this morning?"

"Few, and mostly service calls," I replied, which meant a customer wanted service of some kind, but not a mortgage.

"Keep at it. I'm sure you have some previous customers you can call to rustle up some business."

"Sure, that's what I had in mind," I said. But if you were trolling for business on your phone line, you'd miss the call of a customer looking for a mortgage; definitely a coin flip. I continued, "I just wanted to see how you were doing under the circumstances."

"It's been tough. I'll be glad when it's all over, and they bring whoever did this terrible thing to justice. I thought Jamison would have this wrapped up by now, but now I wonder if we'll ever find out what happened."

"My big concern is about Rodney Wilkins," I said. We can't do anything for Homer, but I thought if the police found something by now, maybe they could find what happened to Rodney, and at least let Mrs. Wilkins know one way or the other that he didn't just run out on her."

Al looked at me across his desk, but it might as well have been across an ocean. "That's the worst of it," he mused, and looked back at his computer, dismissing me.

I went back to my desk and flipped the coin that told me to wait for the phone to ring and cross off a few items on my to-do list.

I had three appraisals come in via e-mail. I wanted to review them before I called my customers to let them know whether we could go forward with the loan—if the value was what we needed. The first appraisal I looked at was for a man and his wife in Tennessee. The value was there, but I checked to see that there was nothing glaring that would obviate closing the loan. Once that was done, my favorite part was looking at the photographs of the home; it was always fun to see how others lived. The salient feature of this home was the tripod with video camera pointed at the master bed. Oh, my!

The next appraisal I reviewed was of a beautiful home in South Carolina owned by Mr. and Mrs. Slider. Mrs. said she was a real estate broker, but there seemed to be uncertainty as to whether she actually earned the $125,000 she said she did, because she hadn't filed taxes on that income. She couldn't figure out why a mortgage lender would care if she filed taxes or not. This misreading of the law of the land went hand-in-hand with what I saw on the appraisal: In each and every room, except the three bathrooms, were distinct portraits of Mr. and Mrs. Slider displayed on large easels. If you're that pleased with yourself, I guess you don't see the need to pay taxes.

When my phone rang, I was unhappy to hear it was Mr. Bhakta, who had been attempting to refinance what he said was his primary residence. All indications, i.e., driver's license, telephone bills, utility bills, indicated his primary residence was in Chicago, but he insisted he lived here in Cincinnati and that his second home was in Chicago.

"What is the problem, Miss Fillmore. Why is someone questioning my residence?" he asked. The processor had apparently called him to ask him if the Cincinnati residence was, indeed, his primary.

"Because, sir, all of your information you receive on a monthly basis like your telephone bills and your utility bills are mailed to the Chicago address. It would seem that the Chicago residence is your primary and the Cincinnati home is your second home," I said.

"Oh, no, madam, this is my first home. I live here with my wife."

"But your driver's license also has the Chicago address on it," I pointed out.

"Yes, madam, you are correct. It is just for convenience that we use the Chicago address," he explained.

"I'm going to need some definitive information that the Cincinnati home is your primary home, and not the Chicago residence. If you cannot provide me with that, I'm afraid we are not going to be able to continue with the refinance."

"Why is this so difficult? I want to refinance my home; that is all," he whined.

"Mr. Bhakta, there are guidelines that say you may not misrepresent yourself or your dwelling; if you do, you will be turned over to the Fraud Department, and you will not be able to refinance with EFB."

"This is a very bad policy, very bad indeed to tell your customers they are misrepresenting themselves. I don't like this," he complained.

"I don't like it either, Mr. Bhakta; but we will now have to wait to see what the Fraud Department finds out."

"You have a bad policy, Madam," he said and hung up.

At about 11:15, Al called out to the floor, "See you guys, I'm going home to do my taxes."

Oh, geez, with all the murder and havoc, I'd forgotten all about my taxes. I would have to get to that on Sunday.

I took a walk to the Bra to see what goodies were stocked in the automatic machines. Generally, the auto coffee was swill, but I had found that the cappuccino had enough sugar in it to mask the sourness. I dropped my coins in, grabbed my steaming cup of cappuccino, and walked down the hall, up the stairs and all the way to the Grand Entry.

I climbed the red-carpeted stairs with my free hand holding the ornamental railing that led to the third floor where Homer's office had been. Well his office was still there, but Homer was no longer holding court in it. I wondered if there was a way to get into his office. I know he took the hidden elevator to the third floor, but you needed a security card for that, and I didn't want anybody to know I was snooping around. This is the kind of thing that makes no sense to me: you need a security card to enter the elevator, but you can traipse up the stairs to the same place at will.

Homer's office was across from the staircase. Actually, his office was off the back of Alice Mayview's office, which one entered through an alcove off the hall. The view of Homer's office was obstructed by two enormous carved doors. I walked as quietly as I could into Alice's office because I didn't know if anybody might have been working up there that day. The coffee-colored carpet was thick enough to mask my footsteps, but my heart felt like it was beating to a Sousa march. It was dark: no windows, no natural light. I didn't want to turn on any lights even if I could find them. I made my way around her desk to the "Columbus Doors." I reached out my hand for the knob, when someone grabbed my wrist. "What are you looking for?" said a man's voice.

My heart stopped its patriotic thing and stopped completely. I turned quickly to see it was Troy.

"What the hell are you doing, trying to scare me to death?" I asked.

"What are you doing up here?" he retorted.

"What are YOU doing up here?"

"I followed you from downstairs, and I wouldn't mind checking out Homer's office."

"I know I shouldn't be snooping, but it's so slow down there, and I just wanted to take a look around Homer's office," I explained.

"Hmm," he murmured.

"You interrupted me as I was trying to turn the knob to his office."

"Turn away, I'm right behind you."

But the knob didn't turn. "It's locked," I said.

"Maybe Alice has a key in her desk," Troy suggested.

"I don't think we should be looking through Alice's desk."

"Why? It's okay to look in Homer's things, but not Alice's desk?"

"Homer is dead. Alice is alive," I said.

"It doesn't matter. I have to get into that office. I want to make sure he hadn't already pulled the plug on me. There might be paperwork on his desk."

"If there were paperwork, Detective Jamison would have taken anything and everything in it and on it; so if he did pull the plug on you, it's too late."

"What are you looking for if you think everything is gone?" he asked.

I sure wasn't going to tell him I was looking for a combination to the lock in Homer's Pandora's Box.

"I just wanted to see his office. I'm not looking for anything."

"What the hell? I think I just saw a light on that wall in the hall," he warned.

As quick as a couple of prairie dogs we dived under Alice's desk, and while ample enough room for me, Troy was a tall guy. He took up too much space, with his feet sticking out under the chair. We held our breath, at least I did, until we saw there was a security guard on duty making his rounds. We stayed put until we heard the sound of the elevator and assumed that the guard had left the third floor.

"I'm getting out of here. If you want to stay and meddle, have at it, but I'm gone," I said, tiptoeing across the carpet toward the stairs. I peeked around the corner of the alcove wall to make sure the guard was gone.

I walked as quietly as I could down to the second floor. When I made it to the Grand Entry Hall I started breathing again. Too soon. Out came the guard from behind one of the three Corinthian columns that embellished the hall.

"Hey, miss. What were you doing upstairs?" he asked.

"Me? Upstairs? Oh, no, I was just taking a break and doing my stair exercises. You know it's good for the heart," I replied with an amiable grin.

"You better use the stairs at the other end of the hall if you want exercise," he stated.

"You're right, it makes more sense, but these stairs are so much nicer."

"Nicer or not, you're not allowed upstairs, especially until this mess is done with. Upstairs is off-limits, unless your office is up there, until the police give us the go-ahead."

"I don't know what I was thinking," I muttered as I moseyed down the hall to the plebian stairs.

My phone started ringing as soon as I opened my door.

"Annie, hi. It's Marilyn. I found out who took Archie's collars off."

"Oh, good. Who?" I asked, although I don't know if it was really good,

"The kid who lives next door and his delinquent friends," she said.

"Delinquents? Your neighbor's kid who's going to West Point next year?"

"His friends probably put him up to it."

"What did they say?" I asked.

"He came over to apologize and said they just thought Archie needed to be able to wander a little, not thinking he wouldn't come right back. Josh said they followed him, but they lost them in the woods, and he hasn't seen him since."

"Well at least we know he wasn't eaten by a squirrel or made into a doggie pie," I said.

"But he still could have been killed, or worse, is living with another family."

"He isn't exactly Lassie; he's a pest; not everybody would love him as much as you do."

"I don't know if that's a good thing, or not."

Neither did I.

Next to ring my phone was Crystal. "Hi, Annie. It's Crystal. I just wanted to tell you they are letting me go home on Monday."

"That's great, I'm sure you'll be happy to sleep in your own bed again," I said, envisioning the gilt four-poster bed with the curlicues on headboard and baseboard.

"It will be good to be home, but I'm still scared to think whoever killed Homer might want to kill me."

"Did Detective Jamison say he will have police on duty outside your house for a while?" I asked.

"Yes, but you know how in the movies they kill the policeman outside a hospital room to get into the room. They get whoever they want."

"I can understand why you're worried, Crystal, but I'm sure Detective Jamison will make sure nothing happens to you," I said, not knowing at all how he could prevent her from being killed if the killer wanted to get to her.

"I was thinking, maybe I could drill through the big box in the fireplace to get to the little box," she proposed.

"I don't think that's a great idea. From what you said, he was a little crazy, so you don't know if he has that safe wired, or something like that. I would leave it alone. I'm going to try to get into his office at EFB this week, and let's wait to see if I can find the combination or something that will give us a clue as to how to proceed. Okay?"

I was probably being overly cautious, but it didn't sound like a good idea to me for Crystal to work a drill.

The last call of the day was Neil, not a usual suspect, but a welcome one.

"Hi, Annie. It's Neil."

"Hey, what's up?" I asked.

"If you aren't doing anything tomorrow, do you want to take a drive up to Yellow Springs with me?" he asked.

"I was kind of setting aside tomorrow to do my taxes," I said. "But I guess I can do that tonight," I quickly added.

"Great. How about I pick you up about ten o'clock, and we can grab some brunch at The Winds," he said.

MUTE: *Oh, goody, goody.*

"That will be fine. See you tomorrow morning," I said.

Chapter 13

Sunday, April 14

NEIL SHOWED UP AT 10 on the dot in an antique yellow convertible Jeepster, which was a big surprise to me, because he usually drove a black Nissan pickup truck.

"Wow. What's with the yellow submarine?" I asked.

"It's my Dad's. You know he collects antique cars. I thought we'd put the top down. We're going to hippieville, and this is kind of a hippie car," he replied.

"More of a surfer, beach bum car, but it's great. Let's put the top down, break out the love beads, and head for Yellow Springs," I said.

Yellow Springs was about an hour north of Cincinnati, east of Dayton, and the home of Antioch College, one of the foremost liberal arts schools in the country. Or it was until around 2008, when it closed its doors. Kids and parents aren't exactly knocking down the doors of liberal arts colleges these days. It seems they prefer to study only the subjects that lead to dollar signs—the more the better. Antioch reopened in 2011 to a very small class of 30-odd students. I don't mean the students were odd, but, hopefully, they were odd enough not to want to make their life's goal to end up with the biggest pile of coins. If you're a billionaire but don't read anything but annual reports, can you really have a full life?

Sometimes when I leave EFB for the weekend, some of my associates say jokingly, "What are you going to do this weekend, go home and read?" The answer usually being "Yes," it was delightful to be going to Yellow Springs with someone who also read. The hipster car and the laughs were icing on the cake.

We made our way through a countryside that was similar to the one Marilyn and I saw on Friday, but this drive was farther east and the land was flatter, and in some areas the horizon more distant. Wussy, Echo and the Bunnymen, The Jesus and Mary Chain, and Wilco were the soundtrack on the CD player Neil's father thoughtfully installed. Neil liked Indie Rock, and it was fine with me; it fit the mood of driving in a yellow convertible with the top down, in 70 degree April weather with a cool guy. It made me feel that I was about twenty years old. All promise.

We had to pass through Xenia on our way north to Yellow Springs. Xenia is a town tragically hit by many tornadoes, and I always cringe when I drive through it. It is said that the Shawnee Indians referred to it as the place of the devil wind. It was nearly destroyed in 1974, and again in 1989 and 2000. I wasn't pitching my tent. We passed through the town on Rte. 68, keeping pace with the bikers to our right, and followed it into Yellow Springs.

Finding a parking place can be a challenge, especially on a lovely day like that Sunday, but we managed to find one not too far from The Winds. As much as I enjoyed the ride and the music, the blare of both precluded conversation, and I was interested in hearing what Neil had been doing when he hadn't been keeping Delhi Deli afloat.

He had made reservations, so the wait wasn't too long.

We settled in over his trout with scrambled eggs, with fries drizzled with something that looked and smelled luscious and my huge English Muffin topped with some mushroom concoction and poached egg. We looked at each other and smiled.

"So how is your Sherlock Holmes thing going?" Neil asked.

"It's not *my* Sherlock Holmes thing, it's the police's thing. People just tell me their business whether I ask them or not. Remember from the video store days?"

"All I remember from the video store days were those couple of times you say we had too much to drink, and you know, the kissing and stuff part?"

"Didn't we have this conversation about never bringing that up again? It's so embarrassing."

"So you've mentioned. Embarrassing isn't the word I would use. I might say mind-blowing. That's why I'm still hanging around. I can't forget that."

It was eye-popping to realize those kisses made me feel as I never had before, but the guy was 20 years younger. How self-respecting could I be? The heat and blush on my face must have been a tip off that I agreed with him.

"I knew you felt the same way even though you've clammed up about it ever since."

"Back to my Sherlock Holmes 'thing' from the video store days."

" Oh right, I forgot about that. So, even though you are not trying to solve the crime or aren't collecting information, what do you know so far?"

MUTE: *"I know nossing. I see nossing."*

"Here are the facts, just the facts, sir." I don't know if he got the *Dragnet* reference. "Homer was found dead under the balloons on Friday, April 5. The coroner thinks he had been dead since about midnight, or that's what I heard she thought. Rodney Wilkins, one of our maintenance staff, has been missing since that night. The two guys who were following me turned out to have had an insider trading deal with Homer that cost them fifty thousand dollars. Three people who were in the building around the time Homer was killed were Troy Whitman, Jan Mulligan, and Rodney Wilkins, who is now missing. There's other stuff that I know, but I don't know if any of it is relevant or not."

"Like what?" he asked.

"I know you wouldn't tell anybody I told you this, but what if you were abducted by the killer, and they threatened to waterboard you if you didn't tell them what you knew? What then?"

"What if that happened? If that happened, I'd overtake

them with my Indian voodoo and stuff their throats with all the plump, newly made cannoli I could get my hands on with the plastic wrap still on them. That would take care of it, don't you think?" he said.

I've had his cannoli (Samali's cannoli really), and that wouldn't be a bad way to die, plastic notwithstanding.

"All right, I get your point. One of the women at EFB knows about a list of people that Homer kept, kind of like J. Edgar Hoover. A list of people he 'had' something on. You know what I mean?" I asked.

"Yeah, I get it."

"If they knew what he had on them, that would be a motive for murder; but I don't know who is on the list, except Crystal Doukas, and I don't think she killed him. One of the strange things is that it looks like somebody from inside did it, but the only people I know of who were inside according to security cameras and security badges were Troy, Jan, and Rodney; so if it wasn't one of them, how did the killer get into the building without being seen?" I queried.

"How do you know those three people were the only ones in the building? Couldn't there have been others?"

"Yeah, but if there were, the only person who knows is Detective Jamison. The woman I know might be able to find out, but that's a long shot," I said.

The waitress came over to ask us if we would care for anything else.

We decided to pass on coffee to enjoy a walk around the town and the "crunchy'" stores. As soon as we stepped onto the cobblestone path, I realized we had talked all about the murder and I had found out nothing of what Neil was up to. More coffee might be needed after all.

With some of the doors open because of the welcome early spring, patchouli wafted out into the street, and the song *If you're going to San Francisco, be sure to wear some flowers in your hair* played in my mind; that was the background music for the rest of the day.

I followed Neil into Dark Star Books, which does sell books but also comics and fantasy kind of stuff that seemed to attract him.

"Do you like fantasy?" I asked him.

"Only when it's really, really dark," he answered. "You know the stuff that's so dark and scary it makes life seem not so long."

"Are you kidding? That's pretty depressing."

"I'm kind of kidding," he admitted.

Whoa. We needed to have that coffee talk. The San Francisco song stepped up its volume in my head: *All across the nation, such a strange vibration.* Oh, boy, I was stuck with this for the afternoon.

We stopped next at a store with Birkenstocks, natural dyed t-shirts, head wraps, and fabric sling bags, so I must have been among the *gentle people there, with flowers in their hair*, and I felt great because it reminded me of a visit I had made to Haight-Ashbury that went along nicely with the music in my noggin. Neil insisted on buying me one of the hippie sling bags that was olive green bursting with orange flowers. I love it when people buy me things spontaneously, and I insisted on taking my leather bag back to the car, where I swapped contents, and we happily continued our store-hopping in style.

We next checked out a Tibetan store, a Peruvian store, another Indian store, and an herbal and spice shop where I bought some passionflower tea for Neil to go with a crazy black donut-shaped teapot I bought for him at a pottery store.

By that time both of us wanted to sit down and have a cup of coffee, or tea, or whatever else we could find at the Underdog Café.

"I know you have this Richard Lewis thing going, but are you really depressed?" I asked.

"Yeah, I am. I take meds, though, and they seem to help. And a day like this helps, too."

"Have you always felt like this, even as a kid?"

"It's hard to say, because when you're a kid you think everybody feels the same as you. You know what I mean?"

"Yeah, I do. Well, whatever I can do to help, I'd be happy to," I offered.

"Thanks. The music also helps, I mean playing music and

listening, but especially playing."

"Good. Keep at it," I advised.

"Enough of this boring shit," he said. "What makes you think one of those three people who were in the building didn't kill the boss?"

"I don't know for sure, but when you know someone, it's hard to conceive they could actually do something like that."

"Very naïve for someone of your age, don't you think?"

"Can you imagine anyone you know killing someone?" I asked.

"I can imagine all of them killing someone, especially me," he joked.

"I guess it could be one of them, but unless there is something I don't know, it seems like their dislike for him wouldn't be deep enough for them to wield a letter opener."

"That's a shitty way to die, by letter opener, don't you think? So ignominious."

"Ignominious?"

"Yeah. I've always wanted to use that word in a sentence," he explained.

"Well said then."

"Are you sure there is no other way into the building: Windows in the back, or a basement? Because it seems like the inside trader dudes would be the obvious suspects," he offered.

"There are windows in the back, and windows in the basement, but there are bars over them, and the windows are locked," I said.

"What about chimneys? Is there a chimney?"

"That's right, you haven't seen the place. There are five chimneys, but I can't imagine how anybody could scale them; they soar about fifteen or twenty feet above the roof. And I'm not even sure they are not sealed."

They probably are closed off, because I've never seen a fire in any fireplace; it's not like the mortgage bankers get together for a brandy at 5:00 and talk of the day's social events or take a game of billiards in the billiard room. I'm sure there was a billiard room originally. It looks like a grand mansion, but now it is definitely a place of corporate business; a true facade.

"What about access below the basement?" Neil asked.

"What are you, a Hardy Boy?"

"Who?"

"It's an old book series about two teenage boys who were amateur sleuths," I explained.

"Kind of like you," he said.

"I'm not a sleuth. I don't purposely go out and try to solve murders."

"And De-Nile is just a river in Egypt," he quipped. "If it wasn't one of the people already in the building, it had to be somebody who got into the building undetected from outside, right?"

"I saw Detective Jamison with a huge floor plan on his desk at EFB before he left the bank. It looked like an original, because it looked hand-drawn and the paper was yellowed. There were several pages, and I loved the way it sounded and looked as he turned the pages. Actually, it looked cool enough to frame. So if there were a way to get into the place, I'm pretty sure Detective Jamison would know about it," I said.

"It has to be solved because of the janitor guy."

"Rodney Wilkins, right."

"Yeah, him. They can't just let that go even if they never found out who killed the boss."

"Agree one hundred percent. We have to find out what happened to him," I said.

"How about a few more stores?" he asked.

"I'm up for it."

We walked around the corner off of Rte. 68, and found a funky little store with crystals, tarot cards and readings, and Faerie paraphernalia. I'm well acquainted with all of these artifacts because my "parents" (my two aunts) believe in much of it and used these metaphysical gadgets to conjure, negate, and protect—mostly me, I think.

The store was manned by a strange-looking guy in faded jeans, a baggy black t-shirt, and long grey hair tied back in a ponytail. The place smelled of incense, but I'm pretty sure I could pick up a hint of weed as well.

"I like the smell of this joint. No pun intended," joked

Neil.

"Good afternoon, how may I help you on this fourteenth day of April?" the guy asked.

"We're just looking around," I replied.

"I've just returned from a faraway planet, and I delighted in new experiences I'd be happy to share with you," he suggested, leaning over the counter conspiratorially.

Neil whispered in my ear, "The Planet Cannabis."

"Thanks, we're fine," I said.

"How about a complimentary tarot reading for the lady?" the intergalactic traveler offered.

"I don't think so," I replied.

"Yes, I think you should. It'll be fun," said Neil.

The spaceman guy called for Joan in the back. "I have a complimentary reading for you, dear." Joan emerged in garb that would not disappoint the tarot: long black velvet skirt with some kind of red peplum over it, and a lacey blouse that showed her ample décolletage, silver filigreed earrings that touched her shoulders, and rings on every finger. Her hair was pinned high off her shoulders, with evocative tendrils spiraling down.

"Come with me, miss," she said. I don't know why my heart started to thud as I followed her to the back, which turned out to be a storage area with one small round table festooned with several table coverings, none of them looking fresh and new.

"Is this your first reading?" she asked, once we were seated and almost close enough for our noses to touch.

"No, I've had tarot readings before, but this is the first one with you," I answered.

"Of that, I'm certain. I would have remembered." She looked at me from under her heavy-lidded and made-up eyes, making me wonder why she would have particularly remembered me.

My aunts read the tarot all the time, but they are happy tarot readers, and I got the impression from Joan that she favored the dark side. Neil should have had his cards read instead of me.

"Please place your hands on mine," she requested, holding her hands face up, so mine faced down on top of hers.

"Hmmm," she murmured.

She released my hands, splayed the cards out in a fan shape, and said, "Pick five cards and give them to me facedown, please."

I did as she asked, and I kind of held my breath. Why was I so nervous? I hadn't killed anybody and wasn't a bad person—a little impatient and could be snarky if I was pushed, but on the whole I think I am a pretty reasonable person. So why the shakes?

"I'm using the five card spread today that will tell you what's going on in your Present, Past Influences that may have brought you to this point, what lies ahead in your Future, the Reason behind your present condition, and what the Potential is for you today," she explained.

The first card she turned over was a guy lying with ten swords in his back. I drew in my breath, and she looked up at me. "Have you seen this card before?" she asked.

"I don't know, but it looks kind of scary."

"It can be. This can mean a disaster in your life that came on suddenly or is to come, but I think it has already entered your sphere. Am I right?"

"It could be, I guess," I said, seeing Homer with only one "sword" in him, and facing up, not down.

The second card she turned up was the Devil. What a great reading.

"The Devil card can signify greed, anger, and tyranny, but I'm not feeling those in you. Do you know somebody close to you who might engender these qualities?"

I didn't want to unfold the Homer story for her, but I did want to know if by some miracle the next card she turned up would have a picture of the murderer.

"I work in a corporate bank, so I don't know about the anger, but the greed and tyranny would seem to fit some people," I said.

The World card appeared next, thank God. I knew from my aunts that this was a good card, so I was eager to hear what

Joan had to say about it.

"If I had to pick one card in the deck that is the most optimistic, I'd say it's the World card. It says what you have undertaken will come to fruition in the best way. You will enjoy fulfillment and success with what you have undertaken," she predicted.

What could this mean? I really hadn't undertaken anything. I had to remind myself that I didn't believe in any of this baloney.

She turned up the Magician, which at first blush looked like it might be a good omen. I was wrong. She said, "The Magician can indicate deception, trickery, abuse of power. Once again, these don't seem to apply to you; but they are present in your life. Do you know why?"

"I may," I said.

"The last card in the reading is the Wheel of Fortune."

Surely this was a good sign, maybe not as good as the World, but good, I thought.

MUTE: *You are incorrect, madam.*

"Reversed, as this card is, can mean a time of misfortune and unpleasant surprises. But let's keep in mind that the World card that is telling us the outcome is positive, so the Magician may be just a passing phase," she explained.

I didn't say anything. I didn't know *what* to say. This seemed pretty bleak to me, if any of it were true.

"I hope I have answered your questions today," Joan said, standing up and taking my elbow to direct me to the front of the store, where Neil and the planet guy were in deep conversation.

I gave her a $10 tip for the bad news. Neil said his goodbyes to his new best friend from another world.

"Geez. I'm not doing that again. It was dismal," I moaned.

"Do you believe it, or do you think it's a party trick?" Neil asked.

"I guess I don't believe it, but she sure was dead-on about what was happening right now with the murder and everything. She did say that anything I have undertaken will come out positively, so, if I did believe her, that's good."

"What next?" he asked.

I looked at my watch; it was 3:30, and an hour to get back home would mean I still would have time to finish my taxes and get that off my chest.

"I guess 'Home James, and don't spare the horses,'" I said.

"Huh?"

That's the problem about knowing people much younger than you. They don't get your jokes.

"It's something my aunts say. I think it was from an old movie; something a guy says to his chauffer," I explained.

"I like it. I'm going to use it and confound my friends. Another great word, confound, don't you think?"

"Yes, very Sherlock Holmes," I answered.

We drove back down Rte. 68. I felt sad that this great day was going to end, and from experience knew that I had to circle these days in my mind, because they don't come that often.

He pulled up at my condo, and we sat in his car chatting for about 15 minutes because I don't think either one of us wanted to part. I finally said, "I absolutely have to go to finish my taxes."

"Yeah. I'd better get up to the deli to make sure there are no poisoned customers. But this was fun. Can we do it again soon?"

I've known Neil for some years, and that slight frisson has always been in the air between us, and we've been out with friends and alone. We had even shared a couple of tipsy kisses; but, for some reason, this was different.

"Sure. I enjoyed it, too, and thank you for lunch and my trippy bag," I said. Then he leaned over to give me an awkward hug, and I kissed him on the cheek.

"You're a tough nut to crack," he said.

"What do you mean?"

"You know what I mean," he said, as he gently rubbed my shoulder.

I peeled myself out of the wonderful yellow car; and started inside to do my taxes.

Chapter 14

Monday, April 15, 2013

MONDAY MORNING WAS USHERED IN by April rains, grey and steady. Once again, removing myself from a warm bed to don weather gear and slog down 71 was not a thrilling prospect, but it had to be done if I wanted the comfort of the bed instead of a box on the street. True to form, Monday 8 a.m. traffic was bumper to bumper and as slow as a bill in Congress.

It was business as usual on the mortgage floor, and it seemed that to most people Homer's demise was only a vague memory. I think Al, Alice, Sophie, and I were among those who still had it uppermost in our minds—and, I suspect, the murderer, if it was indeed an employee of EFB. I settled in by reviewing e-mails, and the one that popped up first was titled Changes in Guidelines. These changes, whether from EFB or Fannie Mae or Freddie Mac, were the most challenging part of the job for me, along with remembering all the changes from day to day to tell customers. Even if Fannie Mae and Freddie Mac, the VA, or HUD have guidelines that are fixed, lenders can set their own rules that can affect whether a customer is eligible or not. If a credit score is set at 580 by FHA, but the lender thinks that's too low, they can set it at another number like 620 or 640. There are hundreds of these guidelines, called Over Lays, to remember. My first call came in at 9:20:

"EFB, This is Annie. How may I help you?"

"Yes, dear, this is Agnes Heppelworth. I do my banking

business with you on Evergreen and Shauncey streets. Do you have my records in front of you?"

"No, Mrs. Heppelworth, I don't have your records. But I could look you up with your Social Security number if you would like."

"Heavens, no. I wouldn't give a stranger my Social Security number no matter how nice they were," she said.

"I can look you up with your full name. Can you please spell it for me?"

"I'm not sure I want to give that information either," she replied.

MUTE: *Work with me here, Agnes.*

"If I have no way of looking you up in our system, no information about you, I won't be able to help you with what you are looking for today," I said.

"Oh, dear. What to do, what to do?" she asked herself.

I tried Heppelworth, then Heppleworth, then Happleworth, but I couldn't find her.

"Okay, look it up under Agnes H. Brown. That's my married name, but he died some years back, and I go by Heppelworth now. But it probably is under Brown come to think of it, but you know time has gone so fast since Edgar passed on that I can't remember if I'm under Brown or Heppelworth with you people. It was such a quick death that it was hard to make any sense of it. One minute he was here stoking the fire, and poof, the next minute he was dead in front of the fire. It just took my breath away."

MUTE: *Not to mention Edgar's.*

I got Ms. Heppelworth/Mrs. Brown taken care of and took a few more calls before our team's 11 a.m. meeting with Chad in A-8.

Sophie and I walked down the hall together, and she nudged me saying, "Anything new on who killed Homer?"

"Not really. I just wonder if Detective Jamison is any closer; but if he is, he isn't telling me," I answered.

"Poor Gladys. I stopped by on Friday, and she is a wreck; between knowing she is going to have to move and not having Rodney around, who I gather pretty much did everything for her but feed her, it's going to be tough," Sophie said.

"That's all I can think of, is Rodney. Where the hell is he? Even if it's just his body I think it would help, as terrible as that sounds," I stated.

"Agree," said Sophie.

The meeting was short and sweet the way Chad liked it: He told us of changes coming up that were to improve our lot. This, of course, was not coming from Chad; he was the messenger of the messenger of the messenger. When business took a downturn at all, we would get these flimflam promises. Or the messenger might be a step up from Chad, and it would be an even bigger deception: "We have something in the works that is going to change your life," or some bullshit like that. Nothing really changed, and it was okay, because we were still helping people and our paychecks kept coming, but it made me wonder who came up with these ideas and why did they think they were necessary? The doozy of all incidents came the day before we received word that our commissions were to be "changed" (read cut). Management heralded that notice by treating us to "Pizza Day" that the executives served us dressed in suits and latex gloves. One of the guys in line called out, "Hey, Homer, I'm allergic to latex."

Back at my desk, the first e-mail was from Alice asking if I could join her for lunch "off campus."

We drove over to a local pizza place where Alice chose a table way in the back. Over big Greek salads, she started to talk in a panicky voice as she added to her story. She wasn't ready to share the "Hoover" list, but she said, "I have to get this off my chest, and I didn't tell the police, but Homer kept recordings of all of his meetings."

"Where are they? Were they in his office?" I asked.

"I don't know where he kept them, but I looked in his desk before the police came, and I didn't see them. He was so shifty, who knows where they could be?"

"Did you want to hide them from the police, is that why you looked for them?"

"I wanted to listen to them to see if he had anything on there that would be bad for me," she admitted.

MUTE: *Good grief, aside from a peek at a thong, what would she have to hide? Whips? Chains?*

"What on earth could he have on you that you would be afraid the police would find out?" I asked.

"He was constantly accusing me of taking things. One time he even asked if I had taken a hundred dollar bill out of his top drawer. Of course, I hadn't, but I couldn't tell if he was accusing me of these things to keep me on my toes or if he really thought I took things," she said.

"Even if Homer recorded one of those conversations with you, I doubt the police would take much interest; they have bigger fish to fry. Wait. Was this what you were referring to the other day when you said Homer 'fixed' it so he did have something on you?"

"Yes, that's what I meant that I didn't want to share with you. But, still, I wonder where those recordings are."

"Do you think he kept them all?" I asked.

"Most assuredly. He was that kind of a person."

I wondered if they were in Pandora's Box, or wherever the combination to Pandora's Box was.

"Can you let me into Homer's office?"

"No, of course not. The police said even *I* couldn't go in there," she said rather huffily.

"There's nothing in there anyway. You said they carted everything out, didn't you?"

"Yes, they did take a lot out. I don't think there's anything left to see," she said.

"Right. So what difference if I take a look. Who's going to know? I'm not going to tell them, and you won't."

"What about the security guards? What if they see you go in there?" she asked with a shaky voice.

MUTE: *A in adventure might stand for Amelia, but definitely not Alice.*

"You can stand guard at the front of your alcove, and if you see somebody coming, I'll dive for safety," I said. I didn't mention I had already done the dive to safety thing the previous Saturday.

"Gosh, Annie, I don't know; you're putting me in a bad

position," she claimed.

"Listen, Alice, you're already in a bad spot. The only thing that my getting in that office is going to do is to find something that might help you," I said.

"Let me think about it on the way back to work," she said, with her brow all puckered up again.

"Fair enough," I declared, settling the bill for both of our salads.

MUTE: *I'm not above bribery.*

We made our way back to EFB in total silence except from some serious sighs emanating from the passenger seat.

"Are you okay, Alice?" I asked as we pulled into a parking space.

"Yes, I'm just trying to decide if I should let you in the office, and I just can't think it through," she replied.

"Let me help you. You should let me in the office. If the decision is that difficult, the scales are balanced I'd say."

"Oh, you're probably right. But when can you do it most safely?" she asked.

"There aren't any security guards roaming the halls while business is in operation. Why don't you send an e-mail that you need to see me, so that I can gain entrance to the Grand Stairway and your office?"

"Very well. I'll e-mail the guard station in about a half an hour so it doesn't look suspicious," she said. "I hope I'm doing the right thing," she added.

We stepped into the cloudburst under our umbrellas and went our separate ways. I got back to my desk and logged on for a few calls before I was called to Alice's office.

My phone didn't ring for about 15 minutes after I logged in, and I spent the time noodling over the rumor that had gone around the floor since I had been there that some of the higher funding loan officers got the good calls, and the rest of us didn't unless it was very busy. This was solid brass gossip based on the fact that some days there were only a few people who would get loans while the rest of us wrestled with service calls. The "word on the street" was that slam-dunk loan marketing code would go to the big funders and the marketing codes for a general question would go to the rest of us. Was it legal? Probably. Was it moral? You judge. Was it corporate business? Absolutely.

I checked my e-mails again, and the security desk appeared in my e-mail queue saying that I was free to go to Alice Mayview's office any time after 2:30 p.m., and that I should stop at their desk for a security pass. I quickly sent a copy to Alice with a note that I would be up to see her at 2:45.

As I made my way up the baronial staircase, I ticked off in my head what I needed to see in Homer's office, and number one was to see if I could find 120 boxes in which he could have stashed a combination to Pandora's Box, and, maybe, a key to the smaller box. I didn't know what number two or three would be, but I assumed I'd know it if I saw it.

Alice was waiting at the alcove entrance as twitchy as Don Knotts with a gun. "Are you sure you have to do this, Annie? I'd feel a lot better if you didn't."

"I'd feel a lot better if somebody hadn't murdered Homer and, maybe, Rodney Wilkins," I answered.

I stood at her desk for a few minutes listening for anybody coming down the hall, which was difficult to discern because the carpet up there was plush and hushed, as opposed to the industrial carpet in the mortgage department, which was meant for wear and spillage.

"We should have a signal in case something happens while I'm in there. Why not keep your phone open to Homer's office and say something if somebody stops by. I'll keep very still."

"Okay. How about, um, um, how about, 'Isn't it nice to see the sun again?'" she suggested.

"Interesting," I said. "Where do you see the sun from in here? And as you may recall, there was a torrential downpour when we came back from lunch. Did the sun come out?"

"Oh, I don't know. Let me know when you get into the office and look out the windows," she replied.

"How about you say, 'I can't wait until Friday,'" I offered.

"Okay. I can't wait until Friday," she echoed.

"Right. So say that if you hear somebody coming."

"Just when I hear them, or when they are already in my office?" she said.

"If you hear somebody coming. Once they are in the office, and you are talking to them, I'll be able to hear them."

"You are like a detective," she declared.

"A regular Sam Spade, and Sam is going to need a key to the office."

She said, "Turn around."

Good grief. I heard a few drawers open and close, I guess in an attempt to cover up where the key was; then Alice said, "Okay, you can turn around now."

I took the elaborate key and slipped it into the elaborate lock, but the door didn't open.

"The door isn't opening? Is there a trick?" I asked.

"Oh, no. You have to use the key, and once it's in the lock, I have to buzz you in," she said.

"How did Homer do this if you weren't here?"

"You can also buzz the buzzer, and then use the key, and that's what he would do. The buzzer is hidden as well as they key. So, turn around again so you can't see where the buzzer is," she instructed.

MUTE: *Patience? What's so virtuous about that?*

"Okay. Can you buzz me in now that the key is in the lock?" I asked.

She did. I entered.

Wow! It was very impressive. The walnut paneling and curlicues with cherubs and details on every piece of furniture was intense. But as notable as all of the workmanship and artistry was, they didn't trump the thrilling view through the huge Palladian windows of the Ohio River meandering its way from Pittsburgh to Illinois.

I sat down at Homer's desk, which must have been every bit as big as the Resolute desk in the Oval Office, but the room was big enough to accommodate it, even if it wasn't oval in shape. I started pulling out drawers, but, except for a few paper clips and other oddments, the drawers were empty.

I looked in two credenzas and a drawer in a table set between two wing chairs in front of the fireplace: more detritus.

I eyed the large books on the bookshelves on either side of

the fireplace. They had words like Equity, Leverage, and Dynasty in their titles. I couldn't read them. I wouldn't read them. The one I wanted to read was how it really all worked. Who had that book?

I sat on the window seat and admired the mighty Ohio River—even through the downpour, it looked stately—and I thought that this view was the only thing that Homer had had that I would like to have.

I started in earnest to look for 120 boxes, but I couldn't see anything that might replicate those square boxes indicated on that slip of paper. I sat down in his ergonomic chair, which was the only piece of furniture in the room that wasn't embellished with any froufrou, and swiveled to view the river again. I leaned back and closed my eyes and took a deep breath. What was I doing? Was I fantasizing that I could in any way help find out who murdered Homer and find out what happened to Rodney? You know, you get on a path and keep going, thinking you're headed for something magical, and then you stop, look around, and realize you're in a parking lot.

I leaned back in the chair, stretched my legs out, and looked up at the ceiling. I don't know if it was the chair that sprang up, or if it was just me, but there on the ceiling were boxes. The whole ceiling of Homer's office was comprised of a geometric pattern of wooden panels. I leaned back again and started to count, yep, twelve across, ten down. On the second look, I took stock of the height of the ceiling, it must have been 18' high. How was I going to get up there? Borrowing a ladder from the maintenance staff and walking it up the grand staircase wasn't going to work. I'd have to think of something.

I said good-bye to the spectacular view, left the office, bid Alice adieu, and went back down to the mortgage floor with its charming fluorescent vista.

After several calls, one loan, and a peek into one of the maintenance rooms to see if I could find an acceptable ladder, I clocked out and made my way back up 71.

I had no food in the house, so I decided to stop at Delhi Deli for dinner, and if I had to see Neil, oh well.

Again, I had to park at the other end of the strip mall and

make my way close to the buildings to avoid the rain.

The place looked crowded, and I could see Neil toward the back talking to some guy. He looked up and waved, and I wended my way toward him until the guy turned around and I saw it was Marlon. I stopped dead in the aisle, but I didn't think I could turn around and walk out. Neil motioned for me to come back, so I felt I had no choice.

"Good evening, Annie. I was just explaining to Marlon that we had reunited this weekend after our breakup last year," said Neil raising his eyebrows in some kind of code while Marlon was looking at me intently.

"That's right. After we saw each other here last week when I was having dinner with you, we realized maybe we should give it another chance," I said.

"Aren't you a lot older than he is?" Marlon asked.

"How gallant," I replied.

"Why are you on Match if you were interested in somebody already?" Marlon pouted.

"I guess I didn't know I was interested until I saw him again."

"All this is beside the point. From now on she's not going to be seeing anybody else but me," Neil interjected.

"Well, I think it stinks, that's what I think. I think you should have been up-front with me," Marlon said.

There was no use going further with something that was already not true, but nicer than letting Marlon know I just wasn't interested in him—a fact he obviously couldn't grasp.

"It does stink, I agree," I said, hoping that would be the end of it.

"I think I'm owed a further explanation," Marlon continued.

"There is no other explanation, and now I think it's time for you to leave so Annie and I can enjoy our dinner," Neil said.

"I'm going to report this," Marlon said, face reddening.

"That's a good idea, Marlon. That's what I would do," said Neil.

I had no idea Neil was such a take-charge kind of guy. I

was kind of stunned.

Once Marlon was actually out the door, Neil said, "Do you want to eat? Or has that spoiled your appetite?"

"It would take a lot more than that to spoil my appetite. I do think we should sit down and get straight that while that conversation was a very helpful way to show Marlon the door, it was just a ruse," I said.

"A ruse. I'll have to remember to use that in a sentence this week," he said. "Now, what would you like to eat?"

"Whatever you are serving that you think I would like," I said.

"How hungry are you?" he asked.

"Starving," I answered.

"I'll bring you the vegan cheese pie; it's really good. And, I'll join you for a glass of wine on the house," he said.

"Shouldn't I be buying you dinner after the Marlon fiasco? I'm going to have to block him from my Match page so he doesn't know I'm still looking."

"*Are* you still looking?" he asked as he left the table.

MUTE: *Search me! Wait, maybe that's not such a good idea.*

The minute I got home, I called Marilyn. "Marilyn, does Mike have a very lightweight thirteen- to fifteen-foot ladder?"

"I haven't measured his ladders, but I'm sure he's got what you need. Why?"

I unfolded the story for her about the panels on the very high ceiling in Homer's office.

"How would you get a ladder in the building without being seen?" she asked.

"I need some time to think about that. But if he has a ladder that will fit the bill, I'll figure out how we can do it," I said.

"We?" she asked.

"You don't think I can haul a ladder that size into EFB by myself, do you?"

"Good night BFF," she said, and hung up.

Chapter 15

Tuesday, April 16, 2013

THE CONTINUING DOWNPOUR MUST HAVE been payback for
the unseasonable warm and sunny weather on Sunday, and the
longer it rained the harder it was wresting myself away from
fragrant downy pillows to jump into a shower.

I dried off and checked out the hair situation, which wasn't
good. I needed an hour to make it look reasonable, and once I
did and I walked outside, the coiffeur chaos would no doubt
reign once more. I grabbed some pomade, or gel, or whatever it
was, and smooshed it down so it didn't look like I was wearing
a clown wig. Dear lord, I looked like an old-timey bartender.

On the way down 71, I went over what I had to do to
move forward on finding something out to bring in the nasty
piece of work responsible for this crime.

I *had* to find out from Alice who was on the "Hoover" list.
I didn't know how I was going to do it, but she did let me into
Homer's office, and that was strictly off-limits as far as the police were concerned. And the police didn't even know about
this list. The list had to be a priority, after working my job, of
course.

By the time I got to my desk, I was late and wet, and I
sensed the eyes of my co-workers on my hair.

MUTE: *Will that be your regular, Chauncey? Whiskey with a beer
chaser?*

I logged into my computer, checked e-mails, and jumped

on the phone queue.

"Good morning, EFB Mortgage. This is Annie. How may I help you?"

"Are you real? Are you a real person?" asked the caller.

"Yes, sir, I am a real person. How may I help you?"

"You can help me by telling your boss it's bad business to have customers call and get nothing but a machine, for starters. Then you can take my name off of your call list. I've received six calls from you this week, and I don't appreciate being harassed," he said.

"I'm sorry you have had a bad experience. Let me see if I can help you now," I offered.

"I don't want help. I want you to take my name off your goddamn list, and I want you to stop calling me," he insisted.

"Very well, sir. What is your name?"

"Joseph Green."

"Sir, can you please spell your name for me?"

"Jesus, you don't know how to spell Joseph Green?" he bellowed.

"Some people spell Joseph with an 'f' at the end, and some people spell Green with an 'e' at the end," I said.

"My name is spelled the usual way people spell Joseph in the United States, with a J in the beginning of Joseph and an h at the end, and without an 'e' on the end of Green," he said.

MUTE: *Yes, sir. Is that "J" as in Jerkowitz?*

"I have two full pages of Joseph Green. May I look you up with your Social Security number?" I asked.

"No, you may not. I want to speak with the president."

MUTE: *Of the United States? Where we all spell your name the same?*

"One moment please, I'll transfer you," I said, transferring him to customer service.

An inauspicious start to the day, but the odds were good that the next call would at least be somebody whose mother raised them properly.

I gave my usual spiel to the next caller.

"Hi, Annie. This is Jared Smyth from Lexington, Kentucky, and my wife and I are looking to see if it's a good idea for us to refinance our home at this time. Can you help me with this?"

MUTE: *See how pleasant and civilized people can be?*

It turned out it was a good idea for the Smyths to refinance their home and to save about $305 a month. It seemed like it would be an easy loan to get closed as, according to the findings, they didn't need an appraisal and all else looked in order.

I had been on the phone for about an hour before I took a break and e-mailed Alice, asking if I could come up to see her and if she could get me an okay from the security desk.

She e-mailed me back: **What do you need now?**

I answered: **I'll let you know when I see you.**

I received the security desk go-ahead, and I made my way down the commoners' hall to the aristocratic lobby and up the stairs that any bride would be happy to have come down.

Alice was sitting at her desk doing I don't know what without Homer barking directions at her.

"How are you passing your time, Alice, without Homer?" I asked when I arrived at her desk.

"I'm filling in when other admins are away or twiddling my thumbs until they can decide what to do with me. I guess they're waiting to find out who murdered Homer."

"Have you gone to HR to ask them about another position?" I asked.

"No, but I guess I should."

"The sooner you are out of here, the better for you, don't you think?" I asked.

"I guess so," she said.

MUTE: *I guess she knows what she's doing.*

"One way to be sure you are safe, and out of harm's way is to let me know who is on the list Homer kept; you know, the list like Hoover kept?"

"Oh, no. I'm not divulging that information. You got into his office, but you're not going to get me killed," she said, looking like she was in an acting class and the teacher said 'portray indignant.'

"Look, Alice, don't you think those people know that you

know what Homer had on them?"

"No, why would they?"

"Because they knew Homer, and Homer would have made sure he wasn't the only one who knew about them; you know, back up blackmail."

"You just want to see that list. You don't really want to help me," she said.

"Nothing could be further from the truth, Alice. If we find out who killed Homer, you are out of the woods, and these people couldn't do a thing to you," I said, not making one whit of sense.

"What? You are not even making sense," she said, twisting her hands as if every twist made her even more earnest, which was pretty near impossible.

"Look, let me put it another way. If one of these people is the murderer, that lets you off the hook. If one of these people is not the murderer, you go on to get another job, and whatever Homer had on them would make no difference. You're not a blackmailer. So as long as the murderer is found, you have no skin in the game."

That was confusing enough that even I thought I might have a point.

"You're not going to go to these people, are you?" she asked.

"Of course not. Then *I* would be in danger."

"What would you do if you knew who is on the list?"

MUTE: *Damn good question. Damn good.*

"If I knew who was in the building that night, and one of those on the Hoover list was here, that would be mighty suspicious, don't you think?" I asked.

"Yes, of course. But we don't know who was in the building that night, only the police know that, and you absolutely cannot tell the police the names because if they found out that I told, I might be the next victim."

"You are getting way ahead of yourself, Alice. Have you had any luck with your friend who is the head of the security cards?" I asked.

"It seems like I'm the only one with any information that

is going to help find out who killed Homer, so I'm taking all the risks here," Alice said.

"You're the only one who worked closely enough with him to know all this stuff. You're the person with the information I need, but you aren't taking any risk, I am."

"How do you figure that?"

"Because you are just speaking words, and I am going out and doing something about those words, trying to put together a case against somebody, and the more I know, the sooner I can stick a fork in it and it's done."

I hate these sayings like "put a fork in it," but it's used so often by my colleagues that if I'm around them enough, I start using those terms. In this case, "stick a fork in it" might have been overcooked. Ugh.

"You have to swear on your mother's life that you will never tell anybody that I was the one who gave you the names."

"My mother has passed on," I said.

"Well then, you have to swear on her grave," she countered.

MUTE: *Why do people want me to swear on my dear departed mother's grave? Maudlin lot.*

'Okay, I swear on my mother's grave that I will never ever mention that you were the one who told me the names on Homer's list," I said.

"Okay. I have them memorized. The actual list is in a very, very safe place."

MUTE: *I wish I couldn't visualize where a very, very safe place might be.*

"The first one on the list is his wife, Crystal. He doesn't say what he has on her, but it has to be something. Number two is Jan Mulligan. Oh, my God, you're not going to believe it, but she's a man," she said, grasping her neck.

"Wow. She's pretty beautiful for a guy. I mean he's pretty beautiful for a guy. Wow," is all I could say.

"Do you know Mr. Richter?" she asked.

"I know who he is, but I don't know him."

"He's an executive VP and has something to do with mergers. He does other stuff too, but that's the thing I think of when I think of him. He and Homer were called in front of the board for suspicion of insider trading. Do you know what that is?" she asked.

"Oh, yeah, I know what it is."

"Well, they got off the hook with the board, but Homer's notes say that they actually did some stock purchases on information Mr. Richter had. Homer said he paid Mr. Richter ten thousand dollars for the information. I don't know how they got out of it, but they did."

If Homer got $50,000 from the loan sharks for that bit of information, he was still $40,000 ahead.

"It doesn't make sense why Homer would hold it against Richter since he would be liable, too," I mused.

"True, but he was such a worm that he would hold that over Mr. Richter if he ever had the idea of turning on Homer. These people just didn't know who they were up against."

"And yet they are alive and Homer's dead," I said.

"Oh, right."

"Who else?" I asked.

"You're going to hate this one: Charlie Harrison."

"Charlie? What did he do?"

"Homer caught him fixing the call queues to benefit his team. You know Al is the only one who can do that or Homer if he decided he ever wanted to get at someone. I think he fixed that guy Troy Whitman's queue one time because I heard him cackle, 'Take that, Whitman, you asshole, try to make a salary with no calls.' Anyway, when Charlie's team had so many more loans one week than the other teams, Homer looked into it and found out about it. Typical of Homer, he didn't care that Charlie did it. Any way there were more loans was fine with him, and he didn't care who got them; but he then had something on Charlie. It was like something was wrong with him to want dirt on everybody. What do they call that, I wonder?" she asked.

"I don't know, paranoia, insecurity? It doesn't make much difference now, but it may have contributed to his murder. Who else?"

"That's all I have, but I'm sure there were more. They may be on those tapes he kept."

"Do you think you'll get a chance to talk to your friend in the security department?" I asked.

"George Tidings *is* the security department. He has people working for him, but he's the guy who could tell me who was in the building that night. I think he kind of has a thing for me, so maybe I could get it out of him."

Well, well, well, Alice was a full-fledged female after all, unlike the gorgeous Jan Mulligan. And for all I knew, maybe Jan was a full-fledged woman as well.

"Thank you so much, Alice. You're a champ, and I know this is going to help bring this to an end," I declared.

"I sure hope so. I'm a nervous wreck," she said, collapsing back in her chair.

Back at my desk, I logged on my phone, rewrote my to-do list both for work and Homer's murder, and took a call that turned into the second loan of the day after the Smyth's. It wasn't a slam dunk like the Smyth's because the Eddingtons thought their home in Elkhart, Indiana, was worth $150,000, and our value estimator thought it was more like $106,800. They owed $85,400 on their current mortgage, so if the house was appraised at $106,800, they'd be okay, but if it were too much lower, they would have to pay private mortgage insurance. They were adamant about the value of their home, but everybody is. It was a W&S loan, aka a "Wait and See" loan.

I know I shouldn't have, but I couldn't resist walking past Jan Mulligan's desk. She was standing, talking to a loan officer on Charlie Harrison's team, and I could tell he was fairly drooling at the experience of talking to such a beauty. I wondered if she had the whole sex reassignment surgery along with whatever hormones she must certainly be taking. I just couldn't figure out why it would have been so bad if people knew she was a man, unless she had sights on moving up the corporate ladder. She was smart enough, maybe too elegant for the bank though. EFB was liberal with their views of, at least, cross-dressing, because we had a guy who worked on the floor who was Simon during the week, but if he had to work on the weekends, he would be Patsy all dolled up down to his press-on fingernails. It was a bit off-putting at first, and the guys seemed to have a lot of trouble with it, but my attitude was, who cares?

Erwin Richter. What was the back story on Erwin Richter? That I would have to find out to see if it led anywhere pointing to him as a murderer. But it would have to wait until the end of the day at my home computer because I needed to put in some quality work at EFB for a paycheck this month.

I worked on a list of loans I needed to close that month in order to hit my $1.5 million necessary to commission, and went to Chad to see if I could marshal him for some help. Because it was to Chad's advantage to have as many of his team members' loans close as he could, he was aggressive in pushing our loans.

"What's the holdup with this one?" he asked.

"I'm waiting for the processor to get an updated pay stub from Mr. Gianakos' employer," I said.

"Why don't you get it?"

"Because I'm on the phones trying to get loans, and the processor said she was calling on Monday to get the pay stub, but today she said the employer isn't calling her back."

"Call the employer yourself, and see if you can get it this afternoon, and then let me know what the outcome is. I'll touch base with her manager to let her know her processor's not doing her job," Chad said.

I would call and probably get the pay stub, but it was frustrating to continually get e-mails demanding we be on the phones, and then be told we need to do somebody else's job. Sadly, it was the way the mortgage world worked.

"Anything else?" he asked.

"Do you know Erwin Richter?"

"Why, are you doing a loan for him?"

"No, I just wondered if you knew him."

"Yes, I know him, or I've met him a few times. But if this has nothing to do with your commission this month, I'd let it go," he said turning around to his computer.

I went back to my desk, called Mr. Gianakos' employer, VVR Fishery, to get an updated pay stub. Mr. Gianakos was a captain of a fishing boat out of southern Florida, and this particular company didn't think it necessary to hold to tried and true business practices vis-à-vis accounting. The real story on the pay stub turned out to be that Mr. VVR gave his employees handwritten accounts of their time, and our Underwriting Department wouldn't accept that. I had to beg Mr. VVR Fishery to have a pay stub for Mr. Gianakos printed up on his computer.

"I got no computer," he said.

"Do you have a Kinkos in town that you could use and have it printed there?" I asked.

"What's with kinky? I don't know about kinky," he said.

"Thank you for your time," I said, knowing I would have to have Mr. Gianakos straighten this out if the loan was to close, and saving money is always the best incentive.

The rest of the day flew by, but by 6:30 I was ready to call it quits and bumper-to-bumper my way back home.

I pulled into my driveway about 7:20, got my mail, sat down to take a breath, got up and looked into my refrigerator, which looked depressingly like Gladys Wilkins' refrigerator the first day Sophie and I visited her.

What the hell. I made myself a bowl of oatmeal, poured a small glass of red wine, and called it dinner. I know you're not supposed to drink wine with breakfast, but this was really dinner, right?

I sat at my computer and Googled Erwin Richter. It turns out Mr. Richter had worked previously as CEO of Gemini Mortgages in Tennessee. Prior to that he worked at a few other small banks in New Jersey and West Virginia. He received his undergraduate degree from Rutgers University and his MBA from Wharton School of Business. Unfortunately, there was no link to Crooked Bankers.com with his profile on it, so I'd have to find out that part on my own.

Of course my phone rang as I was cogitating about how I might find out more about him.

"Hi, Annie. It's me," Marilyn said.

"Hey, what's up? Did you find out from Mike if he has the ladder we need for Saturday?" I asked.

"That's what I'm calling about. Can we do it the next Saturday? We found a litter of beagles out in Hillsboro we're going to see Saturday evening."

"Oh, no. Can't you put that off until the next Saturday? All I can think of is Gladys not knowing what happened to Rodney, and the sooner she knows, the more quickly she can get on with her life even if it's the saddest outcome she can imagine.

"I'll have to think of something really good for Mike. Not that he wants to get another dog right away, but he thinks I'm depressed without Archie, and a new puppy would help. What am I going to say we need the ladder for?" she asked.

"Um, let's see. How about you say I have a leaky window? You know the one over the space that goes through to the living room from my bedroom loft? You can tell him my neighbor is going to help us, so he doesn't think he needs to come over. How does that sound?"

"Yeah, that sounds good."

"What about dinner? Do you have to make dinner first, or can we leave around six-thirty?"

"Katy was coming over to watch the kids and make dinner, so having Mike to cook for too will only make her happier, so that's fine. How are we going to get into the building without being seen on the security cameras?" she asked.

"I don't know. I guess we can cover our faces, but my security badge will let them know the next day if they are checking, and I bet Detective Jamison checks every day. I know I would."

"So how can we get around that?" she asked.

"Maybe I can say my badge was stolen on Monday morning. But let's dress as butch as we can, so if we cover our faces and swagger, maybe they'll think we're two guys," I suggested.

"Swagger and carry a fifteen-foot ladder—that's going to be interesting," she said.

No sooner had I sat down to my book than the phone rang again.

"Hi, Annie. It's Crystal. What's up? Have you found out anything? I can't wait anymore, I have to get into that Pandora music box thing," she said.

"It's a safe, and I'm working on it. I have a question for

you. Have you ever met Erwin Richter?"

"That asshole. Yeah, I've met him."

"What happened that you have such a dim view of him?" I asked.

"He was always grabby at any of the EFB functions, but not bad enough for me to say anything, just bad enough that I kept away from him. But the time Homer invited him and his wife—what's her name?— oh, yeah, Bitsy, or Blitsy, one of those country club names, over to our house, that was when I let him have it."

"What happened?" I asked.

"I went to get more ice in the kitchen, and he came up and grabbed my ass. I turned around and asked him what the hell he thought he was doing. I smacked him across the face and turned around again; then he started humping me, and said, 'I thought you were a Hooters' girl.' And I turned around as quick as I could and kneed him, and said, 'I thought you were a country club old man.' He didn't say much after that, just kind of shuffled off to the bathroom. I never had a problem with him after that. God, I hated that guy. Why are you asking me?"

"His name came up while I was trying to find out what happened. Were he and Homer old friends or just work friends?" I asked.

"Homer never said, and I was never interested enough to ask him, but I did hear them snickering about college times, so they might have been friends back then," she replied.

"Where did Homer go to school, do you know?"

"Some place in New Jersey. I think that's where he came from," she said.

Some marriage; she wasn't even sure where he was brought up or where he went to college.

"What kind of conversations did they have? Was it Rutgers University?" I asked.

"Maybe. Hey, back to the reason I called you in the first place. When can I get into the safe, or whatever it is? I took off the tiles from the fireplace and see what you're talkin' about, and yeah, it's not the box he put in there. The box he put in there was small, like a little bigger than a shoebox."

151

"I hope to have something for you by Monday. Monday night, probably."

"God, Annie, this is taking forever," she said, groaning.

"I'm doing the best I can. You insisted that I be the one who does this, so you'll just have to be patient," I stated.

"I'm paying you good money, you should be done by now."

"You're paying me? How much? I forgot about that conversation," I said.

"I don't think we actually talked about how much, but how much do you want?"

"I don't think I can take money from you for this, Crystal," I protested.

"Why not, who doesn't want money? I was thinking about ten grand, is that enough?" she asked.

MUTE: *Say what John Beresford Tipton?*

"Let's talk about it if I find something, okay?"

"IF?" she screamed in my ear.

"When," I said and disconnected.

And so to bed and crazy dreams.

Chapter 16

Wednesday, April 17, 2013

IT HAD TO STOP RAINING at some point, but that point hadn't come, as I once again needed galoshes for my feet and pontoons for my car. When it rains in Cincinnati, it seems every car slows to a baby crawl. There's no obvious reason why it takes an hour to go where fifteen minutes usually takes you, but the raindrops seem to put a stop to peoples' will to drive over 10 mph.

I arrived at my desk both wet and late, and both Troy and Sophie popped up to talk to me as soon as I sat down.

"Annie, Gladys is back in the hospital," Sophie said.

"Oh, no, did she have a relapse?" I asked.

"I don't know if you'd call it a relapse; her diabetes is acting up again. I asked her if she had been drinking plenty of water and taking her insulin; but I think she's so worried and perplexed about Rodney that she forgets both the water and the medicine."

"It's just crazy that they can't find anything, not even a hair of his, anyplace," I said.

"When she gets out again, somebody is going to have to stay with her 'round the clock until we know what happened to Rodney. She just can't go on this way," Sophie stated.

"I agree. She needs a plan for her future with or without Rodney. And without Rodney sure looks like the way it's heading."

"You ladies finished?" Troy asked, leaning over my desk.

"I guess we are now," said Sophie, sitting down.

"What's up, Troy?" I asked.

"What the hell is going on with this thing?"

"What thing?" I asked knowing full well what he meant. "Why are you asking me?"

"You know more than anybody except the police. I'd put money on that."

"Troy, I don't know anything the police don't know, and I don't know anything the police do know."

"Well, your friend Jamison is still on my back. I have to go back down to District One today for more questions, and if he's still asking me questions, he doesn't know anything," he said.

"Unless, of course, you are the murderer," I said, stopping myself just short of twirling my make-believe mustache.

"Funny," he said, and sat down.

I checked my e-mails to see if anything extraordinary popped up. You'll be surprised to know I didn't get one that said: Re: Murder. I know who did it.

I logged on to the phone, and transferred people to 1) the auto loan department 2) a branch in the Nashville area 3) customer service (after the guy said "you bitch" when I asked him if I might be able to help him). I should have just hung up, instead of letting somebody else take that nastiness. I didn't think fast enough.

Out of the next five calls, I managed to eke out a $90,000 loan that was iffy at best with a required appraisal in the mix, but it was in a part of North Carolina with homes that seem to have held their value. Of course, all it took was one foreclosure on the street to make that irrelevant.

Then I got a call from Alice sounding terror-stricken. "Guess who has been at my desk for the last hour? Can't guess? Erwin Richter. I know you went right to him after we talked yesterday. I can't believe you would do something like that," she sobbed.

"Alice, Alice, I didn't speak to him. I wouldn't even know what he looks like if it weren't for the thumbnail photo of him on Google and seeing him from the last row when he was on the stage with Jamison. I kept my promise, and I will continue to keep my promise," I swore.

"What was he doing here asking me all these questions?"

"What did he ask you?"

"He wanted to know if everything was out of Homer's office and if I had ever seen the recordings Homer had of his meetings," Alice replied.

"Hmmm. He must be getting a little antsy not knowing if anybody else will get the information about the insider trading, don't you think?"

"Yes, I'm sure that's why he wants to know. But why is he questioning me?" she asked shakily.

"Because you're Homer's administrative assistant," I offered.

"I know, but it's such a coincidence so soon after we spoke."

"I don't know him. I didn't say anything to him," I repeated.

"I told him I didn't know anything about recordings. Do you think that was wrong?"

"No, I think that was smart."

"What am I going to do?"

"Why did your conversation take so long?" I asked.

"He just wanted to talk about Homer. He reminisced back to their college days at Ruggers? I think he said Ruggers. It's a college in New Jersey, he said."

"It's Rutgers, but he is definitely a Jersey boy."

"Why?"

"They pronounce it Ruggers," I explained.

"Oh. Well he had a lot of memories."

"Like what?" I asked.

"Like they had a business back then and made some good money."

"What was it?"

"I don't know exactly. I think he said they sold bootleg tapes and recruited other students to sell them, too."

"Sounds like a pyramid scheme. So they were crooks from

the get-go."

"He didn't say it was crooked," she said.

"Right. I don't think he would do anything to you; he's just snooping to make sure that Homer didn't leave information about him in his office."

"You know Homer did leave information about him."

"But he doesn't know for sure, so that's what we have to pin our hopes on right now. I'd go about your business as usual, but if you see anything out of the ordinary, you can call me on my cell. You have my number, right?" I asked.

"Yes, I have it. I'll enter it on my speed dial right now. I just can't wait until this is over. And, oh, I'm having lunch with George today, the security guy. We're eating off campus so there won't be any prying eyes."

Just as I was ready to hang up, Al Markey came by, and in his usual fashion knocked on my desk twice, and said, "Can we have a word in my office, Annie?"

Had I forgotten to lock a loan? My concentration probably wasn't as focused on my job as much as it should have been. I felt a pang of guilt as I made my way to the "death box."

I knocked on the glass wall, and Al motioned me to come in. "Shut the door, Annie, please," he said.

He looked terrible, even worse than a week ago; I wondered if the police were on him or if he was living in fear that what happened to Homer would happen to him.

"I'm just touching base with the gang to see how everybody is doing in the wake of the terrible tragedy that befell us. I've been looking at numbers, and yours seem to be down a little, Annie. Are you okay, or has this rattled you to the point where your work might be suffering?"

MUTE: *Befell us? Al's sounding very Shakespearean since Homer's demise.*

"I think it may have had an effect on my work. I mean just seeing him there like that, and not knowing who could have hated him that much. And even worse, I feel guilty even thinking it, is what happened to Rodney Wilkins," I replied.

"I know what you mean," he said, with a far-off look. "I feel bad that it happened on my watch, in my office, you know?"

"It really wasn't on your watch, Al. You weren't even here."

"Oh, right," he agreed, seeming totally distracted.

"I'll try to keep my mind on the work and not the murder," I said, as I rose and left his office.

"Thanks, Annie," he called after me.

~

Sophie and I went to visit Gladys at lunchtime, again taking more time than we were allotted for lunch. We were okay with that and would make up the time at the end of the day.

Nobody likes to visit hospitals if they don't have to, or at least I don't; it's like going to a different planet, where all of the sick people have been sent. I can't even watch TV shows where the entire series is set *in* a hospital. Why can't they have the vibes of say, a day spa? I am thankful that they are there to care for us when we're sick, but I wish they could at least burn vanilla-scented candles.

Our heels clipped down the industrial green hall to Gladys's room, and we found her dozing. We didn't want to disturb her, so we arranged the flowers that we had bought in the lobby gift store on a small table where she could see them, and Sophie sat in the only chair in the room while I stood at the side of the bed.

Something either in her sleep or in the hall must have startled Gladys, because her eyes popped open. She looked vacantly first at Sophie, then over to me, probably thinking, What are these white ladies doing in my room? They're not nurses.

"Hi, Gladys. Do you remember me? I've been to your apartment a few times with some other folks to make sure you were doing all right. Do you remember?" Sophie asked.

"Yes, you look familiar," Gladys said.

"I'm Sophie, and this is Annie. She was at your home one time, too."

"Thank you ladies for coming to see me. I'm feeling kind a poorly right now."

"We're going to arrange for someone to be with you when

you get home to make sure you are being taken care of properly," Sophie stated.

"That's fine, just fine. I'm thankful to you."

"Do you need anything right now, Gladys? We can run out and get you anything you need," I offered.

"No. The nurses are doing a good job of taking care of me. I'm just so sleepy," she replied.

"We won't stay. We'll let you get some rest. I'm going to write my phone number down on this piece of paper, Gladys, and if you want anything or need anything, you call me, okay?" Sophie said.

"Bless you, miss; you are so kind."

"No problem, we are happy to help," Sophie stated.

I patted her hand, and Sophie kissed her on the top of her head, and we left the room.

"Let's stop at the nurses' station to make sure they know Gladys has people looking after her. It can't hurt," I suggested.

We waited at the nurses' station for either Mrs. Showalter or Mrs. Dinkens, as their name tags said, to look up from their conversation.

"Hi, we are Gladys Wilkins' friends, and we want to be sure she has everything she needs, and if there is anything she does need that you can't provide, perhaps somebody can let us know," I requested.

"Are you on her list to be called in an emergency?" Mrs. Showalter asked.

"No, we aren't, but we don't know if she has a family or if they are looking after her," Sophie replied.

"Wait a minute, I'll look it up," the nurse said, logging on to the computer.

"Her husband is named as next of kin, Rodney Wilkins?"

"Yes, but he's missing right now. Is there anybody else listed?" I asked.

"A sister, Bettina Johnson."

"Do you know if she has had any other visitors?" Sophie asked.

"There's no way I have of seeing that. She just got here yesterday morning."

"Okay, thanks," we said in unison, and departed dispirited.

We grabbed salads at Panera to eat at our desks and sat down again at about 2 p.m. Again Chad said he would put the extra hour gone as work.

My first call was from Alice. "I have some news for you. Can we meet for coffee about three o'clock in the Bra?" she asked.

"I just got back from seeing Gladys Wilkins at the hospital. It will have to be more like four-ish. Is that okay?" I asked.

"I guess it has to be. See you down there at four," she said disconnecting.

After five more calls, and a promise of a call back, I logged off and walked down to the Bra to meet Alice.

I saw her at the coffee machine, and started toward her when a man cut me off and walked up to her instead. "Good afternoon, Alice. Twice in one day, it must be my lucky day," he said.

I thought he looked like the thumbnail photo of him on Google and the guy on the stage, but I wasn't 100% sure until Alice said, "Hi, Mr. Richter."

I walked around the other way to see if he would have moved on, but he didn't. He had his arm around her shoulders, and said, "Get your coffee, I'll wait, and walk back upstairs with you."

I tried to catch her eye, but couldn't, so I had to deep-six the operation.

Yoga night couldn't have come soon enough especially after the hospital visit and now the unctuous Mr. Richter.

I finished up at work at about 6:30, changed into my yoga togs in the ladies room, and drove up to Lotus Yoga—where I met up with Marilyn, who was looking like I felt: Downward Facing Dog.

"What's up? You look a bit under the weather," I said to her.

"I just can't shake Archie's absence. And the boys must feel it, too, because, frankly they are acting up and are a pain in the ass."

Three boys even without the Archie trauma would send

me up a wall, too, so I had plenty of sympathy for her.

I started to whisper to her about our Saturday plans to enter EFB with a ladder when Debbie Markey came over to join us. And, I have to be honest, she looked as bad as her husband.

"Hey, Debbie, how are you?" I asked.

"Terrible. I will be so happy when they find out who was responsible for this horror. It's not bad enough that one, and probably two, people are dead, but our lives are in shambles. You might have heard from your associates who were in the building that night that the police have been talking to them over and over again. Al wasn't even there, and they keep insisting on asking him more questions. I know it was his office, but he wasn't there. They must see that from the security cameras and the security cards. And, aside from that, he was next to me in bed.

"I'm so sorry, Debbie. It must be a nightmare for both of you," I replied.

"The worst part is that Al can't sleep, so he drives off at ten o'clock just to drive around and think, he says. Driving always did soothe his nerves, but this is a little crazy if you ask me."

"I think it's going to be over pretty soon," I said, just to calm her jitters.

She grabbed my arm, "Do you really think so? Do you know something? It would make Al feel so much better, I'm sure."

"I can't swear to it, but I have good reason to believe I should have some information by Monday," I stated, putting all my hopes in the ceiling of Homer's office.

"Thank God," she said.

Our Yoga instructor, Melissa, called us to our Ananda space, and we assembled in our usual places on our mats.

After an hour of breathing, stretching, and bending, I felt a lot better, and Marilyn and Debbie said they did too.

I checked my cell when I got to my car; I had four calls from Alice and three texts.

"Where are you? Call me as soon as you can." The message didn't say I'm in a panic, but the number of calls and texts said so.

"Alice, it's Annie. What's up?"

"Where have you been? I've been calling since I got back to my desk from the coffee machine. Do you see what I mean now? He's following me. Even when I go to the ladies room, he's slinking around," she said.

"Yeah, I see what you mean, but I'm not sure what I can do about it. Is that why you called me so many times?"

"No, no. The reason I wanted to meet you at the coffee machine was to tell you I had lunch with George, my security friend, and to tell you what I found out. Wait a minute, you don't think Mr. Richter can be tracing my calls, do you?

"Not unless he works for the NSA."

"No, I don't think he does," she stated.

MUTE: *For some, sarcasm doesn't make it west of New Jersey.*

"So what did he say?" I asked.

"George said the only people logged in that night were Troy Whitman, Jan Mulligan, Charlie Harris, and Erwin Richter. I believe you said you thought it was only Troy and Jan, and, of course, Rodney Wilkins," she said.

"Good lord, that's all the names on the Hoover list except for Crystal. Did he know the times for Harris's and Richter's entry and exit?" I asked.

"Yes, Charlie left at six-thirty and came back to the office at eight oh six, and left again at ten twenty-three from the exit by the Bra. Mr. Richter left at ten forty-three from the front exit. He also told me that Jan Mulligan left at ten thirty-three from the Bra exit, too, and that Troy Whitman came in at nine thirty-one and left at ten forty-five from the Bra exit. Oh, and the real mystery is that Rodney Wilkins came in at ten twenty-seven at the Bra entry, but hasn't been recorded ever leaving."

What if somebody removed his badge and walked him out at gunpoint? Or knocked him out and carried him through the exit? Or wove some magic curse and made him disappear?

"How did Troy not see Charlie Harris at his desk if they both were on the floor at the same time? They sit an aisle away. He may not have seen Jan Mulligan because she sits in the back, but he must have seen her leave, or she must have seen him when she was leaving. Why are they not telling the truth?" I asked rhetorically.

"I don't know. You're the detective," Alice said.

"Jan purposely didn't tell me who was on the floor; she said it was none of my business, but I'm pretty sure Todd said he was the only one there. I'm going to have to grill him a little more," I stated. "Anyway, that's great information, Alice. Thank you so much for that."

"It's okay, I got a date for dinner out of it," she replied.

MUTE: *Oh, that Georgie.*

~

I was ravenous as I made my way up Montgomery Road, which runs almost parallel to 71-N. I couldn't face the speeding trucks. I was pretty mellow after my Yoga workout and wanted to stay that way. I wanted to wait at least one respectable day to bring out my middle finger wave to the eighteen wheelers pounding around me. I passed Delhi Deli thinking how delightful a bowl of some kind of organic soup would be instead of a bowl of oatmeal, and I turned around at the corner and headed to what I told myself was a healthy meal.

"Hey, Annie. You're later than usual. Can I get you a glass of wine?" Neil asked, showing me to one of the empty tables.

"No, I've just been to Yoga. I think I'll just have some water with lemon."

"Something light to go with it?" he asked.

"That's what I was thinking. What kind of soup do you have?"

"I think we have something that you might like tonight other than soup," he said. "I'll bring it out, and if you don't want it, I'll bring you a bowl of broth."

"Okay, that sounds good."

MUTE: *"No soup for you." A true Seinfeld fan.*

A few minutes later he set before me a baked yam topped with Greek yogurt, sprinkled with some kind of nuts and drizzled with honey, with a side of field greens with vinaigrette.

MUTE: *A gastronomical whiz, and adorable to boot. I needed at least my head examined.*

I tried not to moan with delight with every bite, but I'm not sure I pulled it off. I paid my bill, bid Neil goodnight, and was genuinely happy to pull into my garage, and be home.

I finally found my bed and my book about 9:45, and my head hit the pillow about 10:15. It was going to take the resolution of this murder for me to get through the rest of *Bangkok Tattoo*. I don't know how long I had dozed before a sharp sound from downstairs startled me. I always hear house noises and expect the worst, but this was different, unless I was dreaming. I often dream things and think they are as real as this April rain. Sofia Vergara's death by icicle for instance. I sat up in bed and heard it again, somebody was at my back sliding doors. The door is securely locked to keep rapists and pillagers away, so I thought it might have been one of the pesky squirrels trying to get to my window bird feeder. I looked out my upstairs window under which the doors sat, but it was too dark to see anything. I stood beside the window, behind the curtain, to watch if anything moved as my eyes became accustomed to the dark. I didn't see anything. When I heard one of my outside chairs being bumped into, I jumped. I couldn't call my neighbors at 11 o'clock. I got back in bed and listened. The last time I looked at the clock, it was 12:03. I was going to be tired the next day. I need my full eight hours of sleep in order to be in my best form, well, mentally at least. A sprightly walk around the lake before work would help with the mental and the physical. I'd get to that right after I found a killer.

Chapter 17

Thursday, April 18, 2013

I AWOKE THINKING, I need a break from this. The noise downstairs the previous night worried me. Who would want to get into my house? Oh, unless it was the murderer with sights on murdering me, too. But nobody knew what I knew. My imagination was in overdrive. The only two people who knew about Pandora's Box and the other mysterious boxes were Marilyn and Crystal. It was 6:30 a.m., and my head already hurt from trying to tie up the mental strings scattered haphazardly in my brain. Had I dropped any hint that Homer might have kept a stash of threatening information that could be used against Jamison's list of possible suspects? I couldn't think, so I shook and cleared my head and got in the shower.

The weather had cleared: Perfect night to head down to Mainstrasse with Jim Grate to listen to some soothing jazz and sip scotch at the bar at Dee Felice. That happy thought lit a fire under my butt and got me hopping. When I opened the door to fetch *The New York Times,* I saw a plastic Coke bottle on my walk. On garbage pick-up day there might be an occasional paper wrapper or receipt decorating the lawn or a shrub, but this condo complex is the antithesis of the South Bronx litter-wise.

I just stood there staring at it, wondering what to make of it. With the noise at my back door last night and a possible bottle bomb at my front door this morning, I'm not going to lie, I was scared. A call to my local police was met with a morning yawn at the other end.

"Can you please send someone over as soon as possible to see if this is an actual bomb?" I pleaded.

"Yeah, we'll get someone over there as soon as someone is available," the dull voice announced.

I called Detective Jamison next, and he was much more accommodating.

"How close is your house to your next-door neighbor?" he asked.

"It's a condo, so their condo is attached to mine," I replied.

"You and he and whoever else is nearby need to vacate the premises until the police get there," he stated.

"He said they'd send somebody over here as soon as somebody was available," I said.

"They'll be there in ten minutes. I'll make sure of that," he said.

I knocked on my neighbors' door. The Hoffmans were a retired couple of whom you could ask anything and nothing was too much of a bother: The perfect neighbors.

Len came to the door in his pajamas, and I explained the situation to him.

He said, "You'd better wait across the street, while I wake Nancy."

Two minutes later they came out to the grassy knoll across from our condos to join me, with three canvas folding chairs.

"Let me at least buy you two a copy of coffee," I offered, making my way back into the house to fetch three cups of coffee.

Len had set up a folding table, and we were all set.

"It's like being witness to a tornado. Do you think we're far enough away?" I asked.

"I guess it depends upon what's in the bottle, if it is a bomb, and not just dropped by some careless kid," he said.

"There are very few kids in this neighborhood and none that I've seen walking around drinking Coke," I pointed out.

Just as we were about to discuss which kids did live in our area, we heard sirens wailing nearby, no doubt waking all the lucky late sleepers. Two cruisers careened around the corner of our street with two policemen in each, followed by a huge white truck that said BOMB SQUAD on the side.

The police hopped out of their cars. "Who's Annie Fillmore?" asked an officer.

I stood up, and the officer came forward to speak with me.

"When did you first notice this bottle?" he asked.

"This morning about 7:15 when I came out to get my morning paper," I said.

It was then 7:35, so they did make pretty good time after, I'm sure, Detective Jamison escalated the matter.

"Do you know anybody who might have it in for you, hold a vendetta?"

"Not that I'm aware of; but I thought I heard somebody at my back door last night," I replied.

I turned to Len and asked, "Did you hear anything last night about ten-fifteen or ten-thirty?"

"I did hear something—and then saw a shadow on the grass walking in the back toward the horse farm."

Said horse farm sits off to the right of our backyards: Near enough to look bucolic, far enough away not to smell the horse dung.

Len was the neighborhood sentry and didn't miss much, even if some of it was a figment of his imagination.

The officer walked away, conferred with one of the bomb squad guys, and walked back over to our hastily assembled neighborhood gathering.

"We're going to grab it with the robotic arm and detonate it back at headquarters. We'll let you know what happens. My captain said you are involved in the case of Detective Jamison. We're passing all of our information on to District One, but we'll be handling this investigation ourselves. Please write down your name, phone numbers—work, home, and a cell phone if you have one," he said.

And badda bing, badda boom, they were out of there, leaving our little group drinking coffee in our canvas sling chairs.

"Have you got time for a bagel?" Len asked me.

"Why not, I just escaped getting blown up," I answered.

"There's some salmon cream cheese in the refrigerator," said Nancy. "Bring that, too."

Len came out and set the tray with the bagels and cream cheese on the table, and turned to me, "We should have known a city girl like you would bring havoc into our neighborhood!" he said jokingly.

MUTE: "*An Expat Without a Clue.*"

"I have no idea what's going on. I do work in the building where that executive was murdered downtown, but aside from working in the same department I don't have anything to do with it," I prevaricated.

"Something is going on; unless somebody had the wrong house," Nancy suggested.

"It's not good no matter what. I'm going to see the detective on the EFB murder case today. Maybe he knows what's going on. In the meantime, please keep your eyes peeled for anybody lurking around while I'm not here. I'll keep all my outside lamps on tonight to intimidate any intruders. I won't be home, but I'll be back tomorrow, and I'll check in to see if you've seen anything, or if I've found out anything."

"Sounds like a plan," Len said.

"And thanks for breakfast and the company. I'm still pretty shaken by all of this."

"No problem, kiddo, take it easy, and try not to let it get to you."

Easier said than done. I called Chad from my car to let him know I was headed down to District One to talk to Detective Jamison about the possible bottle bomb. I also called Marilyn.

Marilyn's reactions are always the most encouraging, imbued with just the right amount of horror and sympathy—one reason why we're such good friends. I hope my support of her is equally comforting.

Per my car clock, I reached District One at 8:50, plenty of time to have worked myself into a frenzy. Detective Jamison wasn't about to help. "Ms. Fillmore, do you remember our conversation at the beginning of this investigation when I told you I didn't want to be having a conversation about *your* murder?" he asked.

"Yes, I remember," I said, feeling totally culpable.

"But for some reason you've ignored my warnings to not get involved."

"I haven't purposefully gotten involved; people have come to me asking me questions that I couldn't answer, and I've just tried to offer them some peace of mind," I argued.

MUTE: *Surprisingly he didn't break into a rendition of "Annie's Song."*

"And in the meantime putting yourself and your neighbors in danger. What kind of peace of mind do you think you're offering your neighbors?" he asked, and I could sure tell he was upset with me.

"I had no idea I was in danger or putting my neighbors in danger; no idea at all. Do you think I want to die?" I retorted, getting a bit hot under the collar myself.

"Then today, right now, you have to tell me everything you know that I might not know," he demanded, with his Frank Sinatra eyes cutting into mine.

"I don't know what you know," I said, pushing the envelope way off the desk.

He just stared at me; I guess my answer didn't warrant a reply in his estimation, but how could I go back on my promises to Crystal and Alice? I just couldn't do it.

"Seriously, I do not know why anybody would want to put a bottle bomb on my walk, if it even was a bottle bomb," I said.

"It was definitely a bottle bomb, and one that would have been very unpleasant for you if it had detonated. If you had even kicked it, you would probably be minus a foot." He continued, "Let's go down the list of people you have spoken to about the investigation, no matter how trivial the conversation might have been," he said.

"I've spoken to everybody I come in contact with during the day at EFB and a few of my good friends who have asked me if the police had found the murderer."

"I'm trying to help you, but you seem to not want to help either me or even yourself. That is perplexing and illogical," he said.

MUTE: *Illogical? I didn't know he knew my middle name.*

"I don't know anything that would help you or me, Detective Jamison, but if I do find something out that might lead to the arrest of somebody, of course, I'd let you know. Why wouldn't I?" I asked.

"That's what I'm trying to figure out. In the meantime, we'll be working with the Lakeview police to determine who might have been behind the placement of that bomb this morning. And, one more time, you are not snooping around anybody who might want to eliminate you? You haven't had a suspicion you were trying to follow up on that might be the reason for the bomb?"

"No. I have no idea who might have killed Homer or who would have it in for me for any reason. Wait, what about those loan shark guys, could it have been them thinking that I might be responsible for their being arrested?"

"They have not been arrested yet, and they would have no reason to link you to their dealings with Homer Doukas now that they know you are not Mrs. Doukas," he replied.

I stood to leave, but he continued, "I have no option but to believe you; but I don't," he said.

MUTE: "*You despise me don't you, Rick (Detective Jamison)?*

~

The mortgage floor was in chaos when I arrived back shortly before noon.

"What's going on? Please, God, not another dead body," I said to Sophie.

"No. They escorted Charlie Harris out of the building about an hour ago. He's been fired."

"Why?" I asked. I wasn't going to let on that I knew he had been playing fast and loose with the phone queues.

"I don't know for sure, but word is that it had something to do with Amanda Dimpling."

Amanda had been at EFB almost as long as I had, and she did quite well, but she left the department and went to work for a mortgage lender closer to her home.

"Somebody said she sued the bank for some reason and that it had something to do with Charlie, but it's only a rumor,"

Sophie said.

Another twist in the plot? Maybe. Maybe not.

I checked my e-mails to find the usual hundred or so that I either deleted or tagged for further attention. Not surprisingly, my now daily e-mail from Alice Mayview had asterisks in bold italics in the subject line to get my attention.

Annie, this guy will not leave me alone. He's been at my desk three times today, and he's making me very nervous. What do you think he wants? I don't have anything to say to him. I've tried to call you several times but you are not answering your phone Are you avoiding me?

Good grief, the woman is driving me bonkers. I'm dealing with threats in the form of bombs, and she's dealing with somebody hanging around her desk.

I answered her: **Alice, maybe he's in love with you and can't stay away.**

She retorted: **That's not even remotely funny.**

MUTE: *If you saw Erwin Richter, you wouldn't think it was funny either.*

The first call I picked up and started to give my spiel to was Debbie Markey.

"Annie, it's me, Debbie Markey. I'm sorry to be calling you at work, but have you seen Al this morning?"

"I got in at about noon today, and I don't see him in his office, but there's been a bit of a brouhaha with the firing of Charlie Harris, so maybe he's in meetings," I said.

"Charlie Harris? Fired? Why?"

"I don't know, Debbie, but I'm sure Al can fill you in," I replied.

"That's just it, he's not answering his office phone or his cell phone, and I'm worried about him," she said.

"If he's been in meetings all day, he probably wouldn't answer his phone," I offered.

"It's not just that, he got home late again last night after one of his drives, and he was up and gone before I got up this morning. That's so unlike him."

"Debbie, this has been tough on a lot of people, but probably nobody more than Al. Even though Al wasn't in his office when Homer was killed, he was killed in Al's office, and, naturally the police want to know why," I said. "And they've probably been grilling Al about that very subject, putting him on edge. Did they have any connection other than work?" I asked.

"No. We didn't even socialize with Homer and Crystal unless we had to. To be honest, Al didn't like Homer that much, and I, of course, had nothing in common with his young wife."

"If I see him, I'll let him know you're worried about him, and I'll ask him to call you as soon as possible," I promised.

"Thanks, Annie. You do make me feel a little better about why he's been acting so strangely, and you are probably right, it must be the strain of continually being grilled by the police."

Despite all the tidal waves of emotion on the floor and from Alice and Debbie, the rest of the day went smoothly, except for a closing that was scheduled for that afternoon for one of my customers' refinance loans. The title company had assigned a closer, Billy Dean Grubbins, to be at the customer's house at 3:30. But my customer, Mr. Benz, called me to let me know that Grubbins hadn't shown up by 4 p.m. I called the title company, the title company called Billy Dean, who eventually called me in what sounded like a drunken stupor. This meant we had to cancel the closing and rewrite the closing papers, which would increase the costs slightly because of the added daily interest—a situation that wasn't easy to explain to a customer whose loan didn't close through no fault of their own. I prevailed upon the title company to make it up to the customer, and they said they would with a $100 gift certificate, more than the added interest. These are the kind of complications that drove me, and every other loan officer, to distraction. In my case, to a scotch on the rocks.

After that pluperfect mess, I was even happier to be driving south and over the wonderful blue Roebling Bridge into Covington, Kentucky, to meet my friend Jim for a night out without any vestige of pandemonium.

Jim lives in the historic Licking River district of Covington and, as I said, in a two-family house, built circa 1889. Not only is he gracious enough to allow me to stay on his top floor on evenings I find myself out late in northern Kentucky, but he treats me to one of his stupendous home-cooked breakfasts in the morning. His specialty is grits, eggs, and fried oysters. What's not to like about that?

I parked my car, and we drove over to Dee Felice in his spiffy, antique, grey Porche 356a. I like to think I'm not a car person, but I have to say, that car turned my head. Jim is about 73, so 23 years older than I. And I might remind you that Neil is 30, 20 years younger than I. Can't I find a nice middle ground? I have no idea if Jim might have been interested in me if I showed interest in him, but he was a catch at any age: great-looking with grey hair and goatee, wide at the shoulders, narrow at the hip, and with courtly manners you don't run into much anymore. I'm blabbering, but just want to keep you apace of the confusion that reigns in every corner of my life, not just in work and death.

Dee Felice is a New Orleans-type restaurant with live jazz, good food, and a group of regulars who are friendly partyers. In short, a great place to go to take your mind off a dead body.

We found a seat at the bar; Jim ordered a Manhattan, and I ordered a scotch. The place was jumping, and we decided to eat at the bar so we could be up close to enjoy the Lee Stolar Trio, who sat on a raised dais behind the bar, and to be as far away from the tables as possible so we could listen to the music instead of the chatter.

"So, what's shaking in the world of Annie Fillmore?" Jim asked.

"Everything's shaking, unfortunately," I started to say, when I felt a tap on my shoulder.

Erwin Richter. Good God. Couldn't I escape the malevolence?

"Annie Fillmore, isn't it?" he said, looming over my shoulder.

"Yes?" I answered, trying to pretend I didn't know who he was. I wished I didn't know who he was.

"I thought I spotted you over here. Erwin Richter, executive VP of EFB," he said, attempting to be congenial, "and this is my friend Missy," he said, introducing me to a thirty-something woman with fried blond hair and boobs as fake as

Richter's smile.

I knew he was up to something, because generally anybody above team manager or floor VP would do anything they could to avoid one of us loan officers. I've seen them practically jump into a bush or a shrub to avoid saying hello, and this guy was tapping me on the shoulder "off campus."

I pulled myself up to my full sitting-down height, and said, "Mr. Richter, I never mix business with pleasure. I'm sorry." I turned around and started talking to Jim again.

"I just wanted to ask you a question," Richter persisted.

Jim stood up and said, "Sir, I think you should go to your table now. The lady does not wish to engage in conversation with you. We are out enjoying ourselves after business hours."

"Hey, no need to get pissy with me. I'm just trying to be cordial," Richter spat out.

"Why don't we be cordial tomorrow at work? Tonight I'm trying to forget work and all the unpleasantness that has happened over the past few weeks," I said.

MUTE: *Move your ass and take your skanky girlfriend with you.*

"This is crazy. I can't talk to you? Is that what you're saying?" he asked.

"The manager is a good friend of mine," Jim said, "and I know he won't have any problem showing you the door."

Richter took Missy by the hand and snaked his way to the back of the restaurant to his table.

We continued to try to enjoy each other and our friends, but just knowing that Richter was there took the gleeful edge off.

Ten o'clock was my bedtime, but I made an exception on Thursdays, and we bid our farewell to everybody and headed out the door into the back parking lot at about 10:35. Just as we reached Jim's car, I noticed Richter and Missy getting in his car, a little red Mazda, one lane over.

"Jim, I don't know if it's a coincidence or if that guy from work is going to follow us," I said.

"No problem, I'll lose him," he said.

We made a speedy retreat, and Jim took a right where he usually went straight. After that I was lost, so I hoped Richter would be, too, if he was following us. We drove around for about 15 minutes before we took the corner onto Jim's street.

"Jim, isn't that his car in front of your house?" I asked. "How would he know where you lived?"

"He probably asked someone at the restaurant. They all know where I live," he replied.

Jim pulled over and called 911 to report being followed. He pulled up his car next to Richter's and opened his window. Richter leaned over Missy's boobs, risking impaling himself, clearly drunk. "I need to know what you know, lady," he slurred.

"I know you're a jerk wad and that the police are on their way," I said.

"You'll pay for this," he muttered, screeching his wheels down the street, not bothering to stop at the stop sign.

"I wouldn't worry about him," Jim said as we entered his house. "He probably won't make it home alive."

I bid Jim good night and walked up the stairs to a bed where I knew I would be safe and sound for at least one night.

Chapter 18

Friday, April 19, 2013

THE AROMA OF BREWED COFFEE and bacon beckoned me down the stairs as I made my way to Jim's kitchen, where he was puttering around with the bacon, a cheese omelet, and some kind of flaky rolls he had baked the day before. I forget any dietary restrictions I might have when I breakfast with him. That stuff is too good to pass up.

"The police came by last night for your good buddy," Jim said.

"Too bad he left so speedily," I replied.

"I wrote down his license plate, so he may be getting a call anyway," he remarked, pouring coffee into the cup he had set out for me next to the plate that was heaped with a fluffy omelet and roll.

"How about some homemade strawberry jam with that?" he asked.

MUTE: *One more dollop of jam, and you would see my picture under "Zaftig" in the dictionary.*

"Why not," I said, mentally counting the calories I was about to take in. Probably, about a day's worth.

He walked me to my car and on the way plucked a red tulip out of his side garden, "Here, take this to brighten your desk," he said, giving me a hug and a peck on the cheek. After last night and the charming breakfast, I wanted to forget the peck on the cheek and bend him backward in an old-fashioned

Hollywood kiss.

Driving to EFB from northern Kentucky instead of Lakeview was a journey to savor: ten minutes door to door. I was at my desk at the astounding hour of 8:30 a.m. Even more astounding was finding Troy at his desk and not in the same state of morning perkiness that I was enjoying. He was slumped over.

"Troy. Troy. TROY. Are you okay?" I asked leaning over the divider between us and tapping him on his shoulder.

"Huh? What," he said, looking up with red eyes and a five o'clock shadow that made George Clooney look clean-shaven. His rough appearance was in no way improved by the reek of ganja he was emitting.

"What the heck are you doing? You have to get out of here, or you're going to be fired!" I exclaimed.

"Hah. I got information," he mumbled.

"Come on. I'll walk you to your car where you can grab a snooze before you go home and change, and you can tell me your big secret."

"It won't be a secret for long," he said, trying to get on his feet.

We walked down the hall to the back entrance by the Bra, and Troy lumbered to his car with me holding his arm. I got him settled in his black Ford Ranger, and I went around to the other side and climbed into the passenger seat.

"So what's the big news that warranted what must have been a big doobie?" I asked.

"Doobie, doobie, that's great. How do you know about a doobie?"

"How old do you think I am? Come on. I have to get to work. What's the news?"

"Okay, it's not really news, but what I saw that night Homer was killed that I didn't tell you before or the police," he said, looking like hell.

"What?" I asked, trying to sound casual but wanting to shake him to hurry up and tell me.

"I told you I ran into Homer, and he was his usual asshole self, right?"

"Right," I said.

"I walked off down the hall, and Jan Mulligan was coming toward us, right?"

It was going to be one of these conversations. "Right," I agreed.

"I pretended to go in our door, but I hid behind the alcove and peeked around it to see what he was going to say to Jan. He was in a lousy mood, and I wondered if he was going to bust her balls, too. If she had balls."

MUTE: *Oh, she had balls.*

He continued. "They spoke for a few minutes; then he grabbed her and kissed her. It looked awkward because with those high heels she's so much taller than he is; I mean, than he used to be; I mean, was. She took his hand and put it on her private parts, and he kind of jumped back. Then you won't believe this, he clocked her. He hit her like she was another guy!" he exclaimed, sounding astounded.

"Gosh," I said.

"I didn't tell anybody, because I thought it would make her look too guilty, but I seem to be Jamison's favorite suspect, so I think I have to say something, don't you?"

"Yes, I think you definitely have to say something; but did you see her leave the building after he hit her?" I asked.

"After that she pushed him so hard he lost his footing, but I did see her walk down the hall to the exit by the Bra, so I assume she left. I didn't see her actually go out the door," he said.

"Are you sure she didn't see you?" I asked.

"Why? Do you think she did it, and will come after me?" he asked looking very concerned.

"I have no idea, I'm just asking if you think she saw you," I said.

"No, she didn't see me. I'm sure of that," he said.

He was wrong.

"One more thing. Why didn't you say Charlie Harris was on the floor that night, too?

"I don't know. When I passed his desk he turned and did the 'shh' thing, meaning, I think, to keep my mouth shut about him being there."

I waited until he fell asleep, extricated myself from the truck, and ankled my way back to the scene of the crime, aka work.

~

After a slow day in the mortgage department even by Friday standards, I walked over to see one of my processor friends.

"Hey, Susan. What's up in this part of the world?" I asked.

"Hi, Miss Annie. Nothing but sunshine over here. Can't you see it beaming through the ceiling tiles?" she asked, rolling her eyes.

"You know, I think I missed it until you mentioned it," I said.

"What's going on with *Law and Order* up there in the front?" she asked.

"I wish I knew. Nothing seems to be happening, but, of course, Detective Jamison isn't checking in with me for my opinion or to share clues."

"Too bad. I thought you were good at solving crimes. Did you tell me that, or did somebody else tell me that about you?"

"Definitely somebody else, not me," I replied.

"Hey, did I show you my photos of our vacation in Mexico?" she asked, rummaging through her purse.

Just as she pulled a packet of photos out of her bag I heard, "Annie? Annie, can you come over to my desk for a minute? I have an issue I need to discuss with you," Jan Mulligan called, standing at her desk two aisles over.

"Ooops, I've been called to duty," I said to Susan. "Catch your pix later."

"Hi, Jan. What issue do we need to discuss, the Hammond loan?" I asked. "I knew that was going to be a bugger."

"No, actually it has to do with Homer's murder. Since our conversation about the cleaning guy's wife, I get the feeling you know more about this than anybody besides the police, and I have a question for you."

"I don't know anything about the murder investigation, Jan. I just asked you if you saw Rodney Wilkins that night.

That's the name of the cleaning guy, by the way," I said, even though I knew she knew his name.

"When you asked if I had seen anybody else that night besides the cleaning guy, I said I hadn't, but actually I did see somebody, and if the number of times that detective has asked me down to see him is any indication, I'm beginning to think he thinks I might have murdered Homer," she stated.

"So I assume you haven't told this to Detective Jamison?"

"Not yet. That's what I wanted to ask you—if you thought it would be a smart thing to do. I don't want to get Troy, oh, um—" She stopped in mid-sentence.

"So it was Troy you saw here that night?" I asked.

"Yeah. He was hiding in the alcove by the door watching me and Homer talking, I guess," she said.

"You definitely have to tell Detective Jamison, the sooner the better. He's trying to solve a murder case without all the facts. You must want this to be over as much as anybody, seeing as you had to go downtown so many times."

"I absolutely want it over," she declared.

"Call him now, and tell him you need to speak to him about that night. I'm sure he'll make himself available."

"Yeah, that seems right," she said. "Thanks, Annie."

I fiddled a few hours away, made some calls to customers who had previously refinanced with me to see if I could entice them to do it again. No luck. I spent some time organizing my desk and to-do list for Monday morning, and by 4:30 it seemed like a very fine time to leave for the weekend.

Chad had already left, and four out of ten of my team members had left, too; why not make it an even five?

I knew Delhi would be busy on a Friday night but, probably, not as early as 5:30, which was about the time I figured I'd get there.

For the first time ever I had trepidation about going home. I felt dread at the end of the day in place of the delight I felt at the beginning. I should have gone home to let the Hoffmans know what I knew about the bomb. Delhi Deli seemed so much more comforting. I called the police from my car first to see if they found out who planted the bomb, then called Len and Nancy to let them know the police didn't have any suspects yet.

The place was already full, and I looked around for Neil, but didn't see him. There was a table for two in the middle of the floor, but I never liked that much visibility no matter where I was. I always liked the back of the classroom, too, but I didn't want to hog a table for four or more, so I sat.

Jeff came over with a glass of water with lemon, and a menu. "Hey, Annie, how are you?"

"Good, thanks. How are you doing?" I asked.

"I'm here," he said.

"Where's Neil?

"I think he had a date this afternoon, but he thought he should be in by about seven," he replied.

"A date?" I asked, my heart sinking.

"Yeah. I think he said it was a friend of his cousin's."

"Oh, that's good. It's nice to know that he dates," I stated, heart beating double time.

"I know. He works too hard. What can I get you?" he asked.

"I'll have a glass of cabernet, whatever you think is nice, and I'll look at the menu," I said.

MUTE: *A date? Whaaa?*

I sipped my wine, feeling sorry for myself, although I had no rational reason to be feeling that way. What was wrong with me? I ordered a cup of garlic broth and the fish tacos and wished I had brought a book along so I didn't find myself looking at the other diners and wanting to join in their conversations. The soup was perfect, and the fish tacos with cilantro and lime aioli and avocados, delightful—even if I did end up with a handful of filling in my hand before I finished.

It was about 6:35 when I looked up to see Neil come out from the kitchen. I pretended I didn't see him, but somebody must have told him I was there because he walked right over to my table and sat down.

"How was it?" he asked.

"Delicious, as usual. How was your date?" I brazenly asked.

"Date? Oh, not really a date. I just helped out my cousin's friend with her band."

"What kind of band?" I asked, feeling much better.

"You know, they're in college, rock and roll in a garage. They're okay, but you know how many kids want to make a living at music."

"Is she that much younger than you? Any vibes?" I asked even more brazenly.

"I'm not interested in someone younger. I'm interested in someone older. You're not usually here on a Friday night; what's going on?" he asked.

I told him about being followed by Erwin Richter in Covington the night before, and that Jim called the police and wrote down his license plate.

"What does he want with you?"

I was about to answer him when I looked up to see the specter of Erwin Richter. What was with this guy? What did he think I knew that he didn't think Alice knew?

"Neil, you can ask him yourself. He just walked in. Please call the police," I said, starting to sweat.

"No problem. I'll take care of it," he promised and left the table.

Sure enough Richter the Horrible came over to my table. "Hi. Annie. Your friend Alice told me you hang out here, so I thought I'd stop by to see if we could have a chat. Mind if I sit down?"

MUTE: *Alice better be tied up and gagged somewhere, or I was going to do it myself.*

"Yes, I do mind. The owner of this place is with me, and I told you last night if you have something to say to me or to ask me, do it on company time. I'm off of company time now," I said.

He pounded ahead. "Do you know Teddy K, the loan shark from northern Kentucky?"

Neil came back to the table. "What's going on here? Do you know this gentleman, Annie?"

"Yes. But I don't want to talk to him, and I've told him so," I said.

"Why don't I show you to a nice table in the back, sir, so you can enjoy yourself," Neil offered.

"I don't want a nice table in the back, I don't want a table here at all," Richter said looking around.

"Is there anything I can help you with?" asked Neil, I assumed trying to stall him until the police came.

"I doubt it. I work with you people every day—all you know is computers, and that's not the kind of information I'm looking for," he growled.

"'You people'? What do you mean by 'You people'?" Neil asked.

MUTE: *A triple threat: a jackass, a philanderer, and a racist.*

"You talk pretty good for an Indian," Richter commented.

"But you don't talk pretty good no matter where you or your family comes from," Neil shot back.

I saw a policeman enter the front door; he spotted Neil and came toward us.

"Let's see if this policeman thinks you talk pretty good," Neil said.

The officer came forward and said to Neil, "What's the issue? Is this gentleman causing a problem?"

Richter started to walk away, but the officer grabbed him by the arm and held him there, and I couldn't help but notice that the officer's big black hand had no trouble circling Richter's bicep.

"He's been harassing my friend here, Annie Fillmore. Apparently he was tailing her last night in northern Kentucky, and it was reported to the Covington police, and now he shows up here continuing to bother her," said Neil.

"Come on, pal. Let's go to my car. We can have a little talk, and I'll call down to Covington to see about that report last night," the officer said.

"Do you know who I am? I'm an officer of EFB. I'm sure you've heard of them," Richter boasted.

"I don't care if you're Jay Z. Come on," he said, easily steering Richter out of the restaurant.

Neil turned to the tables. "I apologize for the disruption. Please enjoy the rest of your meals. If you would like, your waiter will bring over a dessert on the house when you are ready for it."

"I should pay for the desserts. It's my fault," I said.

"You city girls are just plain trouble," he said, ruffling my already ruffled hair.

MUTE: *Hey, that was the second time I was called a city girl this week. How nice.*

"What does he want with you?" Neil asked.

"I didn't know, but tonight he asked me if I knew Teddy K, who I guess is a loan shark in northern Kentucky. Did I tell you I was followed by those two creeps who thought I was Crystal Doukas, the dead guy's wife? She told me that the loan shark guy had called her and said that they had paid Homer fifty thousand for insider trader information that never paid off and they wanted her to pay up. She reported it to the Cincinnati police, and those gangsters are probably going to jail. The connection is that that ass who was just in here, Erwin Richter, was the one who sold Homer Doukas the insider trading information, so he's running scared, and for some reason thinks I know all about it."

"You do seem to know all about it," he stated.

"Yeah, well, I don't know anything that can get him off the hook, so I'm not sure what he thinks I can tell him."

"He's panicked, and men do crazy things when they panic," Neil observed.

"Men? Not women?" I asked.

"I think women are more level-headed about things like that."

"I don't feel level-headed right now. I feel like I'm in an eddy, or is it a vortex?"

"It's got to come to an end sooner or later. At least this guy Richter is out of your hair."

I shuddered. "Richter, I don't even like his name, it reminds me of the word rictus," I said.

"Rictus? What does that mean?" he asked.

"The way I think of it probably comes from one of the hundreds of crime novels I've read, when the dead body has a smile they would call the 'rictus of death,' and I can't get away from that word when I think of Erwin. Arghh," I said, ever so eloquently.

"Hmm. I like that word, rictus."

"Well, I'd better get going. I have a long day tomorrow. I just hope I can sleep what with Richter following me together with that bottle bomb outside my house yesterday morning."

"Bomb? You had a bomb outside your house?"

Oh, I guess I didn't tell you about that. I didn't have time."

"You're not staying at your place tonight, are you?"

"Of course. Where else would I stay?" I asked.

"You can stay at my apartment. I'll sleep on the couch," he replied.

MUTE: *And, hopefully, you walk in your sleep, and I'd be too drowsy to stop any canoodling.*

"Thanks, but I'll be okay," I said.

"Or why not stay at Marilyn's?"

Sleeping at his apartment or at Marilyn's meant no sleep, but for totally different reasons.

"Not Marilyn's," I said. "I'll be fine at my place."

"I'm sleeping on your couch. I insist. I'll be over after we close up. I know you'll be asleep, but I know where your key is. It is still there isn't it?" he asked.

It's only been hidden in one place since I've lived there, and he knew where that was. So that was it, Neil was staying at my house, and I did feel better about it after all.

As soon as I got home I called Len and he said, "Come on over. I'll bet you'd like a little nightcap."

"Thanks, Len, but I just had dinner and a glass of wine. Have you seen anything I should know about since yesterday morning?" I asked.

"No. All quiet on the condo front. Any more news since we spoke earlier this evening? Do they have an idea who did it?"

"I don't think so, or at least they haven't told me if they do know."

"Well, sleep tight and try not to worry about it."

"I have a friend who insisted on sleeping on the couch to-night, just in case. So if you hear someone at my front door, it's him," I warned Len.

"Okay. I'll put away my shotgun," he said, I think jokingly, but it amazes me just how many people have told me they sleep with a gun in the drawer next to them or under their pillow.

I soaked in the tub with some Epsom salts, thinking about the day and how it started so charmingly and, actually, didn't end so badly either. It was all the in-between stuff I could have done without. Once I was detoxed and scrubbed, I got into my lovely bed, waited for the front door to unlatch, and hoped whatever good sense I had lurking somewhere would material-ize like a nice respectable head of foam on a beer.

I lulled myself to sleep with my ipod playing John Prine. As soon as I heard the last words, "This love is real," I hit replay.

Chapter 19

Saturday, April 20, 2013

NPR AWOKE ME ON SATURDAY morning at 6:30, early enough for me to hear a repeat of *Fresh Air* with Terry Gross and go back to sleep. It must have been the aroma of coffee wafting up to me that awakened me for good at about 8:45: Men making me coffee two mornings in a row; I must be doing something right.

I felt compelled to make breakfast for Neil no matter how much I knew I was going to embarrass myself. He, of course, was gallant as I placed before him two eggs "over easy," three slices of bacon, an English muffin, and half a grapefruit that all together looked like a Francis Bacon portrait bleeding off the plate. Well, I couldn't screw up the grapefruit, but the eggs and bacon didn't exactly have that Bon Appetit charm.

"This is going to taste great," he said, I guess, being cautious enough not to say, "This looks great.

"What are you up to on your day off?" he asked.

I didn't want to tell him I needed to rest up for my night of breaking and entering EFB with a 15' ladder. "Cleaning. I haven't cleaned this place in about a month, and, as you can tell, it needs it," I lied.

"Looks fine to me," he said looking around.

MUTE: *He's a bachelor, living alone. He wouldn't be giving my place the white-glove treatment. His apartment probably smelled like dirty socks.*

"Thanks, but it does need a good going over," I said. We finished our breakfast, said our good-byes which amounted to a hug and a kiss from him on my cheek, which would have been on my lips had I not turned my head.

"Annie Fillmore," he said shaking his head as he walked to his car.

I actually did take a dry mop to my hardwood floors and one of those duster things to the furniture tops. I eyed the windows, which I hadn't gotten to the week before, but I felt like one of those giant arm-waving balloon guys you see at the side of the road trying to get you to buy tires or rent an apartment; I had the energy, but it wasn't going anywhere, so I went to my couch to find out what Sonchai Jitpleecheep was up to in *Bangkok Tattoo*.

Naturally, this couldn't last all day. The phone rang at least five times from various folks looking for money for causes (diseases, politics), an announcement that I had won a cruise, and, of course, Crystal.

"When are you going to Homer's office to get the combination and the key?" she asked.

"Marilyn and I are going tonight, but don't put all your money on our finding what we're looking for. It's a stretch," I said.

"But I *am* counting on it. I'm paying you to find it, and you have to find it," she stated, while I pictured her stamping her feet like a four-year-old in full tantrum.

"I'm going to do my best, Crystal, but if it isn't there, it isn't there, and you wanting me to find it isn't going to change anything."

"Mmmm," she whined. Yes, a thirty-something woman was whining in my ear like a four year old, a sound I couldn't take even when it had come from my own children when they *were* four.

"Okay, Crystal. I'll call you tomorrow," I said, and hung up.

I shouldn't be so judgmental. I was as antsy as a kid waiting for the ice-cream truck to ring its bell. I just wanted to get down to EFB, check out where I thought the goods were, and be done with it.

I drove to Marilyn's about 6:30, figuring it would give me time to say hello to Mike and the boys and give Marilyn time for three or four trips back into the house because she forgot something.

As usual the lights were aglow along the walk even though it was still daylight. The front door was open, and the Monroe cacophony greeted me. It was hard to distinguish if it was from the boys, the TV, video games, or a little of each. It sounded like a place I would have liked to have been when I was a kid.

"Hello, hello," I announced myself.

"Annie's here," I heard one of the kids bellow.

"Annie," said Norman, running at my legs and hugging them.

"Hey, Norman. How's my guy?" I said, picking him up and giving him a kiss on his round, soft, boy-smelling cheek.

"Are you going to play games with me?"

"Not tonight, sweetie. Mom and I have to go out for a little while, but next week I'll come and we can play anything you want," I said.

"Uno," he screeched.

"Not Uno," one of the other guys yelled out.

"We'll play whatever we decide next week, okay?" I also yelled; you had to if you wanted to be heard.

I went into the kitchen, where Mike and Katy were still sitting at the table.

"Hey, guys. Thanks for letting Marilyn out with me tonight," I said.

"Where did she say you were going?" Katy asked.

"Oh, one of my windows is leaking and needs re-caulking, and my neighbor said he'd do it for me, but he didn't have a ladder tall enough, so we're borrowing Mike's ladder."

MUTE: *The lies just trip off of my devil-forked tongue.*

"Why isn't Mike doing it? You know he can do anything," Katy said proudly.

"I know he can, but he does it all week long, so we want him to relax and have somebody else do the heavy lifting," I lied.

"Let's go," said Marilyn, walking into the kitchen dressed like a cat burglar.

"What's with the black outfit, Mar?" asked Mike.

"If I have to climb the ladder, I'll be flexible," she replied.

"Yes, black does help with pliancy," said Mike, smiling.

"Whatever," she said grabbing my arm and steering me to kiss the boys good-bye.

We climbed into Mike's van, which was a workshop on wheels. He had everything exquisitely organized in the back—in the event he had to build an entire house at a moment's notice it seemed. I wonder how much he would charge me to organize my closets.

"So what's the drill?" Marilyn asked. She even sounded like a cat burglar.

"The drill is we park the van in the back, walk the ladder down the hall, up the first flight of steps, down the other hall to the Grand Entry, go up those stairs, and into Homer's office. There's a buzzer you can man while I work the key, because it's as secure as Bernie Madoff's office probably was."

~

As soon as we drove up and parked, it hit me how nuts this was. My heart started pounding, my palms got clammy, and I just sat there.

"What are you waiting for? Let's go," Marilyn said.

Clearly, she didn't have a grasp on reality.

"Okay, okay. I'm just getting my bearings." I took a deep breath.

As we were unfastening the ladder from the ratchet straps on the top of the van, Marilyn said, "Scaredy-cat." It took a few steps to get in sync and to walk the ladder to the door. We set it down, I swiped my badge at the Bra entrance, held the door, and in we went like Butch Cassidy and the Sundance Kid.

"Okay, Sundance. It might be a little tricky getting the ladder up the first set of steps. I hadn't really thought of getting it around that tight corner," I said.

"I want to be Butch Cassidy," Marilyn whined.

MUTE: *I want to 'have' Butch Cassidy.*

"All righty, Butch. Down the hall until the first set of steps; then it might get tricky."

"Nothing's too tricky for Butch Cassidy," she said, the old Newman gleam in her eye.

We got to the end of the bottom hallway, and it was touchy getting that cumbrous ladder around the bottom of the stairs and up them. We had to bring it over the rail, and then manipulate it an inch this way, an inch that way, scraping the wall until it looked like a cat had clawed its way to the top.

"I hope the other stairway isn't going to be this difficult," Marilyn groaned.

"It won't be difficult getting it up, but may be a hitch if we have to turn it. I can't remember if Alice's office is straight ahead at the top of the stairway or off to the right a little, but I guess we'll find out."

Marilyn hadn't been in the EFB building before and was rewardingly open-mouthed at the grandeur of the Grand Entry.

"Oh, my God. Did someone actually live here?" she asked.

"Yep. I think they lived here during the Prohibition, so in the 1920s. I'm not sure how long they were here, but it sure is a party palace."

"How long has EFB been here?"

"I think about fifteen years, so about 1999, 2000," I said.

"Did they change the whole thing, or just the bottom floor?" she asked.

"Let's get up the stairs, and we can talk about history later," I suggested.

"Fine," she said resignedly, picking up her end of the ladder again.

"Wait. Let me run up to see if the office is off to the right or straight ahead. If off to the right it's going to be a problem. But somebody must have to get ladders in there to change lightbulbs and stuff," I said.

I sprang up the stairs, saw that Alice's office was right across from the top, and genuflected for who knows what reason—kind of like spiritual sign language, because I was never Catholic.

"Okay, we're good, Butch. Let's rob this train," I said.

We navigated the ladder up the stairs and into Alice's office, having to rest the first half of it on her desk. I rummaged through the desk, finding the key to Homer's door, and locating the buzzer.

"Marilyn, I'm going to turn the key in the lock, and when I say go, you press the buzzer," I said.

"Butch," she jokingly reminded me.

We got into Homer's office, and I realized there wouldn't be that much natural light, and I didn't want to turn a light on that might be seen from outside by some snooping security guard. I was sure Alice was the kind of person who would have a flashlight in case of emergencies so I went back out into her office to look in her desk. No flashlight.

There were a few closets to check, and, bingo, it was in the first one on a shelf next to a pair of those clear rubber shoe covers old ladies put over their shoes. Alice wasn't that old, but, apparently, vigilant about wet shoes.

I unfolded the sheet of paper from Homer's book and stood behind the desk where he would have sat. I looked up at the wooden ceiling squares and tried to decide if he would have hidden something from a standpoint of where he sat, or would it have been more likely he hid something up there from the vantage point of the door?

"Marilyn, what do you think? Would the hidden stuff be in a square he counted off from his desk or from the door or someplace completely different?"

"I'd guess from his desk," she replied, and that's what I thought, too; so we positioned the ladder in front of his desk under the square that was five over from the left wall and five down. The ladder was tough to get in place, but Marilyn seemed to know more about it than I did, so she got it arranged just where I needed it and we opened it to its upside-down V position.

I mounted the ladder to the third from the top step and tapped on the square. I didn't know what I thought was going to happen, but it didn't budge.

"Marilyn, hand me the flashlight. I need something to tap the square to see if it will move."

She climbed the ladder and handed me the flashlight, and I tapped as vigorously as I could, but the square didn't move.

"Do you want me to try?" Marilyn asked.

"Do you think you're that much stronger than I am?"

"I'm that much younger, and maybe I can apply a little more elbow grease."

"Fine," I said, in the same tone she used earlier and climbed down the ladder.

She had no luck either, so, disheartened, we moved the ladder to the vantage point of Homer looking at the ceiling from the door.

We again positioned the ladder accordingly, and again I mounted its steps and groped for the wooden square. This time it didn't take more than a tap for the square to move. I reached in with my eyes closed, because who knew if a rat or a bat was waiting in there? But it wasn't a bat, a rat, or even a rabid squirrel; it was a small manila envelope folded over and stashed as far into the square hole as possible. I stepped up another rung, held the flashlight in the hole, and squinted to see if there was anything else in there; there wasn't. I stepped down to the safer rung and opened the envelope to find a slip of paper with a combination and a small key. "Yea! This is it," I squealed with delight.

"You might want to get down from there pretty quick. I think I saw a high beamed light from outside scaling the building," Marilyn warned.

"Are you sure you're not imagining it?" I asked.

But no sooner were those words out of my mouth, than I saw the beam cross the ladder and the wall.

"Shit," I said. "Hit the floor."

"What about the ladder," Marilyn whispered.

"We need to get it flat, and we need to crawl out of here."

We maneuvered ourselves into a position so we could close the ladder, and I pulled the legs out while Marilyn caught the other end and laid it flat. I definitely had the easier job, but, as she said, she was younger.

We crawled out of the office, and Marilyn started for the stairs. "I think we had better hide in an office up here until we think the coast is clear," I said.

"Are any of the offices unlocked?"

"I don't know, but we're going to have to try."

As it turned out, the last office down the hall was unlocked, and we stepped in and flattened ourselves against the wall. I inched myself toward the window to see if I could see who was controlling the light that seemed, in Homer's office, to be one of those Bat Signals peeking in the window, but it was more likely a guard with one powerful flashlight. I didn't see anything, but thought it would be wise to leave the ladder where it was and escape the building out the front door. We would have to come back the next night to retrieve the ladder.

"We're going to leave the ladder in Homer's office and get it tomorrow night," I whispered. "We'll make our way down the stairs and out the front door."

"Mike needs his ladder," Marilyn said, not in a whisper.

"Shhhh. He'll have it tomorrow night. He doesn't work on Sundays does he?" I continued to whisper.

"No. But if he doesn't have it by tomorrow night, he's going to go to your house to get it first thing Monday morning, so it has to be back tomorrow."

"It will be."

We kept low and exited the front door, crawling around the side of the building on our hands and knees. The only sound I could hear was the pounding of my heart. When we saw the coast was clear, we made a beeline for the SUV.

We never did see the guard with the flashlight or any other guard for that matter, and I was mightily relieved to be pulling into Marilyn's driveway.

It was about 10 p.m. by the time I got home, too late for anybody to call me, but I figured Crystal would be up and partying, even if it was only by herself.

"Crystal, hi. It's Annie. Good news. We have the combination and the key," I said.

"Jesus. Thank God," she said.

MUTE: *Jesus? God? I never would have guessed she was so devout.*

"Come on over," she said.

"What? Now? No way. I'll be over tomorrow when I'm awake."

"Why can't you come now?" she whined.

"I'm too old. I'll see you tomorrow," I said, and hung up.

Chapter 20

Sunday, April 21, 2013 (morning)

WHEW, IT'S OVER, I thought as I rolled over in bed on that sunny Sunday morning. What was over? I asked myself. Retrieving Homer's combination and key was just the beginning. Who killed the bugger? Where was Rodney? How were we going to get the ladder out of EFB without flashlights searing our eyes, and worse, being arrested? I dragged myself out of bed, feeling more tired than when I fell asleep the night before at about 11:30. Adrenaline kept me awake. Now it was all used up.

I padded down my steps and outside to pick up the Sunday *New York Times*, something that always cheers me up; but that morning the front page was covered with the Boston Marathon bombers' story. What could be more heartbreaking and dispiriting than another mass murder by some misguided, unbalanced young men. No matter how much *The New York Times* or every other newspaper in the world wrote about it and parsed it, they couldn't write away hate. It kills me that newspapers and magazines ask, "Why? Why did they do it?" Why? Why isn't going to shed any light on crazy.

My phone rang around 11:30, the clarion call that I had other stuff to pay attention to, stuff in my own backyard.

"Where are you?" said Crystal.

"I'm in bed," I lied.

"In bed? It's 11:30," she said.

MUTE: *Like she never stayed in bed until 11:30.*

"What time would you like me to come over?" I asked.

"Now. Right now," she said louder than she needed to.

"Okay. See you in an hour."

I took my time having breakfast, read the parts of *The New York Times* that didn't make me want crawl back in bed, and I headed out of my garage an hour later.

Crystal was acting like a brat, and I was going to take my sweet time. I give a personal pass for brats thirteen or under because it's hard learning how to fit into the world without always getting what you want, but after that you have to suck it up and realize McDonald's is wrong, you don't deserve a break today.

I pulled into the Doukas estate about 1:45. Crystal was standing at the door, with her hand on her hip, in short shorts showing a pair of impressive legs.

"Hey, Crystal. How's it going?" I asked.

"It's going you're late," she said.

"You know, I'm not your maid, although you shouldn't be using that tone of voice even on the girls who clean your house if you don't want rat poison in your sugar bowl," I retorted.

"What are you talking about?" she asked.

"You're being rude, and I don't appreciate it."

"Okay, sorry. But I'm just nervous about what we're gonna find in the box and all, that's all," she said kind of like a thirteen-year-old.

I followed her through the house of hanging pink crystals and leopard print throws into the dining room, to the fireplace and the removable tiles under which Pandora's Box lay hidden. "Let's take out the tiles so we can get to the box," I said.

We removed all the tiles, and I took out the piece of paper with what I assumed was the combination for Pandora's lock. My hands were shaking a bit as I read the instructions: Right 3x to 23. Left past 23 to 12. Right to 32.

"Okay, Crystal. Here goes." I turned the lock right three times to 23, left past the 23 until I got to 12, and once again to the right until I got to 32. Bingo, the spring on the lock pinged open. I think we both withdrew our breaths at the same time. We just sat there on our haunches looking at the box. Finally,

Crystal flung the top up to reveal a slew of voice recorders of all shapes and sizes. From older versions with tape, to the newer versions. There were also some old newspapers, photographs, and a small metal box that could be opened by a key.

"What the hell is all this crap?" Crystal said, flipping through a newspaper. "This one is a Cincinnati paper from, um, 1953. What was Homer doing with a Cincinnati newspaper from 1953? He was from New Jersey."

"I wonder how far back these recordings go. They can't just be from since he was at EFB. I guess the police will have to listen to them to see if they are related in any way to his death," I said.

"Oh, no. Not until I listen to them," Crystal insisted.

"Well you better start, because now we have information that might point to his murderer, and we can be cited for obstructing justice if we don't turn them over to Detective Jamison post haste."

"I'm not mailing them to him. I'll just tell him to pick them up after I'm done listening," she said.

"Huh?" I said.

"Didn't you say we had to post them to him," she asked.

"Who's on second?" I said, quickly adding a "Never mind" to put an end to our unintended routine.

"Where's the key to the metal box, that's what I want to see. He must have kept *really* secret stuff in there," she said.

I handed her the key, and she took the box to the dining table with her back to me. "What the heck is going on with him? Or was going on with him?" she said. "Do you think this is his birth certificate?" she asked me handing me the document.

"It says 'Homer Christos Markos, born November 9, 1944 to Athenia Doukas Markos and Christos Homer Markos at General Hospital, Cincinnati, Ohio.'"

"It must be him. He must have changed his name," I said. "But why? And why did he tell you he was born and brought up in New Jersey?" I said.

"Whoa!" We exclaimed at the same time.

"General Hospital? That's the soap opera. Do you think he

had something to do with the soap opera?" Crystal asked.

MUTE: *Whew. Too bad her brain wasn't as gorgeous as her body."*

"No. I think whatever hospital he was born in here in Cincinnati was called General Hospital at that time. Maybe University Hospital now?" I asked to no one in particular, because I sure knew she wouldn't know.

She rummaged through some other paperwork, read something, and stuffed it into her pocket while saying, "Bastard."

"What?" I asked.

"Nothing," she said.

"Oh, here's the thing that says he changed his name from Homer Christos Markos to Homer Doukas, back in 1959, and it's signed by someone called Eleni Doukas in New Jersey," she said.

"What else is in the box that you feel comfortable sharing?" I asked.

"Wait, let me see what else that douche bag had in here about me," she said.

She read two other documents, looked at a few photographs, and said, "Here, you can read them," handing them over to me.

"Here's the plan. You listen to all of the tapes you want to listen to, and I'll take the rest of this stuff home and read it to see if I can come up with something. How does that sound?" I asked.

"Like a lot of work if you ask me."

"I know, but we may find out who killed your dear, departed husband," I reminded her.

"Yeah, right," she replied. "The dear part I mean."

"Got it."

I drove home via the splendid Indian Hill countryside, thinking, as I reveled in the landscape, what was in Homer's past? Why the secrecy? Why the name change? I couldn't wait to get home to see if I could unravel something with the paperwork and newspapers I had in my trunk.

I laid out the newspapers on my dining table; there were three of them all dated the same day: April 7, 1953. The headlines for that day were that Dag Hammarskjöld was elected the second United Nations secretary-general and that the first west-to-east transatlantic nonstop flight was achieved; neither one having anything to do with Homer Doukas, or Homer Christos Markos for that matter.

I turned each yellowed page, and the nostalgia of another time washed over me. What was it like to be alive in 1953? Moms in aprons serving dinner as soon as their husbands got home from work, with their children not having much TV to watch, and certainly no video games. How would Andrew, Jackson, or Norman Monroe have survived? I envisioned huge elm tree arbors branching over midwestern streets where there resided nothing but goodwill, until I remembered the Hungarian Revolution, the cold war, Joseph McCarthy, and the other horrors that blackened that decade.

I was thinking that people who died that day, or shortly before, have been dead for sixty years. When suddenly I saw it—the obituary of Athenia Doukas Markos. It seems she died when giving birth to Alexander Christos Markos on April 5, 1953. She was the wife of Christos Homer Markos who owned Christos Chili in Cincinnati, both of whom had come to the United States in 1950 from Thessaloniki, Greece. They had two other children: Homer and Chloie, besides the infant, Alexander. There were some old photographs I guessed were of Athenia and her elder son, Homer, but no photos of Christos or Chloie.

I knew Christos Chili was still in business, because I had once been to one of their locations on the west side of Cincinnati. It never found the popularity of Skyline Chili, also owned by a Greek family, but it kept afloat for these past 63 years.

I googled Christos Chili and found the owners to be Mike and Chloie Papadopoulos. Surely Chloie was the daughter of Christos, and she had married another Greek.

I checked my watch. It was 1:45, and if the gods were favoring me that day, maybe I could find Chloie, ask her a few questions, and be back in time to get to Marilyn's, get the van, and retrieve the ladder.

The west side of Cincinnati was like another country to me, but I knew a few major roads, like Winton Road, and

Google said there was a Christos Chili on that one. I called the number for that store, but it was out of service the voice said.

I tried another one in Cheviot, another west side town in Cincinnati that I can never find, and someone answered, "Christos Chili, where chili lovers meet to eat. This is Justin. How can I help you?"

"Hi, I'm looking for Chloie. Will she be in today?" I asked in the perkiest voice I could muster.

"Chloie? You mean Mrs. Papadopoulos?" he said.

MUTE: *Say that three times fast.*

"Yes," I answered.

"She's not usually in the stores on Sunday, not even that much during the week."

"Oh, of course. It's been awhile since I've been in touch. This is her cousin Eleni from New Jersey, and I'm in town for the day and didn't want to be in Cincinnati and not say hello. Do you have her number?" I asked.

"Yeah, sure," he said, and gave it to me. I was shocked.

"Do they still live over on—oh, my gosh, it's been so long I forgot the name of their street," I lied.

"They live off of Bridgetown Road someplace. I don't know the address," he offered.

"Okay, thanks, Justin. I'll give her a call.

I went immediately to my computer and googled their name, and there she was on Kendry Drive. I suppose I could have just googled them in the first place, but you never know when there's a senior and junior, and I didn't want to show up at the wrong door and waste all that time. I printed the MapQuest driving instructions from my house to Kendry Drive, and it said 22 minutes door to door. Twenty-two minutes if I could follow the directions, if the directions were accurate—which they more than often weren't—and if they didn't have one of those gates I had to climb around or over.

It was a hike, but I found Bridgetown, then watched my mileage to see how far I was going to reach Kendry, which MapQuest said was 1.7 miles.

And so it was. As I pulled up in front of the house I had to stop my fluttering heart. I always had so much nerve until the thing I should have been nervous about in the first place was right in front of me. I sat in the car outside their sprawling property to practice what I was going to say. Maybe I should call her Chloie because I didn't want to insult her and mess up the pronunciation of her last name. So something like: Good afternoon, Chloie. I'm so sorry to bother you blah blah blah. That wasn't going to work, so it was better to just get to the front door and wing it.

The house was impressive, built from a lot of chili money, no doubt. The double doors were, as the Doukas's doors, inlaid with stained glass. I rang the bell, and a little girl of about 7 or 8 came to the door. I figured it must be Chloie's granddaughter, because if Chloie were a little younger than Homer, she would have been too old to have a child that age.

"Hi. Is Chloie home?" I asked.

She looked me up and down in a curious way, not an unpleasant way, and turned her head to say, I think, "Yaya,"or something that sounded like that, that I guessed meant Grandma in Greek.

"Yes, Athenia. What is it?" someone asked.

"Somebody wants you," Athenia replied.

A very lovely woman with dark hair streaked with grey and pulled back into a low bun on the nape of her neck, dressed in a deep purple silk pants suit came to the door and said, "Yes? May I help you?"

"Hi, my name is Annie Fillmore. I work at EFB, and I knew your brother Homer Doukas.

"Oh," she said taking a step backward. "Homer, yes, I read about it in the newspaper that there had been an accident."

MUTE: *Dribbling chili on your shirt front is an accident…*

"I thought that there was no family to alert, until his wife, Crystal, told me she found his birth certificate, and it sounded like he was born in Cincinnati and actually had family here," I said.

"Oh, dear. It's such a long story, and I don't have too many details. But why don't you come in, since you've been nice enough to come.

She showed me into what surely would have been called a

parlor in an old mansion, but this mansion didn't look that old.

She motioned me to a short, white brocade sofa, where we both sat.

"I know it will seem strange to you, but I never met Homer, or at least I don't remember him, because he left our house when he was about seven, shortly after Alexander was born and Mama died. I was only one year old, so you can see why it would be hard for me to remember him."

"I'm so sorry to dredge up these memories," I said.

"What's sad is that there are so few memories, and not many good ones when I was growing up either. Thankfully, I was raised almost exclusively by my aunts, my father's sisters, and they were kind to me and Alexander."

"Where is Alexander? Do you have contact with him?" I asked.

"No. I haven't seen him in some years, and I don't even know where he lives or what he does for a living. I think our childhood was so terrible that neither one of us wanted to see the other and relive any of those terrible days; terrible especially for Alexander."

"Why so much more terrible for Alexander?" I asked, feeling bad to be prying into a person's pain, but hoping something would direct me to a murderer.

"Papa was always volatile even back in Greece my aunt's told me; but when he came here the stress of opening a business, and living in a country with a language barrier just kind of pushed him over the edge.

"When Alexander was born and Mama died in childbirth, he really seemed to lose his mind. My aunts told me Mama and Homer were very close, and they thought Papa was jealous of the little boy. Can you imagine? They said he was never nice to Homer, and after Mama died he decided to send him to live with Mama's sister, Eleni, in New Jersey. Of course, they didn't tell me any of this until Papa died when I was about fifteen. They were scared of him, too; and he did support everybody, even my aunts, so they felt beholden to him.

"Anyway, he blamed Alexander for Mama's death, which was, of course, ridiculous. After Papa died, Aunt Agatha told me that Mama had said the doctor had told her she shouldn't have any more children because she almost died of preeclampsia giving birth to me. But Papa wouldn't listen to her. He said she was making excuses for not wanting to have sex with him and that all she cared about was Homer.

MUTE: *Hearing what he was like, it would have taken a lot less than preeclampsia for me not to want to have sex with him.*

"One night I heard my aunts whispering, and they said that Mama had breast-fed Homer until he was six years old. Even by Greek standards that's too old for a child to be breast-fed. Oh, my goodness, I don't know why I'm telling all of this to a perfect stranger. I've never told anybody most of these things," she finished.

She was so nice, and it seemed like something she should have gotten off her chest a long time ago.

"Sometimes it just feels good to confide in a stranger who has nothing to do with your daily life," I assured her, reaching over and patting her hand.

"You must think Alexander and I are terrible for not being closer."

"No, of course not," I said.

It must have made her feel better because she continued.

"Papa took it out on Alexander that Mama died and started hitting him and whipping him with a belt or whatever was handy any time he got out of line or even if Papa *thought* he was out of line. He was a little boy, for goodness sake," she said, tears now streaming down her lovely face.

"When Alexander was about ten, he just went off on his own, doing God only knows what. He would leave for school in the morning and not come home until bedtime. Unless we were at my aunts' house, he wouldn't be around, and Papa never said a word about it.

"He hung with a group of the tougher boys in school, so I knew they were probably up to no good, but I wouldn't have breathed a word even to my aunts. He had it bad enough."

"When did you say your father died?"

"Let's see. I was about fifteen, so he must have been, I think fifty-four. He was young to die, and God forgive me, but life was better after that. My aunts ran the chili parlors until I was old enough to take over. We asked Alexander if he wanted to run them, being the boy, or man, but he had just graduated from Miami University and said he had no interest. So that's it. I had no idea Homer was living back in Cincinnati, and I don't know where Alexander lives, even if he's still here," she said.

I felt sorry for Homer and even gave him a little wiggle room for his nastiness with such a sad background, but in the end, we're all responsible for our actions. He was a bully in the worst sense of the word, just like his father.

We said our good-byes, and I told her I would let her know when, and if, there was to be a funeral for Homer if she cared to attend. She said she'd talk it over with her husband, but she felt as if she should represent the family and say good-bye to him to make up, in some small way, for his being abandoned by her father.

I arrived back at my house about 4:30, in time to read the rest of the Sunday paper and relax before I called Crystal to see if she had a chance to listen to many of the recordings, and before Marilyn and I had to set out to retrieve the ladder in Homer's office.

"Crystal, hi. Have you had a chance to get through many of the recordings?"

"Yeah. I started with what looked like the newer ones and then got to the older ones with the tapes," she said.

"And?" I asked.

"And what?"

"Did you find out anything incriminating about anyone?" I asked, then reworded it. "Did he say anything on any of the tapes that you listened to that might point a finger at who murdered him?"

"Well, there was the thing about Erwin and the insider trading like those bastards were talking about who called me and wanted me to pay them money for.

"I didn't know what else he was talking about on those things. They didn't make any sense to me cause all I cared about is that he wasn't talking about me, and he wasn't, so if you want your friend at the police department to come get them, he can."

"I think it would be better if you called him and told him you found these things, and that he can pick them up if he wants. I'll drop off the rest of this stuff, and you can tell him you found them all in the same place when you were cleaning up. I'll drop them by tomorrow, so you better not call him until you have all of it, okay?"

"Okay. I'll call him when you drop the stuff off. When do you think that will be?"

"Tomorrow morning on the way to work," I said.

"What time?

"About eight o'clock."

"In the morning?"

"Yep, in the morning."

"I'd better go to bed early," she said.

"Okay, then. I'll see you in the morning," I said, and disconnected.

~

By the time 7:30 rolled around, I was dragging from the emotional hour with Chloie and wished that I could put off the ladder retrieval, but I couldn't.

When energy fails, thank God for a cup of coffee. Times five.

Chapter 21

Sunday, April 21, 2013 (evening)

I ARRIVED AT MARILYN'S AT 8, later than the night before, to ensure it was plenty dark. She was waiting for me in her driveway in her black cat burglar gear, and I had on my jeans and black t-shirt.

"Look, we're practically invisible," I said.

"Ha," she answered.

We got in the van and started out again for EFB. "I don't think we should park near the building this time. We don't want to alert a security guard that there may be anybody in the building," I said.

"We can't park too far away because we have the ladder to deal with," she protested.

"Once we get the ladder out, you can run to the car and pull around to pick me up, and we can attach the ladder on the top of the van again," I suggested.

"Okay, that sounds good."

~

As we were driving around the bend on the road to 71, she stopped the van, pulled over to the side, and let out a yelp, "Oh, look at that sweet scraggly dog over there."

A black dog sniffing around the edges of a tree looked up nonchalantly at the van.

"I'm going to see if he has tags. Maybe the owners are

frantic like I was when Archie left," she said.

She jumped out, walked around the front of the van, and checked the dog for tags.

"No tags," she announced, pushing out her lower lip.

She picked the dog up and brought him over to my window. "He's so filthy, and don't you think he looks forlorn?"

"I'll go with filthy, but he looks perfectly happy otherwise."

"I'm going to bring him with us, and after we get the ladder, I'll take him home, give him a bath, and call around to see if anybody's reported a missing dog."

"I think that's a terrible idea," I said. "We can't leave him in the van to bark his head off and draw attention to us, and we definitely can't bring him in the building with us."

"Well, it's my van, I'm doing you a favor, and I get to do what I want with the dog," she insisted.

At this point she handed the filthy critter to me, but all he wanted was Marilyn. When she got in the driver's seat, he wiggled and whimpered until he was sitting on her lap behind the wheel.

"Oh, look. He loves me," she said. "Sweet puppy, sweet little guy," she said nuzzling him and petting him. "You need a good meal, don't you, you skinny little thing."

As she was petting him, the layers of dirt and mud caking his fur started to come off, and we could see he was actually not black, not even brown, but a much lighter color. I don't know how long it took for us to look at each other and say, "Archie?"

He started wagging his long black tail at me, slinging the muck onto me, while licking Marilyn's face.

"Archie, Archie. Oh, my God, you found me, or I found you," she said, crying tears of jubilation.

"Do you want to turn around and drop him off before we head down to EFB?" I asked.

"No. Oh, no, I can't let him out of my sight now," she declared, still trembling with emotion.

"Oh, geez. Well, hand him over, or do you want me to drive?" I asked.

"Yes. You can drive so I can cuddle with him and see if I can get some of this dirt off him with the rags Mike has in the back."

She retrieved the rags, rubbed him down, and he sure looked like a skinny (very skinny) version of the Archie I once knew.

Marilyn talked to him all the way down to EFB, regaling him with what she went through while he was on the lam. "And then Auntie Annie and I went out into the country, and we met a terrible, terrible man who said he had found you. Oh, it was so awful, Archie," she yammered on.

MUTE: *Eject button? Eject button?*

When we arrived near EFB, I drove around the back way and parked the van in a small grove of trees.

"Okay. I hope you are not considering bringing Archie in with us," I said.

"I'm not considering it, I'm doing it. I'm not leaving him alone," she stated.

So in we trounced with the mangy mutt in tow. We got up the stairs and into Homer's office and were trying to figure out how we were going to carry the ladder while she held Archie.

"Maybe there's some rope hanging around, and I can make a loose collar and leash for him," she said.

"Rope? Why would there be rope?" I asked.

She started opening Alice's desk drawers, then started on the closets. "Look, here's a sash to a raincoat. I bet that will work."

Alice was going to love having the crisp belt from her Burberry raincoat wrapped around this scruffy dog's muddy neck.

Marilyn put Archie down for the first time since she rescued him from a life on the road, and he took off like a flash.

MUTE: *Cujo. On the run.*

She took off after him, screaming, "Archie! Archie!" and I took after her, saying, "Shhh, be quiet, be quiet."

The place was a mansion, so it was going to be a great chase, not to mention a highly annoying one. Suddenly I heard Archie barking frantically somewhere on the first floor. Well, he didn't actually bark, he kind of bayed. We finally found him in the kitchen standing in front of an old cabinet, howling his heart out.

"It must be a rat, or a mouse, or something behind there," Marilyn said.

I walked over to the baying Archie and the cooing Marilyn and noticed that the huge built-in hutch he was clamoring over looked like it had warped away from the wall. It probably was over one hundred years old, so I wasn't surprised, but something made me pull on it, and as I did, the side I was pulling on came out and the other side pivoted inward.

"Marilyn, look at this. It looks like one of those old book-cases in the Charlie Chan movies. There's something behind here," I said, completely forgetting the ladder.

We stepped inside the opening and found a floor-to-ceiling metal door that slid over to the side; it seemed to be on a spring-action mechanism, because once we stepped inside to a wooden step, the door snapped shut. A dim light was coming up from the bottom of old rickety steps that led down to a dirt floor.

"Mister?" somebody's voice said weakly.

We were holding each other, more spooked than Laurel and Hardy, inching ourselves timidly forward on the hard mud floor surrounded by a stone wall until we were staring at a black gentleman sitting in a camping chair and reading a newspaper by the light of a headlamp. "Rodney?" I said.

"Yes, ma'am," he said, as casually as if he were sitting on his front porch.

"Rodney," I repeated.

"Yes, ma'am."

"What are you doing here? How did you get down here? What is this place?"

I'd eventually have to allow him to answer.

"I don't know how I got down here. I can't remember," he said.

"Where did all this camping stuff come from?"

In addition to the chair, there was an airbed on a double cot, a sleeping bag, a radio, what looked like a mini stove with a fuel can underneath, and lots of food wrappers and empty Gatorade bottles. He was dressed in jeans, a red-plaid flannel shirt, and a fisherman's sweater with a rolled collar.

"I don't know that either."

Marilyn piped up. "Did you bring all these things down here for a little vacation, Rodney?"

"No. It's not a vacation. I just forgot how I got here and can't remember who brought all these things," he said, looking around.

"Is this a tunnel? How far back does it go?" I asked.

"It goes back as far as where I go to relieve myself," he replied.

He was so sweet, he was breaking my heart even though I didn't believe a word he was saying.

"I'm going to fiddle with that door we just came in and call Detective Jamison. Although I doubt my cell is going to work down here."

"No, ma'am, no cell phones down here," Rodney said.

I went back up the old wooden stairs and tried to slide the door over, but it wouldn't budge.

"Marilyn, come up here and help me open this door," I called.

We pushed, pulled, jimmied, and tried to get our fingers around the edge, but that thing wasn't moving.

"Where's Archie?" Marilyn said, for the first time realizing she and Archie were separated once again.

"He's out in the kitchen. Can't you hear him howling?"

"Oh, my poor boy."

"Poor Archie? What about poor us, stuck in a dank tunnel with no way to get out," I said.

Back down by the "campsite" I again tried to coax some information out of Rodney.

"Rodney, we've been to see Gladys, and she's back in the hospital again. I don't think your disappearance has helped her condition, and they're rehabbing your building, so you are going to have to move soon, and I think she's worried to death about where you are and what's to become of her," I said.

"I hardly think about anything else except Gladys and what

she must think about my not comin' home," he said.

"We can get you home very soon if you tell us how you got here and who brought you all this stuff."

He was clearly scared and looked at us with those sad brown eyes almost begging us not to ask him anymore.

"You better sit down. You're going to get tired," he said sweetly.

"May I use your headlamp and take a look around at how long this tunnel is?" I asked.

"Sure," he said, taking the contraption off his head and holding it out to me, making everything go dark but a round glow on the hard-packed dirt floor.

I secured the headlamp and headed toward the other end of the tunnel. It was damp and moldy, and if Rodney had been here since Homer was killed, he was braver than I was. As I made my way down the tunnel, I noticed the stone arched ceiling and walls that were holding the place up, and the closer I got to the end, the stronger the smell of Rodney relieving himself became. Almost at the end there was a kind of a small port-a-potty that must have been brought in by somebody for his convenience. But who?

Then I saw another set of steps, these of stone, that led to what looked like a trapdoor. I tried to climb those steps but almost took a header because they were impossibly slick and had something like moss growing on them. Rain must get through the cracks making them treacherous. I ascended them on my hands and knees, hanging onto the wall with my right hand for slight equilibrium, and when I got to the top, I tried to shove the door open, but it, too, wouldn't budge. So this was a place you could get into, but couldn't get out of. Like a roach motel.

I went back down the tunnel toward Marilyn and Rodney and figured someone was coming to feed Rodney sooner or later so we wouldn't have to live down here until we withered away. But then it hit me, whoever was hiding Rodney had to be Homer's murderer, because Rodney more than likely saw the whole thing and had to be hidden. But until when?

"Rodney, what did you see that night Homer Doukas was

killed? Did you see who killed him?" I asked, figuring head-on was the best approach.

"No, I didn't see anything. Nothing."

"If you want to see Gladys again and want her to get out of the hospital and get well, you're going to have to get out of here, and the sooner the better. The police won't let anything happen to you, and you'll be safe once we find Homer's murderer," I promised.

"No, ma'am. I don't know anything," he insisted.

I still had the headlamp on, and I watched as Marilyn decided to tidy up the place, putting all the food wrappers and empty bottles against the wall. She put the new protein bars and full Gatorade bottles next to Rodney's chair.

MUTE: *Interesting. Imprisonment brought out the tidier in Marilyn.*

Out of the corner of my eye, I saw something glinting in the dirt floor partway down the tunnel; I walked over and dug a small silver pistol out of the hard dirt floor. Somebody had buried it there, and it must have worked itself up to the top. A silver pistol rang a bell someplace in my head. Who had said something about a silver pistol? As I was ruminating, I kicked the dirt aside and found a recorder much like the ones in Homer's Pandora's Box. At the same time, we all looked up to hear the trapdoor I had just tried creak open. I quickly put the headlamp on Rodney's head again, and put my fingers to my lips to indicate "shhh" to him. Marilyn and I backed up toward the steps we had come down and hid in the shadows next to the round stone wall.

"Rodney. Dinner's here," said the jaunty voice coming down the tunnel—a voice I clearly recognized: Al Markey's.

"Hi, mister," Rodney said.

"You cleaned up a little," Al said, looking around.

"No, Al. We cleaned up," I stated, walking toward him with the pistol in my hand.

He whipped out a revolver and pointed it toward Rodney's head, "You're not going to make me kill this nice old man, are you?"

"If you were going to kill him, why didn't you do it already?"

"I was never in jeopardy before this. I wouldn't kill any-body just for the sake of it. I'd only kill somebody to save my own life," Al replied.

"Is that why you killed, Homer, to save your own life?"

"To save my own lifestyle I guess you could say. He was a bastard and deserved to die, even you must agree with that."

"So, what now? Are we going to have a shootout?"

"No. You're going to put down the gun and kick it over to me. I'm going to take Rodney out of here, and you and your girlfriend can stay down here and figure out how to stay alive," he snarled.

He sure wasn't the elegant charmer I thought I knew.

"You're going to get caught, Al. You might as well give up now while you have the chance. I'm sure not killing Rodney will help you out in the sentencing department," I said.

"I lived a shitty life until I got out of college and started to make it entirely on my own. Not that I wasn't on my own be-fore that, but I'm not going to live a shitty life again. I'll kill my-self before that," he declared.

"If that's your end game, why take Rodney with you? His wife is sick as you know, and she needs him. You're just going to ruin more lives, and you don't want to do that, do you?" I was pleading by this time.

He just stood there looking from me, to Marilyn, to Rod-ney.

Marilyn stood there motionless, as if she were in Madame Toussaud's Museum. I had never heard her so silent.

"You know what? I'm going to leave you all down here, and you can hope for the best. But no more food, Mr. Rodney, this will be the last time I leave food for you I'm sorry to say. I'm going to hit the road, change my name again, and rely on my street smarts ," he said.

"Change your name again?" I asked, getting a weird feeling that I knew where this was going.

"Yep. I started out as Alexander Markos, and, believe it or not, that bastard Homer was my brother. I can't believe it, so I don't expect you to believe it," he said. "Before I left for vacation, he called me in to tell me he was going to fire me and make my life miserable because he blamed me for killing our mother, for God's sake. She died giving birth to me. The crazy thing is my father, I guess, hated him, and he also blamed me for my mother's death. Two crazy fuckers if you ask me."

MUTE: *Three crazy fuckers, if you ask me.*

With that, he backed up, with his gun poised on us. I'm pretty sure if he pulled the trigger, I was going to be the one to go down.

I had my finger on the trigger of the silver gun, but I was afraid if I pulled my trigger, he'd pull his, and either Rodney, Marilyn, or I was going to be shot, so I let him go.

"Why didn't you let him have it?" Marilyn shrieked.

"If I had shot, he would have shot, and maybe we wouldn't be having this conversation," I said.

"We're going to suffocate down her, or worse, starve to death," she howled.

"I doubt it. We may be down here for a while, but once people know we're missing, they'll find us somehow."

"Who is going to find us?" she asked.

"Do you think Mike will let you starve and suffocate?"

"Oh, Mike. Right, he'll find us if he has to take the building down brick by brick, or stone by stone," she said.

MUTE: *That's a great description of True Love. I wanted that.*

"So, let's decide how we are going to pass the night," I suggested. "Rodney, are there blankets, too, or just the sleeping bag?"

"There are blankets in the sleeping bag, ma'am. You and your friend can sleep on the bed with the blankets, and I'll sleep in the chair in the sleeping bag, if that's okay," he said.

"We don't want to take your bed," Marilyn protested, but I knew she did, and so did I.

"That would be best, ma'am," he said.

Rodney excused himself, took the headlamp, and walked back, I assume, to relieve himself.

Marilyn and I had to do the same after he returned to the site, and I can tell you it might have been relief, but it wasn't a sweet-smelling one.

Once we were settled, feeling strangely cozy with Rodney next to us, I asked, "Rodney, Al is gone for good. He can't and won't hurt you. Why don't you tell us what happened that night with Homer?"

"Oh, it was a terrible night," he started. "I came in late from seeing Gladys in the hospital and taking a nap before I had to work. It seemed like normal when I saw the tall blonde lady walking out. I don't think she saw me, but she's hard to miss with those tall shoes and all. I was doing my rounds, emptying baskets up on the balcony, you know overlooking the floor with all the desks and cubes, when I see balloons coming out of one of the glass offices. Balloons was shootin' over the top and out the door, then I saw Mister was who was getting them out of the office. He opened the door to the hall, and put somethin' under it to keep it open, and in walks another man, I think he works upstairs 'cause I seen him up there one or two times.

"Then the upstairs guy starts shoutin' and yellin' at Mister, and he shoves him into the office with no balloons any more. I can't hear what they're sayin', but I'm peeking around my cart, peeping through the railings. Then I see Mister pull out a gun and hold it on the upstairs man. The upstairs man starts laughing like a loon, and that's when I see Mister pick up something off his desk and shove it at the upstairs man, and the upstairs man didn't saying anything anymore, he just fell down. I must have jumped up and knocked something over, 'cause Mister looked up to see me and pulled out his gun again, and pointed it at me. He said, 'Don't move Rodney, you stay right there. I'm not going to hurt you. I just want to talk to you for a minute.'

"I didn't move and waited for Mister to climb the stairs to get me. I was shakin' like tomorrow, but he was real nice and said he didn't want to hurt me and what did I see?

"I said, 'I didn't see anything, Mister, nothing at all.'

"He said, 'Okay, Rodney, that's good.' He knows my name from me and him working late so many times, but I don't know his name.

"He said, 'Come on with me, you'll be fine. I just have to think what to do with you, but I'm not going to hurt you. I promise.'

"We walked out the door, up the stairs, and into the kitchen they use for fancy parties. It was like a magic cabinet that opened down into this cellar, or tunnel, or whatever it is. We walked down those wooden steps you must'a come down; then he said, 'You can stay here until I get some warm clothes for you,' 'cause it was mighty damp and cold down here that day. Seems to have warmed up a bit since then, or I'm gettin' used to it.

"He went out the end of the tunnel and came back with some blankets and jackets, but I didn't sleep much that night 'cause I was cold, just plain cold. I had some food with me from home, so I wasn't hungry. But the next day he came with all this stuff here, and I been pretty comfortable since then, and he comes once a day with food and papers. I don't know how long he's gonna keep me down here, but he keeps sayin', 'Any day now, Rodney, you'll be outta here.'"

"You'll be out of here as soon as *we* get out of here, and there are a lot of people who are going to be looking for us in the building, so they'll find us, I'm sure of that," I said, not one hundred percent sure they would find us before we were just a pile of bones on a blow-up bed.

We were quiet after that, and I think we even slept a bit before I heard Rodney moving around, to find he was preparing coffee on the little portable warmer. I sat up, and he said, "I'm afraid we're going to have to share. There's only one cup."

"No problem, Rodney. We don't mind sharing if you don't," I said.

Marilyn stirred and sat up, and from the look on her face I could tell she didn't remember where we were. "Oh, my God!" she exclaimed, remembering.

After we took turns walking to the back of the tunnel for our early morning relief, we just sat and waited for something to happen. My watch said 6:47, so I knew nobody was at work yet, or at least nobody who would have thought we were missing. I couldn't even hear Archie at the cabinet anymore. Rodney passed out protein bars, so we sat munching, and glumly passing the coffee cup. I would have started to sing "Kumba-ya" if I had thought anybody would laugh, but even I didn't think it was smile-worthy at that point. Marilyn lay back down and closed her eyes, and Rodney and I made as much small talk as each of us could summon. Trying to keep it positive, I asked him where he thought he and Gladys would relocate once they had to leave their apartment.

"I guess we'll go up the hill. Most of our relatives are up there, so maybe that's where we'll go, too," he said.

"Will that be a hassle for you to get to work from up there?" I asked.

"I'll take the bus, same as now, just a bit longer ride, is all," he said.

I briefly wondered if Rodney could get any money out of the bank for unlawful capture. It might be worth a shot, and it sure would help him and Gladys to have a little money to relocate.

It seemed like a full day before I heard rumblings at the top of the rickety wooden stairs. I jumped up, got to the top of those stairs in what seemed like two steps, and started pounding on the metal door, "It's me, Annie Fillmore and Marilyn Monroe, and Rodney. Help! Help!" I screamed.

"We hear you. We're almost in," said the familiar voice of Detective Jamison.

Marilyn was standing next to me, and Rodney was at the bottom of the stairs when Detective Jamison finally slid the door open. Before I realized what I was doing, I threw myself at him, and flung my arms around his neck.

"That's not necessary, Ms. Fillmore," he said gently, patting my shoulder.

Behind Detective Jamison stood Mike Monroe, Sophie, and some of the rest of my team who started to cheer as soon as they saw us. Marilyn was crying her eyes out as Mike held and consoled her, with Archie nipping at her heels.

When Rodney stepped forward, the gang began to cheer, "Rodney, Rodney, Rodney."

Chapter 22

Monday, April 22, 2013

"YOU'RE PROBABLY GOING TO want this," I said handing Detective Jamison the silver gun. I should have handed him the recorder, too, but I knew if I did I wouldn't get a chance to hear what happened that night, if it was actually on the recorder.

"Thank you. Yes, that will be a definite help; but let's get you and Marilyn and Rodney checked out at the hospital before we start on any breakdown of what happened," he said.

"Marilyn and I haven't been down there long enough to get sick, but you better check Rodney for, God only knows what, maybe chilblains?"

"Chilblains. Interesting. He'll be thoroughly checked out," he assured me.

As we were making our way out of the building to his car, I asked, "How did you find us? I knew you would, but how did you?"

"Your associate Ms. Sugarman called me this morning and said I had better get down here because Mrs. Monroe's dog was racing all over the place with no sign of Mrs. Monroe or you. Surely one of you let the dog, Archie, I believe his name is, into the building. By the way, he was clever enough to find food on desks and even in desks during the night he spent here. He also didn't take it upon himself to relieve himself in corners; just any place he felt like it.

MUTE: *A whole lot of relief going on in that building.*

"Did he finally take you to the kitchen and the movable cabinet?" I asked.

"Yes. We decided just to follow him, so I asked over the loudspeaker for everybody on the floor to get rid of any food they might have packed for lunch or snacks in or out of their desks.

~

Everyone was directed to take their food outside the building so the dog wouldn't be distracted from his mission to take us to you. I have to say, that's an annoying dog—he went all over that place before he went to the kitchen and the cabinet; that's how we found Mr. Monroe's ladder in Mr. Doukas's office. You will have to elaborate on that after your health clearance," he added.

Mute: *Gulp.*

We were taken to University Hospital. Marilyn and I checked out as healthy, and, surprisingly, Rodney was also in the pink of health and had even gained a little weight down in the tunnel.

Detective Jamison released Marilyn and me, since they were concentrating on Rodney and his story as to what happened to him from April 4 until that day, April 22. I had plenty of time to come up with a reason for Mike Monroe's ladder being in Homer's office, but, of course, the only plausible reason for it to have been there was the truth. And as much as I didn't want to, I had to tell the truth. Since everything had turned out well, and it wouldn't have had we not been at EFB with the ladder, I hoped Detective Jamison would give me a pass.

I made my way home to rest, but first to listen to the recorder. It was all on there, from the meeting with Al and Homer before Al went on vacation, as well as the night of the murder. I'm sure you're as nosy as I am, so here it is:

Homer: Al, I've waited a long time for this day.

Al: What's so special about this day, Homer?

Homer: This is the day I'm finally going to pay you back

for killing my mother.

Al: What the fuck are you talking about?

Homer: I've wondered if you ever figured it out, but I guess you are dumber than I thought.

Al: Figured what out? What the hell are you talking about? No offense, Homer, but you sound like you're high on something.

Homer: Oh, I'm high all right. I'm high on revenge at last. I think I've been waiting for this day all of my life.

Al: Homer, I don't know what game you're playing, but it's making me very uncomfortable. What the hell are you saying?

Homer: You really never figured out that we are brothers, did you? You, Alexander Markos, and I are brothers. You didn't even know you had a brother did you? That fucking asshole of a father of ours saw to that, didn't he? He sent me away to live in New Jersey with Aunt Eleni right after you were born and killed my mother in the process. If she hadn't gotten pregnant, my whole life would be a different story. So while you grew up with a normal family, I grew up with crazy Aunt Eleni. I worked my ass off to get to where I am today, while you just slid into home plate. You're nothing but an underling compared to me. You mollycoddle all those worthless loan officers, and look at what you get for it: Nothing, nada, nil, and now you're out.

He yammered on: I know you didn't know it, but Aunt Gaia called me every week from the day I left. She, at least, loved me, and was heartbroken that our father sent me away. I talked to her every week until she died, so I knew all about the trouble you used to get in, going to college at Miami, and then changing your name.

Al: Jesus, are you a psycho? Even if you are my brother, and you'll have to prove that to me, how is it my fault that my mother died in childbirth? I was a baby. Babies aren't responsible for their parents. You do get that don't you? And just to set the record straight, I didn't have any normal family either. My father beat the shit out of me every chance he could get, and between the beatings, I brought myself up while my Dad spent his life in a chili parlor. I was brought up by aunts and neighbors, so my life wasn't a walk in the park either, if it makes you feel any better.

Homer: It doesn't make me feel better at all. I know what happened, and if our father were here instead of you, I'd try to get to him, but, unfortunately he's dead, so you get to take the blame.

Al: What are you going to do, kill me? Is that what you're saying?

Homer: No, I'm not going to kill you; I'm going to fire your sorry ass. I no longer want you under the same roof as me. And it's going to be easy to fire you, because your numbers are way low for the last two months. And, of course, I'll think of something you've done that will make the Board see it my way.

Al: My leadership is what has gotten us to where we are even before you got here. This department funded eleven million in mortgage loans when I arrived in 2006, and you know we funded over fifty million last year alone. I'm sick of walking on eggshells with you, you psycho.

Homer: I'll tell you what, Al. To show you what a great guy I am, to save face, why don't you come in after you get back from Aruba and collect your things from your office. That way you won't have to be escorted out by security next Friday. You can escape under cover of night. Ha ha.Yeah, I like that very…

Al: You sick fuck.

That was from the meeting on March 28, the day before Al went on vacation. Here's their conversation the night Homer died.

Homer: I'm not changing my mind. You killed my mother, and I have to say if one of you had to die, I wish to God it had been you, you little shit. Look where I've gotten to with no help from my family or your Daddy's money. You're nothing but a loser compared to me.

Al: For God's sake, Homer, let's at least talk about this.

Homer: Your numbers stink. It makes me look bad, and you know I don't like being made to look bad, because I'm not.

Al: Let's try to be a little civilized. We can put our heads together and come up with ideas on how to increase the output of the loan officers. We've got those old lists we can have them call between taking the incoming calls. They're hungry, too; they want bigger paychecks, too.

Homer: My ass. Most of those worthless slobs are happy with their medical, 401K, and their base salary, they don't care about our numbers."

Al: They practically make minimum wage without commission; how many of them do you think are happy with earning what McDonald's workers make?

Homer: This isn't about your pathetic loan officers, Al, this is about you getting fired, so get your things together and get the hell out of here.

Homer: What, you're going to shoot me? Ha, that's good, and what do you think the maintenance guys are going to do when they hear your gun go off? And all those other people I passed on my way down here. The loan officers who are working late to suck us out of overtime?

Al: Maintenance is gone for the night, Homer. It's just you and me babe. Everybody else has left the building.

Homer: HaHaHaHaHaHa. You *are* an idiot.

There was some kind of low muffling sound, but no more Homer.

~

I sat there chilled to the bone, and grabbed my warm wool throw from the side of the couch, and I started crying, not even sure for who: Homer, Al, or the sadness of a family so pulled apart by mental illness?

As I ran through the entire thing, it became clear that Al got into the tunnel from outside, but Debbie swore he was sleeping next to her all night. I guess once you're asleep, your partner could take off at night and be back in time to wake up next to you in the morning. Debbie. I can't imagine what she must be going through; that family seemed like the Cincinnati family everybody wanted to be. Not me. They seemed a little too buttoned up. I kind of like the Monroe commotion better. But I'd have to call her and see if I could help her in any way now that her husband is a murderer and has run off to parts unknown.

First call I had to make was to Crystal to make sure our stories jibed when we spoke to Detective Jamison.

"Hi, Crystal. It's Annie," I said.

"Jesus, I heard your name all over the news. What happened, you were stuck in a tunnel?" she asked.

"It's a long story. Did the news say anything about Al Markey?" I asked.

"They said he was a person of interest, whatever that means. The police are looking for him," she said.

"Have you called Detective Jamison yet to let him know you found all the stuff in Pandora's Box?" I asked.

"I called him this morning and had to leave a message. I guess he was up at EFB trying to find you and your friend," she said.

"And Rodney Wilkins. Rodney was being held in the tunnel by Al. Can you believe it?" I asked.

"No. You're going to have to fill me in on the dirty details."

"We're going to have to come clean about how we got into Homer's safe under the fireplace tiles. I was going to lie to him about what happened, but I thought about it on the way home, and we have to tell the truth," I said.

"Oh. No. We. Don't. I don't want to end up in jail," she said.

"Crystal, whatever was in that box of Homer's about you is between you and Homer. You don't have to tell him about that, just that you found his birth certificate, some newspapers, and the recorders, that's all," I said.

"Are you sure he can't worm it out of me?" she asked.

"No, just don't mention that you found anything about you. End of story," I said.

"Okay. When do you want your money?" she asked.

"I don't want any money. You don't owe me anything," I said.

"Yes, I do. I wouldn't feel right not giving you anything for all you did for me," she said.

"Let's talk about it later," I said.

Then I put the phone down, slept and dreamed about tunnels, guns, and trapdoors until the phone rang about 4 o'clock.

"Good afternoon, Ms. Fillmore. It's Detective Jamison."

"Hi," I said.

"Have you had a chance to rest?"

"Yes. I definitely fell asleep, but I'm not sure how rested I am," I said.

"Seeing as all you've been through, I don't want you to make the trip down here. May I come to your house to talk about what happened?" he asked.

"Yes, I guess that's fine. What about Marilyn Monroe, do you want her here, too?" I asked.

"No, I prefer to speak with her separately," he said.

"Okay," I said.

"I'll be at your house about five o'clock if that's convenient," he said.

"That's fine," I said.

I jumped in the shower, and slid into a pair of jeans and t-shirt, then scurried downstairs to see if I needed to tidy up for Detective Jamison even though I knew he'd seen worse than messy before. It was actually pretty neat, save for the dusty floor and furniture tops that took me about fifteen minutes to clean. I realized I was starving and wasn't surprised to see almost nothing in the refrigerator to help the situation. I unfroze a slice of bread, toasted it, and slathered it with peanut butter and honey. I could have eaten about three more slices, but the doorbell rang.

"Were you going to let me know that you were almost killed, or did you think it was okay that I saw it on the news," Neil said, standing at the door with his white apron still on.

"As soon as I got home, I went to sleep. You don't sleep much in a dank tunnel that has no exits. Detective Jamison is on his way here right now to go over what happened. Can I come up for dinner after that?" I asked.

"You might want to wipe the peanut butter off your chin before the detective gets here. And yes, I'll fix something special for the young Miss Marple," he said leaning in for a hug.

MUTE: *He likes me. He likes me. He really, really likes me!*

I hugged him back. "Thanks, Neil, I'll see you about six-thirty if that sounds good," I said.

"Very good," he said.

As Neil was walking down the walk, Detective Jamison arrived, so I held the door open for him and held my breath at the same time.

"Good afternoon, Ms. Fillmore," he said.

"Hi. Come on in," I said.

We sat on my couch practically knee to knee, and he said, "Let's start at the beginning. Why don't you tell me everything that happened from the time Mr. Doukas's body was found until you walked out of that tunnel this morning," he said, readying his pen and notepad.

"I never meant to mislead you. It's just that the people who were involved and came to me made me swear I wouldn't tell the police anything because they felt it would put them in a bad light," I said.

"Excellent. So you felt these people were safer with you looking after them than the police," he said.

"No, of course not. Why don't I just tell you what happened, and you can castigate me when I'm finished," I said.

"Shoot," he said, and I had an unpleasant feeling he would have liked to have done just that.

"I guess it was when Crystal Doukas called me to tell me that Homer had a safe in their house, and she thought there might be information in it that might lead to Homer's murderer. She said she wanted to hire me as a detective to find out what was in the safe. She didn't have a key and didn't know where it might be. I told her she needed to call you, but she was adamant that she didn't want the police involved. What could I do? She wasn't going to call you, and I thought I might be able to help her," I said.

"Why didn't you let me know she might be withholding evidence?" he asked.

"I guess I didn't think of it that way," I said, lying through my teeth.

"Was the ladder in Mr. Doukas's office part of the scheme to get the information out of the safe?" he asked.

"Yes. We couldn't find the combination to the safe or the key to the box inside the safe at Crystal's house, so we thought he might have hidden it in his office. I looked every place and thought we'd give the ceiling a shot, but we needed a ladder. That's why the ladder was there. We borrowed the ladder from Marilyn's husband, Mike, who is a builder." I said not having the heart to go through the whole story of Pandora's Box. It was just too much.

"So you looked under every tile in the ceiling?" he asked.

"Well, not everyone. I just looked until one of them had a combination and a key hidden in it," I said.

"Then what?"

"Then we saw a big flashlight sweeping the walls of the room, so we panicked and left without the ladder. That was Saturday night, and we knew we had to go back the next night to get the ladder because Mike needed it for Monday," I said.

"So you lied to Mr. Monroe as well as to me," he said.

MUTE: *Such a stickler for detail.*

"On the way down to EFB the next night, we found Archie, who had been lost for about three weeks, and Marilyn wouldn't let him out of her sight, so we took him with us; and really, if you think about it, if it weren't for Archie, we may not have found Rodney, or found out that Al Markey killed Homer," I said.

"I prefer not to think that a dog solved my case if you don't mind," he said.

"I understand," I said magnanimously.

He said he would have more questions for me as the investigation concluded without me, but he really needed to know if I had any idea where Al Markey might be. I, of course, had no idea. I swear.

He left my house not totally unhappy I think, but he plays it close to the vest, so I couldn't be sure.

I decided to gussy up out of the jeans into a more feminine skirt and top for dinner with Neil, when the phone rang.

The only sound I could hear was sobbing, so I guessed it was probably Debbie Markey.

"Debbie, is that you?" I asked.

"How could you," she got out between sobs.

"How could I what?" I asked.

"How could you say Al killed Homer." She hiccupped.

"I didn't say he killed Homer. The person who saw him do it did. And, by the way, your husband almost killed me, so I might be the one who should be sobbing," I said.

"What am I going to do without him?" she asked.

Mute: *A few more yoga classes?*

"I'm sure it will all work out, Debbie, once they find him. In a strange way he was kind to Rodney Wilkins even though he kept him prisoner in a tunnel, so that might help," I said.

MUTE: *Keeping a guy prisoner in a tunnel for three weeks is not really kind even if he dressed him up in an attractive flannel shirt.*

"The girls are inconsolable," she rasped.

"I'm sure it's going to take some good counselling for all of you to get through this, but you will," I said.

She hung up, and I was happy she did. Now that it was over, I didn't want to hear one more word about any of it. I wanted to move on, and forget it ever happened.

~

Neil actually did surprise me. He had invited Marilyn and Mike to celebrate a somewhat happy ending. He had set up a table out back in the garden of his restaurant for us even though the garden wasn't officially open until May. But the ivy climbed the trellises. The pots of daffodils and tulips, and the stringing of small white lights made it feel like we were behind a silk curtain in Paris.

On the side table in a bucket of ice was a bottle of Tattinger Champagne that he opened with a festive "pop" as we cheered.

"To the swinging detectives," Neil said as Mike stood and toasted us as well.

"Or, as they are known in some circles, the lying detectives," said Mike.

"Hey, let's not spoil the moment," Marilyn said.

"Can we vow that we will not speak about any of this to-night and spoil a lovely dinner, or any other night for that matter," I said.

"No way, we want details," said Neil.

Both he and Mike prevailed upon us to come clean, so we regaled them with the details they so clearly wanted. Even the swamp man incident, though it made them edgy, was met with requisite approval.

It was a perfect night under the stars with candlelight, delicious food, great friends, and, probably, too much wine.

Neil insisted on driving me home, saying he would pick me up in the morning to get my car. But it didn't happen exactly like that.

MUTE: *Swoon.*

Epilogue

September 23, 2013

A LOT HAS HAPPENED SINCE last April when we found out that Al Markey aka Alexander Marcos was responsible for Homer Doukas's murder, and Rodney Wilkins's disappearance.

There was a small but sedate funeral for Homer Doukas, which his sister, Chloie Papadopoulos, and her family attended, along with several executives from EFB. Marilyn and Sophie accompanied me, and I was delighted Crystal didn't disappoint—showing up in enough black widow regalia to out-widow Jackie Kennedy.

The lovely Jan Mulligan was promoted to VP of under-writing, and rightfully so. Her hard-nosed ways paid off for both mortgage loan officers and for the bank. If she hadn't been as vigilant about adhering to the guidelines, I'm sure many loans would have been dumped back on the bank, and there might have been fewer mortgage loan officers in their cozy cubes today.

Crystal changed her last name from Doukas to Champagne because she thought it sounded "classy." She also sold her house and moved from the old ritzy neighborhood to another in Mt. Adams that was trendier for someone her age. She's called me a few times to see if I wanted to go out bar-hopping with her, but, alas, it hasn't worked out.

Rodney and Gladys Wilkins moved from Over the Rhine to College Hill. They bought a small house with a settlement given to them from EFB, and $10,000 from Crystal, unbeknownst to her, because I just didn't feel right about taking that money and just plopping it in a savings account.

Erwin Richter was escorted out of EFB one June morning and shortly thereafter escorted into jail for insider trading. His sentence was six months. Mrs. Richter stood by her man on the courthouse steps in the photos in the newspaper and the live shots on TV, but I saw his floozy girlfriend, Missy, lurking in the shadows. I wonder how long she'll hang around if he can't find a decent job when he gets out.

Our hero vagabond, Archie, regained all of his lost weight and then some. Marilyn has been practically carrying his rotund self around, but they seem perfectly content with each other, and the boys are happy to have him back as well.

To date, Al Markey has not been apprehended. Debbie Markey has been inconsolable and rues the day he was found out. She doesn't seem to rue the day that he did in Homer, but maybe I'm reading her wrong. She swears she has no idea where he is, and seems to have settled into the idea that she will never see him again. Yet her lifestyle has not changed one whit, and she seems to be taking a lot of extended trips someplace. Being the suspicious broad that I am, I keep picturing him on a lake somewhere fishing and smiling, but much more likely throwing some dice in Monte Carlo.

Detective Jamison says the case will not be closed until Al is behind bars, but I wonder if that's true. The good Detective has covered a lot more cases since April, most of them more grizzly than "The Case of the Skewered Exec." And I feel a lot better about the safety of Cincinnatians knowing that Detective Aaron Jamison is on duty.

What else? Oh, Neil and I have remained mostly good friends. The age difference gets to me even if it doesn't bother him one iota. But when he says, "Stop your caterwauling and get over here," sometimes I go. You have to go with your gut, so I've been told.

The End

Made in the USA
San Bernardino, CA
05 January 2016